2084 - New World Man

Green Deal Quartet, Volume 1

Jim Lowe

Published by JRSL PUBLICATIONS, 2022.

This is a work of fiction. Similarities to real people, places, or events are entirely coincidental.

2084 - NEW WORLD MAN

First edition. April 4, 2022.

ISBN: 979-8201296391

Written by Jim Lowe.

Also by Jim Lowe

Green Deal Quartet

2084 - New World Man

2100 - Crime of the Century

2142 - The Revealing Science

2184 - Twenty-Second Century Man

New Reform Quartet

New Reform

The O.D.C. - The Online Death Cult

With Two Eyes

Fourth Room

Watch for more at https://jimlowewriting.com/.

1.ALL CHANGE

'This is the end of your world.'

The TV screen captivated its captive audience. The last station on-air informed them with authority that it was the end of the world - so it had to be true.

Those lingering in the Communal Recreational area, were momentarily shocked into silence as they watched the statement's confirmation in the flashing images. There were scenes of rioting in the so-called free countries, and there was mayhem in the dictatorships, but of particular interest to this audience was the anarchy in the USA. The smooth-talking TV reporter was harassed but also, maybe a little excited at her scoop. It was a shame about the timing - the last ever transmission.

The leader of the GreenRevs thrust his face into the screen. 'This is it - the Promise has been fulfilled. We are making this world Green again.' He pulled away from the screen to give it back to his fresh-faced interviewer and the jubilant Greens behind her. They laughed as bullets ricocheted off them. They were unmoved by tear gas and other chemical repellents. They didn't even flinch as the grenades exploded around them.

'You are watching Free News, and I'm Rhea Laidlaw reporting from Wall Street.' A female GreenRev pushed past, yelling into the camera, 'Bodhi! We did it!' She hugged her GreenRevs leader, and Glenarvon Cole smiled, but that wasn't enough. There was a message to the people to give. His supporters leapt for joy. Another shot rang out, and the bullet glanced by Glen's face. Rhea screamed, and Glen grabbed her to stop her falling. The GreenRevs cameraman who had commandeered the equipment zoomed in. Glen examined Rhea's wounded arm, before applying some material, 'It has NanoHealing™.' He said, 'You'll be ok - I promise.'

She grimaced, but said with professional urgency, 'Can we carry on with the interview?'

'You're a brave one - perhaps you should join us.' He laughed. 'You've got nothing left to lose. You're broke. Everyone in the world is broke.' He pointed into the camera lens. He was pointing at every Free News viewer - whose ratings had gone from thirty thousand to hundreds of millions in the last two hours; as all its competition, including the Internet, dropped off the airways, 'Even you. Do you still want to carry on?'

Rhea looked to her new lensman. He nodded. It didn't matter if the cameraman was giving her a cue - this was a once in a lifetime opportunity. 'Yes.' She moved the microphone to her right hand and winced at the throbbing in her wounded left arm. 'What my viewers would want to know is - how did you know that the Internet would crash? Did you cause it to happen?'

'Bodhi knew all along. He prepared us for this moment for years. He saw it.'

'What did he see?'

'The future.'

Rhea scoffed, 'Utter rubbish. He might be a GreenTech™ giant, but he hasn't built a time machine.'

'All I know is he said this would happen. He told us that the whole system couldn't withstand the cocktail of viruses within it. He said, "Wait for the predicted 2080 solar storms, and it will collapse irrevocably." We spread the message, and they came.'

Rhea challenged him. 'That was another *end of the world* conspiracy theory.'

Glen smiled and gestured to the rioting crowd and re-stated to the camera, 'The end of *your* world.'

'Surely, this isn't going to be of any use to you or your followers either. There will be mass unemployment and poverty. This is a disaster of global proportions.'

'You don't get it. We've been planning this for years. Sattva Systems™ has been developing GreenTech™ for decades, but the old industries with the governments in their pockets wouldn't let it overtake them. They made all kinds of promises for 2050, but it didn't happen. They lied and cheated and ignored the climate crisis for the sake of their own profits and material wealth. Well, now the wealth has gone. A virtual world of transactions has been wiped. The new currency is going to be Green. Our people earn Green Credits. The Trads will just have to start again and muddle their way through - like they always do. This is the New Green Deal.'

'You can't just take people's savings and belongings from them.'

'Yes, we can. All you've ever owned is gone. Capitalism is dead. Welcome to the new Green World. This isn't a return to feudalism. This is a future of high-tech developments to take us into the twenty-second century. Our friends and early adopters will be well rewarded with new homes, jobs and re-education.' Glenarvon Cole wasn't entirely telling the whole truth - Rhea could tell - but he had to play the political games, like his opponents of old. He knew the places in the new communities had mostly been self-selected already.

'But what if the Trads - as you've named them - as you've labelled me, I suppose - what if they come to claim it all back and storm your Green Communities with force?'

'You've seen what our NanoArmour™ can withstand. It has survived nuclear attacks in Pakistan, chemical weapons in Russia, and everything our government can throw at us. We know how to defend ourselves. The future is not a scary place for those that want to help Mother Nature restore Herself back to health.'

And perhaps it wasn't. But the inmates at the Modern Ridgecrest Supermax Penitentiary would never know.

The interview was cut short as a chair smashed through the TV screen. A Nazi inmate yelled, 'Those Green pigs have stolen my money.'

Brady Mahone, six feet six inches and eighteen stone of muscle made a quick-fire decision to make his retreat. He wasn't scared - he usually enjoyed a good ruck - but he could see where this was heading. He grabbed his diminutive partner, Lucian, aka Lucky Lopez, by the arm and dragged him back to their cell, closed the barred doors and pulled the curtain over. It was a hot, muggy, midsummer day, and tensions among their fellow inmates had already been running high before every prisoner was informed that they had just lost everything. The fucking Green Credit was the new dollar - and they didn't have any fucking Green Credits.

As the inmates were absorbed in the acts of assault, battery and murder, two of the guards had just discovered they'd lost everything they had ever worked - or been bribed for - decided to give them what they should have had all along - death.

The two guards sprayed bullets in all directions. The mayhem continued for minutes. Brady shielded Lucian with his massive frame at the back of his cell. The angle of the firing was upwards, and the hundreds of bullets spilt crumbling masonry upon them. Then the shots took on a more deliberate rhythm. He guessed they'd now entered the execution phase. Brady rooted through the rubble until he found a piece of solid concrete which fitted comfortably in his massive hand. He squeezed it to make sure it wouldn't crumble to dust.

Brady said, 'Lucky, take a peek, and tell me what you see.' Brady saw his animal and insect sketches shot to pieces within the dust and concrete. *I loved those pictures - I spent hours on them*. He thought. Lucian's glamour girl photos were also in the rubble.

Lucian inched back the curtain, 'I see one guard executing the injured prisoners in the Communal Area.' He stuck his head out a little further. 'Shit! Guard Askew is coming up the stairs.'

'Which stairs?'

'To the right.'

'Ok, sneak into Croker's cell on the left, and make some noise.'

'But he'll see me.'

'Shuffle along on your belly, like a soldier.'

Lucian took a deep breath. 'Ok, and when I get there, do I call him or something?'

'Act like you're injured, nearly dead. I don't want him running.'

'Ok.' Lucian slithered along like a snake, not realising that he'd left a trail in the dust from the bullet-ravaged walls.

Askew's heavy boots thudded and clanged on the steel floor. At first, the rhythm was steady as he passed the rows of barred but open cells. They were all empty because their inmates were on Human Communal Time before the massacre - no one stayed in their cells for a minute longer than necessary. Askew spotted the trail in the dust, and he slowed down. He looked warily ahead, and then he heard the groan. He inched forward. *I guess he's dying, but where's the blood?* Askew thought, crouching down to examine the tracks.

That was the last thought he ever had. Brady punched the rock through his skull. He took the antique gun off the dead body of Guard Askew and went through his pockets, removing keys, passes, and even his wallet.

Lucian returned to his side as Brady examined the dead guard. Brady turned to him. 'He's big and overweight - strip him, and we'll use whatever clothing we can. I'll see if his jacket will fit me, maybe even the pants. You can roll the sleeves up and use his shirt.'

'The other one is still down there - and he's a bit smaller.' He smiled. 'His stuff might fit me better.'

'Sneak down the left stairs and watch for me coming down the right. When I get close - distract him - without getting yourself shot in the process.'

'Aye-aye captain.' Lucian whispered, and then he scampered away.

Brady changed into the guard's clothes. They were on the small side but at least the boots fitted. He stayed low as he moved efficiently past the cells and down the stairs. The shorter guard seemed to be double-checking that there was no one left alive. Occasionally, he would fire another shot into a barely twitching body.

Lucian waited for his moment. He watched Brady reach the bottom of the stairs, and he saw him check his weapon. The smaller guard sensed movement behind him. Lucian threw a rock across the floor before the guard turned. The guard's eyes followed the sound - just as Brady jumped him. He put the guard in a chokehold and lifted him off the floor and held him until his last breath left him.

He looked at the Tommy Gun and the Revolver, 'What the fuck are these things?'

Lucian picked them up and examined them, 'Antiques. This is less the twenties - more like the 1920s - and it's out of bullets. That's why he used the old Revolver.' Lucian wiped the guns where he had touched them on a dead inmate's T-shirt, then dropped them back near the guard. He looked over the guard's body and admired Brady's latest kill, 'I think he's new. I don't recognise him.'

'I don't think he was employed for his welfare skills - he was a sick fuck.' Brady issued his instructions. 'We take our time. Think about what we are going to need. Grab keys, money, clothes. If we can't find transport, it will be a long trek. We might have to rough it.'

'You do know this is unfair.'

'What is?'

'That you ended up with the brains as well as your brawn.' Lucian said knowingly.

'I must have come from a good gene pool. Let's move - no time for chatting.' He sighed, 'This is fucked up. I had fifty thousand bucks waiting for me when I got out, and now it's gone. That's my whole life savings - my emergency fund.'

'If we manage to get out of here, at least we'll be free.'

Brady pulled off the dead guard's boots and passed them to Lucian. 'I hate these places. They always stink of sweat and defeat.'

Lucian changed into the small guard's uniform but left the weapons. 'Have you touched them?'

'No. You must be thinking the same as me - we'll be in enough trouble if we managed to escape - don't want to be blamed for a massacre as well.' Brady remembered he still had Guard Askew's gun. 'Wait here.' He took the gun back, cleaned it, and then placed it in the dead guard's hand. From the upper floor, he checked for any further threats before returning to Lucian.

They both left the Communal Area and searched rooms to the left and right. Their newly acquired Guard's key cards were useless, so they used the old-fashioned bunches of keys to open any *Restricted Access* doors. When they found the guards' locker room, they grabbed holdalls. 'There are only two bags,' Brady said. 'These probably belong to the two we just killed. I'm guessing the others legged it when they realised that they were now unemployed and penniless.'

'Those two psychos obviously had other things they wanted to do before they signed off.'

'See if you can find car keys. I'm guessing there will be at least a couple of vehicles outside that don't use fingerprint locks. If not, then we'll have to chop off...'

'Let's hope we can find keys...'

They rummaged through the abandoned lockers. Lucian found some chocolate bars and cans of Coke, and they both consumed them greedily. When they found the car keys, they made their way through the deserted building to the control room. 'That was easy.' Lucian said, apprehensively.

'They didn't think there was going to be anybody left alive. After they've checked their loved ones are ok, they'll start to realise they're broke. That means they'll return to scavenge for anything of value. We'll take a car each if we locate them - then follow me - and don't drive like a granny.'

They moved methodically through the prison. Brady was calm and alert. They filled their requisitioned holdalls with as much as they could carry. In Lucian's case, a little, but with Brady - a lot. They even picked up old toothbrushes and toiletries like an eerie game of the Supermarket Sweep.

Before they reached the outer areas of the building, they came to the CCTV room. Lucian located the keys which would unlock the door, and Brady swept past him, ready to kill any remaining occupants. But there was nobody there. Brady checked the CCTV monitors, and it was clear the place was deserted. He wondered if they had left hours ago. Maybe the last two guards wanted a bit of sport before they left.

He thought about the chain of events leading up to the bloodbath. They hardly ever put on the news, it usually got the blood of the rival gangs or political allegiances up. He remembered Guard Askew yell before switching over from the daytime soaps they were allowed to watch. 'Boys, we got a real treat for you today. We are going to switch on Free News, so y'all can see what you're missing in the big world out there.' At that, Brady had instinctively known trouble would follow.

In the CCTV control room, he asked Lucian to confirm that the Internet was indeed dead. Lucian was in here because he was guilty of being in the wrong place at the wrong time for him, but precisely the right time for a corrupt Police Department to make a positive impression on that quarter's crime statistics. He had worked in Hollywood as a computer graphics assistant for one of the streaming giants. It didn't take long for Lucian to confirm the deceased status of the Internet and the whole of social media. 'Godammit - my education and career has gone down the drain.'

'Talking of drains, make sure you use the toilets before we leave. We don't want someone using your bony ass for target practice when you wanna stop by the side of the road for a dump.'

'At least, they would have the challenge of trying to hit mine.'

Brady laughed. He rubbed his fingers through his stubbly black crew-cut hair - he hadn't shaved it bald for more than a week - while examining the array of equipment in the room. 'Is any of this tech worth taking with us?'

'Only the Dumb Satts™ - Satellite Phones still should work, and they are FusionPowered™. They are supposed to last forever.'

Brady packed them away. They were surprisingly heavy. They both moved out, taking in the heavily wooded areas which surrounded the Modern Ridgecrest Supermax Penitentiary.

There were a few cars in the parking lot, and they soon found a couple of keys that worked without needing fingerprint technology to open them. 'You know what.' Lucian said, 'A lot of products are going to be fucked without the Internet.'

'Not our problem.' Brady found a car he liked, a *Twentieth Generation Ford Mustang*, while Lucian chose a *2045 Mid-Engine Mini*. 'Thank fuck we don't have to trek through the forest.' Brady said, dumping his heavy bags into the trunk. 'I've got a place we can lay low in McFarland. It's about sixty miles west of here. Keep up and keep close.

2.ARCHIE'S RANCH

McFarland wasn't the town he'd remembered. Brady had only been inside for ten years, and McFarland wasn't the sort of place which attracted investors, but it had received quite the makeover. He slowed his driving down to a crawl to take in the details. He wondered how his stolen car could travel on the Highway, but Lucian's car seemed to be blocked by an invisible barrier. Brady had tried, and it worked fine for him, but Lucian was blocked. Lucian drove behind Brady but stayed off-road to the edge of the Highway.

There wasn't another vehicle in sight, but he noticed curtains twitching as he passed people's homes. *Maybe, it's the economic collapse. Or it could be that news of the prison break has reached them*, he thought.

He wondered how many of the prison guards and workers lived here. The prison was only twenty years old. Maybe they had brought a measure of prosperity to the town. He was anxious to get to his old Foster Daddy, Archie. He had a bunker, and he was a sucker for conspiracy theories. As he drove through the town centre, he noticed a common theme of environmental messages and sponsorship by Sattva Systems™ - they seemed to be the most significant player in this place.

He glanced in his rear-view mirror to check if Lucian was still behind, in his Mini, and then indicated right, heading to the more rural east side of town and the small ranch where Archie lived. It was well to the south of McFarland's more populated east side, but not far from the west side. However, Archie was on the other side of Highway 99, which formed a formidable barrier to anyone deciding to investigate his ranch. Archie chose it for privacy from the east and the convenience of the west.

After making their way down a dirt track, past the few cattle Archie still owned, they pulled up just outside Archie's ranch. Brady got out of his Mustang and went to the gate. Lucian wound down his window to check for potential threats. A couple of shots rang out as Brady approached the entrance to the ranch. Brady shouted, 'Hey! You old fucker, it's me, Brady.'

There was a pause before a raspy voice replied, 'Brady! Well, come on in.'

Brady opened the big gates wide open. He turned to Lucian, 'Let me drive in first. He don't like strangers.'

They parked up, got out of their cars, and Lucian stayed back as Brady gave the old man a warm hug. 'Hey, Foster Daddy, how ya been keeping?'

'I tell ya now.' Archie Mahone rasped, 'Some of those young fuckers are gonna git it - if they try to steal my ranch.' Archie was deeply tanned after years of working in the Californian sun, and his thick silver chain glinted in the light, nestled in the bush of his white, wiry chest hair.

'And who's gonna try and do that, with fierce old Archie Mahone guarding it?'

'The Greenies! I knew they'd try and take over the world.'

'You old fool,' Brady teased, 'I thought it was the aliens or the Deep Cons in the government who were going to do that first.'

'I've seen the townsfolk eye up my bunker.'

'I'm surprised you're not down there now - I half expected it.'

'Well, boy, I had to defend the ranch, and I couldn't do that from down there, now could I?' He looked him over, 'Boy, you haven't aged a bit, and there ain't a mark on ya.' He took in his boy's bronze skin. He never did know where he came from. Archie remembered telling him to tell the townsfolk he came from Hawaii to explain it. Archie used to convince himself: *Well, he has got that kinda South Seas islander look about him.*

'I've had my fair share of scrapes, Pops, and you know I take some hurting. And even when I do, I heals real quick.' Brady looked over at the vintage machine gun, ready and waiting with its glittering array of bullets dangling from it. 'You got Old Marvin out. I used to have so much fun playing with that as a kid.'

'The new machines don't work no more.'

'Seven or eight years ago, all weapons had to be fitted with a disabler.' Lucian interrupted, 'You had to activate a stream-switch to use it. It was a compromise with the gun lobby. You could use your weapons as much as you want, but it had to be the owner or authorised user, and all firings were logged.'

'I was inside.' Brady said, 'I must have missed it. Pops, this is Lucian, but I call him Lucky, cos he's my *lucky* mascot. He saved my ass inside Ridgecrest.'

'And for that, Brady here, literally saved my ass!' Lucian laughed.

Archie wheezed, 'I can see that - you're no bigger than a boy, son.' He looked at Brady, 'Really, he saved you?'

'Even I don't have eyes in the back of my head.' He added, 'We need a place to stay, to stay low for a while.'

'Of course. I'll be glad of the company, and you can do me a favour.'

'What can we do for you?'

'You can help me protect the place until things play out.'

Brady placed his massive arm around Archie's shoulder, and Archie almost buckled under the weight of it. 'Be our pleasure. If someone out there wants to play at target practice, then I'll show them that Brady don't miss with Old Marvin.'

When Brady moved his arm from Archie's shoulder, Archie returned to his previous six-foot height. He brushed his fingers through his long, thinning white hair and then stroked his white beard. 'You boys, grab your things and get settled in while I go and get us some grub.'

LATER, AROUND THE TABLE, they devoured the assorted fries and grills greedily. Brady and Lucian talked animatedly about their exploits and near misses in their Supermax home. While Archie enthusiastically tried to claim every conspiracy theory known to geek-kind was correct all along.

'What are your buddies saying about it all?' Brady said,

'I don't know. All my tech is useless. I spent a fortune on it over the years. I kept up to date with every development - but even the Black Web has gone. It shouldn't be able to happen. That's why it must be alien technology. Must be from space to git the whole world in one go.'

'What about mobiles? Surely, the phones still work.'

Archie flushed, 'You gotta understand. That must have been the masterplan, to communicate through the phones. They left them standing for a reason - right?'

'Ok, that kinda makes some sense if it's human overlords taking over the planet - but you said you thought it was aliens - from outer space and all.'

'Couldn't be too careful. The last calls I had said was to prepare to defend yourself to the death, for all that's sacred. They were going to destroy the masts. They ain't gonna spy on us no more.'

'Is that it? That's the plan for the uprising, the fightback?'

'In fairness, it all happened so fast.'

'But you and your conspiratorial buddies have been planning for decades for a moment such as this, surely?'

'We had our bunkers...'

Brady laughed, but Archie saw the warmth within it. 'I notice you ain't in your bunker.'

Archie started to form an answer. 'I got my eyes peeled for them no good, piece of shit Hodgsons. They ain't got no bunker, and they never prepared like me. They just steal what they wants. One man alone can't defend two properties...' But then he roared with laughter, he was so happy to have his boy back again, 'Truth is, son, it's more than forty years old, it stinks and ain't fit for purpose no more. To tell the truth, boy, I'd rather live in Ridgecrest than that piece of shit, hole in the ground. But I didn't think of that when I made it my control centre.'

Lucian spat out the meat he was chewing and erupted in laughter, and Brady and Archie couldn't help but laugh along with him.

AFTER ARCHIE AND LUCIAN went to bed, Brady stood on watch all night. He had never needed much sleep, even as a boy. He wondered if it was because he was always sent from one foster home to another - until he finally settled with Archie and Edie. At least it was quiet here. He thought about his ten years in prison, ten years gone and not being able to sleep. He never did like listening to the sounds of the men inside, snoring, farting, and masturbating all night long - never mind the quiet violence and the noisier rapes. He hoped to erase those thoughts from his mind - given time.

He wandered around the ranch, not too far from the homestead, and looked up at the glittering stars. It was easy to imagine for a moment that the world hadn't changed - but it had. Now was the time for planning not only how he could survive it but also, how he - how *they* might be able to thrive in it. The decking creaked as he rocked in his Pop's old chair. He watched the FusionPlanes™ glide through the skies intermittently. A few of the HeavyLoader™ Planes were coming into land at the nearby Airport. He thought *they* weren't supposed to fly over the town after midnight.

Then something strange appeared. He didn't get up, feeling as though he was catching a glimpse of something that could disappear if he changed angles. *It looks like one of those aurora type things, except I'm sure you don't see them down in these parts.* He knew there was nothing wrong with his eyesight. The prison doctors were amazed at the ease in which he passed his optical evaluation - they didn't have any other charts with smaller lettering to test him. *This ain't like no aurora I've heard of. It's coming from the ground up and not from the skies.* The translucent green glow moved to envelop the town of McFarland at first, and then it rolled, like mist, down the Highways and even the dirt roads surrounding Archie's ranch and the neighbouring Hodgsons. In a matter of moments, the glow faded, and Brady wondered if he had imagined it. *I can't leave my watch, not with the Horrible Hodgsons down the way. I'll check it out in the morning.*

As the first rays of dawn broke over the horizon, Archie appeared with hot coffee for them both. He sat down on the porch next to Brady. 'I still got all your old things, and looking at you boy, I'm guessing you could still get into your old clothes.' He smiled, 'Your little buddy is in the kitchen - says he can't wait to make us all a big, cooked breakfast.'

'Thanks, Pops. I need a shower first, then get changed. I must say I'm looking forward to some proper home-cooked food myself.' He gulped down his coffee. 'The town has changed a lot since I was last here. They didn't let us keep up with the news in Ridgecrest - they considered it a mood agitant. It looks a lot more prosperous than I remember.'

'That was all the corporate sponsorship - part of the New Green Deal. They persuaded the townsfolk to join a scheme where if they let them take over the running of the town, they could get virtually free Green energy and other benefits.' He laughed. 'The Internet ran as slow as if it was moving through treacle, and everybody but the Greens got real mad about it and upped and left.'

'But you didn't go for it - no doubt.'

'Nah, too good to be true, if you start to believe in some corporation's bullshit, then it's the beginning of the end for the freemen of the west like me - like us.' He looked into Brady's face to make sure the years inside hadn't changed him.

Brady smiled. 'I just remembered, we picked up a bunch a Satts™ before we left - could you find a use for them?'

'More Sattva Systems™ stuff - they were worth fucking trillions of dollars, and you can't go barely a mile without seeing a sign of theirs. Having said that, now that the Internet and the Cell Phones aren't working, maybe the old-fashioned Satellite Phones might still work. I might take them, even if it does kinda go against my principles.'

'I need to know more about what I've missed. How did this Sattva Systems™ make their money?'

'It was after the third pandemic of the Twenties and the crash of Twenty-Nine - that fucking crash looks like a walk in the park compared to this one. Anyhows, Sattva was already a highly valued company, even though it was massively in debt - these fucking tech companies never did make financial sense - they must have had something over the government...'

Brady laughed, gently, 'Pops, give me the details first, and we'll talk about the conspiracies later - I promise.'

'Alright, alright. Anyhows, the aviation industry was decimated, but Sattva had developed clean energy with FusionPower™, which solved some of the climate issues. That was probably, just after you were jailed for the jewellery heist in Bakersfield. The trouble with everything Sattva Systems™ did with Fusion-this and Fusion-that is that it was all expensive, slow and total fucking crap, and nobody wanted that shit except the Green Communities - who got it for free - if you call giving up on living *free*.'

Brady guessed that Archie would rather talk about that instead, but he needed to catch up with the rest of the world. 'I thought they were Green, this Sattva Systems™ - surely, the environmentalists would have been happy to see the back of airlines altogether?'

'You said I couldn't go into conspiracy theories, so, let's just say, they musta come to some sort of arrangement.' He smiled as if he had won a point. 'Ya see, boy, they made them all their money by solving the pandemic issues with flying. I'm guessing the Greens still needed to travel to plot against the rest of us good ol' boys.'

'How did they do that?'

'It was their fucking NanoTech™. Trust me, son, if there's an end to the human race planned - it'll start with that invisible Green goo.'

Brady sighed. *I'm just going to have to let him tell it his way, conspiracy theories and all. It's going to be challenging to pick out the facts from all this.* 'Hey Pops, I thought you said it was invisible.'

'Do ya want to hear my story? Or are ya just goin' to pick holes in everything I say? Look around ya, boy, the world has changed. We have new rulers. They just haven't issued their demands yet - but it's coming, you mark my words, and when they do, I betcha we all gonna have to pay a high price - maybe not today, but at some point.'

'Ok, Pops. You're right. Things have changed big time. I can't deny what I see with my own eyes.' He thought again about the green glow he saw last night. He reached over and grabbed his Pop's arm. 'I hear you, Pops.' He could sense Archie's stress levels coming down. 'You were saying about planes and the pandemic issues.'

'Yes, I was, before I was rudely interrupted. Anyhows, they put NanoTechFilms™ - think of it like when you used to blow them bubbles as a young 'un - they put this Film over the entrance to the FusionPlanes™. Passengers had to agree to all this and acquire enough Green Credits from the Sattva Systems™ Reps - to prove their environmental credentials. The devil is always in the fucking details.' He muttered, 'If the passengers did all this, then they would go into the plane and be covered in Green goo...'

'But you said it was invisible. Could the passengers feel the goo on them?'

'Well, I never went on them planes, but apparently, no - they didn't know it was on them. Now, that is scary. It could be all over us right now.'

'Carry on, Pops.'

'What it did was individually isolate them from any viruses or infections of any kind. They were literally in their own bubble.'

'Sounds like a good thing.'

'That's how they get ya, son. They came back from their holidays and their business trips, and they all said they never felt better, renewed, turns out, this Green goo...'

'Do they call it *Green goo*?'

'Sattva Systems™? Of course not. Who markets anything that's the truth? They, and the sheep who follow them to the slaughter, call it NanoFilm™.'

'I didn't think Green goo was a good name.'

'Good enough for me, boy. Anyhows, as I was saying, not only did these passengers say it relieved them of some of their ailments - they also said it acted as a sunblock. Remember the Thirties when the weather got biblical? Record hurricanes, tornadoes, rain and heat - almost all the time?'

'Yeah. Come to mention it. I had noticed the weather calming down since I went inside. Out in the Exercise Yard, I started taking it personally.' He let out a big laugh, but Archie was frustrated because he had made Sattva Systems™ sound good, and that wasn't his intention. He decided to skip telling him about the Intense Renewable Projects and the trillions of investments into Sattva's New Deal.

Archie went for the big conspiracy. 'You know what else these returning travellers said about the effects of the Green goo?'

'What did they say, Pops?' Brady knew conspiracy was coming. Inside he shrugged wearily, but outwardly, he gave his Pops his full and undivided attention.

'That it was also, a contraceptive. Nobody ever got pregnant while they were away, after travelling on those planes.'

'Come on, Pops. How could anybody prove that?'

'I had loads of stuff on it before the Great Internet Crash. There were studies and all sorts.'

'Presumably, people had kids after?'

'Yeah, after, but not during.'

Brady thought about it, even though he thought this was pretty damn trivial for a conspiracy theory. 'Even if this was true. Did the Nano - Green goo just wear off when they returned?'

'No. On arrivals, they would pass through security and the Green goo was recycled. Made more and more people want to fly - for the so-called health benefits and the Green Credits, even though they weren't worth anything, they were just some liberal greenies badge of honour. They were always showing off how many fucking credits they achieved. Sattva Systems™ ruled the skies - and now they want to rule the whole fucking world.'

Brady laughed, 'I don't suppose you've got any of those credits, Pop?'

'Damn right, boy - none. That's my badge of honour.'

3.DISCIPLE

Brady helped Lucian clear up the breakfast dishes - it was the least he could do after Lucian had prepared a breakfast feast of epic proportions. He felt clean, back in his old jeans and a starched white T-shirt and had found the DeNine DeLuxe Sneakers™, he'd hardly had time to wear before his incarceration. And now he was fed and watered; he felt ready to take on the world.

His Pops waited for them next to the log fire. It was spring, warm and sunny outside, but Brady took this as a sign of Archie's oncoming old age that he felt the cold more. It made him a little sad to think of his Pops no longer apparently indestructible.

They all chatted for a while; Brady and Lucian gave Archie all the gory details of their time inside. He especially liked the stories about the old-timers locked up in Ridgecrest - some of them he knew from his old days. By lunchtime, Archie was becoming sleepy. Brady reached out and touched him on the arm, 'Hey, Pops. I'm going to walk over to the town to see how the land lies.'

'Are you sure that's a good idea, boy? Won't folks be looking for you?'

'I can look after myself. Anyway, I don't think anyone's got a job at the prison anymore.' He looked his Pops in the eye, 'I need to check things out for myself.'

'Ok, you be careful, boy. If there ain't no prisons, they might decide to take you dead and not alive. You catch my drift?'

'I've set up a couple of the Satts™.' Lucian said, 'If you take one, we could still communicate. You never know, we could get you to pick up some shopping,' he added laughing.

'Yeah, sure, with no money and none of that green currency?' Brady said. 'I'll ruin my rep if I go from heists to shoplifting.'

Lucian handed him a belt with a holster for the Satellite phone. Brady put it on. 'You'd have thought they'd have made these things smaller by now.'

BRADY MARCHED THE TWENTY-minute walk along the dirt track past the Mahone Ranch and around the Hodgson Ranch. As he came to the first major road - McFarland was his hometown, but this road was new, so he didn't know its name - he saw a couple of the Hodgson Mob, throwing rocks which bounced off thin air. They were yelling as the rocks seem to hit an invisible wall and drop dead to the floor. They threw the stones at passing drivers, who ducked and swerved, expecting the hit, but the rocks never got anywhere near them - until one car veered off the road and headed straight towards Brady. He leapt out of the way just in time as the vehicle hurtled past him, skidding until it came to a halt.

Brady went to rescue the old woman inside, but the Hodgson duo had other ideas. 'Hey, Brady! She's ours - we fucking did the hard work. We want what's coming.' Alan and Gary Hodgson had grown up a lot since Brady had been inside, and they were not the little roustabouts he remembered.

He looked over the old woman. She didn't seem to be injured. 'Are you ok, ma'am?' She looked as terrified of him as she was about the two Hodgson boys.

'Yes, thank you. Please get me to the road, if you would, please...sir.' She thought it might humour him.

'Stay behind me. I'll hold them off.'

He shuffled backwards as Alan danced and dodged his way behind Brady while Gary pulled a knife, ready to attack. The plan seemed to be to distract Brady while Alan grabbed the woman. All the while, Brady fended Gary off while the woman frequently screamed as the knife whipped past.

After a few minutes, Brady reached the edge of the road. Knowing this was their last chance of securing their prize, and whatever this woman owned, they rushed Brady. He staggered backwards and the old woman started to fall. She tried to get out of his way, she twisted and tripped, but it was enough for her to find the edge of the road. An oncoming car swerved to miss her, as did the next car as one only just avoided Brady. He pulled her to the kerbside. He turned back to see Alan and Gary only inches away from him, but they were punching the invisible wall, uselessly trying to get to him. Gary tried to hack and slice at it but to no avail.

They soon lost interest in them and instead turned their attention to the vehicle. Brady watched them closely as they tried and failed to start the car. Then they just took anything of value they could find within it.

He checked on the old lady, but she'd crossed the road while he was watching the boys. She looked back and screamed at him, 'Don't come near me. You shouldn't be able to get in here. I'm going to report this to the Disciple. This isn't part of the deal.'

Brady decided to let her go. *More trouble than it's worth.*

He brushed himself down - he'd liked the feeling of being clean again after his time inside. He wandered around the edge of the new road, which appeared to encircle the town. He thought about testing this invisible wall by trying to leave and then coming back in again but decided against it. *It might have been a fluke when I fell in at the same time as her.*

He came to McFarland Park and decided to remain there while he considered what to do next. People passed him and paid him very little attention. It was as if they didn't have a care in the world - they looked at ease. *How could they feel so safe in the middle of a revolution?* He listened to their chatter until he heard an old couple talking about a meeting for residents at the New Green Hall. *That's as good a place as any to find out what the fuck is going on.*

If he didn't know any different, the town would be going about its daily routines as if nothing extraordinary had happened. He listened discreetly to conversations - mainly about family, friends, and everyday happenings. It surprised him that there were no mentions of prison breaks and murderers on the loose. There were no digital displays or wanted posters to be seen. He took a closer look at all the signs and businesses owned by Sattva Systems™. They all had a theme; how business and environmental activism could come together to save Mother Earth. Brady liked to sketch any creatures he came across, from beasts to critters to insects, and he appreciated the high-quality designs and images of these advertisements.

Physical cash had disappeared from society, even before he went inside, which was why he had turned to jewellery store heists. He had been highly successful until he was undone by pure bad luck. The police were booked to advise on new security measures, just minutes after he and his crew had moved in to rob them.

He watched as people paid for their goods with things that looked like old-fashioned micro-chips - these were in different shades of green. Before handing them over, the customer placed them between the thumb and forefinger and when they glowed, the business owner put them in the top of a small tube, which flashed green as it swallowed it up, as if some kind of transference had been completed.

A new phone store was opening - also owned by Sattva Systems™ on the old First Street. *No surprise there.* The queue snaked back for a few hundred yards, past where the old McDonald's had been, before his time away. He wondered if the whole chain had disappeared. The potential customers didn't look excited - unlike the old days when a new tech product was launched. *This ain't new tech - this is old except for the fancy Sattva logos. They don't want them - they need them.*

He instinctively patted his own Satt™. He spotted an old man sitting on a bench, with a satchel by his side, watching the world go by. It was time to ask one of the residents a few questions, but it would be tricky. The questions he wanted to ask were so fundamental, they'd almost certainly give him away as an outsider. He sat beside the old man and said nothing. He tried to appear relaxed. He rubbed his head. He had got used to shaving it bald when he was at Ridgecrest, but now he felt the stubble sprouting through. The old man watched him. Brady continued to rub his head, fascinated by its rough feel.

The old man spoke first, 'I used to have a lovely head of hair, it was my crowning glory, the ladies used to say, and then it all started to go, almost exactly when I hit sixty. I thought I was going to keep it.'

Brady smiled. 'I think I'm going to grow mine back - make a new start.' He thought about using an assumed name, but he thought it would be a waste of time. He was too recognisable to hide his identity, with his size, pale-brown skin, physique, and dark brown eyes. Only the old natives of McFarland would recognise him, and as he was last here, more than twenty years ago... He reached out his hand, 'I'm Brady Mahone - pleased to meet ya.'

The old man shook his hand, weakly, 'I'm Gus. We're all making new starts, even at my age.'

'I can't get used to this new way of working. What about you?'

'I lost my life savings in this crash. Fortunately, I'd built up a lot of Green Credits over the years...and kept them alive with consistent Green living.'

'What's the deal with those? I've been abroad for the last few years.'

The old man looked at him suspiciously. 'Where could you have been that you hadn't heard of Green Credits?'

Fuck! This really is a worldwide phenomenon. Where the fuck could I have been? He remembered the old wildlife books he read voraciously in Ridgecrest and how he used to copy the pictures and pin the sketches to the wall in his cell. 'I've been deep in the Amazon rainforest, keeping a census of animals which are nearing extinction, like the Pink Amazon dolphin and the White-Cheeked Spider Monkey. If you've got a pen and paper, I could draw you one.'

He expected Gus to decline the offer, but instead, he pulled out a leather-bound notebook and a pencil from his satchel. He handed it to Brady. 'I'd like to see that monkey of yours.'

Brady started to sketch, taking his time - sketching always relaxed him. He began with the monkey's sad eyes. He had to pick out every detail before he could move on to the next feature.

Gus watched on as though he had nothing else to do with his day, and this was worth savouring.

Brady moved onto the grim expression of the monkey's mouth.

Gus laughed. 'Are you sure you're not drawing me there, fella?'

Brady laughed heartily, but then resumed his concentration. After the mouth and the short pencil strokes deployed for the button nose, he opened out the rest of the face, the brandished white hair nearest the main features, and then fanning out extravagantly - the darkening strands which looked like fireworks jetting away in all directions. He handed the notebook back to Gus.

He looked at it closely. 'I love it, thank you.'

'You're welcome.'

'Could you write its' name on there, so I don't forget. My memory ain't what it used to be.'

Brady wrote *White-Cheeked Spider Monkey* in neat, small print, but slowly. He didn't write very often - he added to *Gus from Brady.*

'If you ain't built up any Green Credits, then you'll have to start from scratch. Seems unfair to me. If you've been looking after animals in the rain forests, then you deserve to be a Green Credit Millionaire in my mind.'

'Where did they start?'

'Sattva Systems™ started issuing them for every time you did something good for the environment. They told people to look after them, to nurture them because one day they might be used as an unofficial currency like Bitcoin.'

'I suppose Bitcoin has gone as well.'

'No Internet, no cyber-currency. People started to treat them like a collector's item, a badge of honour in the war against climate change - and because they were a physical thing, it kinda fulfilled an old-fashioned desire. Well, it did for me.'

'Surely, they would try to eliminate manufacturing things first, especially money, seeing as we had already gone cashless.'

Gus thought about this for a moment, 'Sometimes, you only see things with hindsight. It was as if they were planning for the final crash.'

'Do you think they knew it would happen?'

'The GreenRevs and Sattva Systems™ claimed they *guessed* that it would happen - viruses, solar storms - but they've never stated that they were responsible. People tend to admire visionaries - when their visions come true - but not terrorists.'

'So now, people are using these Green Credits as currency. Why aren't people stealing it - or other companies buying them up?'

Gus smiled, 'Because they can only be used by people who believe in helping the environment and have a track record on trying to save the planet, and they can only be given *freely*, and *freely* taken, with an open heart and mind.' Brady laughed, but Gus added, 'And they are only issued in small denominations, a hundred Greenback file is the highest - at least for now.'

'Ok, let's say a mugger robs the purse off an old lady, or there's a stick up at a liquor store...'

'Can't see there being any more liquor stores.'

'Whatever.' Brady took a deep breath. He was starting to become agitated and was in danger of losing the trust of this old-timer. 'What happens next?'

'For the old lady in question, she would be proud of her environmental record, and these, enzymes, hormones, whatever they call them - I ain't a biologist, would be in her body, and when she gives them over to somebody else, she holds them in her forefinger and thumb, and this checks for any stress levels, and sleep agents. The chip glows when it's ready, and the same process happens with the receiver. They said the chips, or Files as they are called now, ensure that we buy what we need, and not through the stimulus of acquiring *things*. It reduces over-consumption.'

Brady knew he would need time to let the implications of this sink in. 'Is there anything that people buy with these Green Credits that aren't just bare essentials?'

'Not that I know of - but I bet it's only a matter of time before somebody finds a workaround. That's what humans do. Someone will spoil it, either for greed or just for the hell of it.'

If I can figure this out first. Brady thought, *then I could make an absolute killing.*

An old woman's voice called out from across the street. 'Gus, honey, I got it.' She waved her Sattva™ Satellite Phone, still in its box, at Gus. 'Now, we can call our baby Claire in Montana.'

Gus smiled at Brady, 'Got to go. Nice meeting ya fella - and thanks for the drawing.'

BRADY WATCHED THE OLD couple stroll away. He wasn't hungry after his colossal first breakfast after escaping from Ridgecrest. He had a sense that his morning world was like a different planet, instead of being only about a half-hour walk from where he sat right now. He was feeling thirsty, though. He looked around - most of the shops were closed, apart from the odd GreenGrocers™. He laughed to himself. *They are actually called the GreenGrocers™.* He checked the area for cops or security, but he couldn't see any. He was in jeans and a T-shirt. *I shoulda worn something to hide stuff. I don't even have the money to buy a carrier - probably don't have none of those either.*

He spotted a sign above a small fountain indicating that this was a drinking station. He stood from his bench and went to check it out. He leant over the little jet of water and drank. As he straightened up, he heard a whirring sound, and at the side of the plinth, which caught the overflowing water for recycling, a slot emerged with a Green chip with a number *1* printed on it. He could only retrieve it by picking it up using his thumb and forefinger. As he did so, it glowed green in his grip. He also noted that the slot glowed green as if it was happy to deliver the One Green Credit File to him. A young teenage boy waited behind Brady - wanting to use the fountain.

Brady moved aside. 'Does this give you free money every time you take a drink?'

'You're funny, mister. It assesses how much you drank already. It read you when you took the Greenback. When it re-assesses that you need rehydrating, and you've chosen an eco-method of replenishment, then it will issue another, as a thank you from Mother Earth.'

'The locals call these Files, Greenbacks?'

'The kids do. My history teacher says this slang originated from more than two centuries ago when the commoners called their paper dollars Greenbacks.'

'What do you kids do for fun now? Y'know, now there's no Internet?'

'It hasn't been down for long.'

'Do you think they will get it back up and running?'

'I don't know. There's no way of communicating with anyone. I lost my friends in the UK to it first, and then we went down. My Dad says it will never recover - he says it's completely destroyed. He used to work in Cupertino. He knows about this stuff.'

'So, what are you going to do?'

The kid looked around. 'When the weather is good, we ride our GreenBikes™ and hang out down the park.'

Brady was determined to pick up intel on what the future markets could be. 'What do you miss doing?'

'Hologames. 3DI...'

'I heard of 3D Immersive games.'

The kid said, 'You haven't heard of Hologames?'

'I'm guessing it's to do with Holographs, Holograms, whatever.' Brady wasn't in the mood for taking grief from a kid. 'What about music, movies, TV, y'know, things like that?'

'Who's gonna do that if they ain't being paid? All the streamers are down - and out. They were all falling foul of the GreenRevs anyway. Love songs are binary - even World Music reinforced stereotypes. There's only the GreenRevs TV station left, and that is showing the Trad riots.'

'Trad riots?'

'The Traditionalists, the Non-Greens. They are outside the Green Safety Zones. It's great fun watching them loot, riot and fight each other over stuff that ain't gonna work no more. I saw this guy stagger out into the street carrying this massive TV - I wish I could see his face when he plugs it in and can only find one channel still going. It will be even funnier if he hasn't had an old-fashioned aerial installed to receive it!' He laughed, and Brady remembered what it was like at this kid's age. He would have found it funny as well.

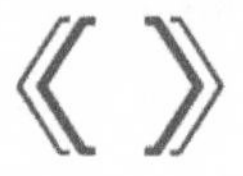

BRADY WANDERED OVER to the GreenGrocers™. He was going to see what One Greenback could buy him. Maybe, he could buy a bag and then steal whatever he needed. Brady went inside. He wasn't inspired. It was full of fruit, vegetables, and most of it proudly *locally sourced*. There were health foods and other essentials. But what there wasn't, was a sales assistant. He went to the pay station and picked up a biodegradable rice bag. He was alone in the store at the moment. He checked for CCTV. He couldn't see any, but he couldn't be sure - they had become tiny over the years. He decided to move quickly before another customer came into the store. He loaded his bag with snacks, drinks, and some assorted fruit and then made his getaway. As he tried to leave, he found he couldn't. He tried again, and his foot stuck at the edge of the doorway.

A robotic female voice said. *This is NanoSecurityFilm™, a trademark of Sattva Systems™. You appear to have forgotten to pay for your goods and services. Please return to the Pay Station to complete your purchase. Have a wonderful Green Day and thank you for saving Mother Earth.*

Brady angrily threw the shopping across the floor, and it scattered across a wide area, with apples and pears rolling away, some under the shop fixtures. He then strode angrily to the exit but was stopped again.

This is NanoSecurityFilm™, a trademark of Sattva Systems™. You appear to have forgotten to pay for your goods and services. Please return to the Pay Station to complete your purchase. This is the second helpful message. If you have changed your mind, then please return all goods to their original place of sale, and ensure they are in the same condition as when you selected them. Consideration of other customers is paramount to us here at your friendly and local GreenGrocers™.

Brady considered destroying the place with his bare hands. For a moment, he wondered if there was another exit out the back. But he was already convinced that these Green bastards would have thought about that. He gathered up the stuff on the floor, checked for damage, and placed them back on the shelves. Then he got down on his hands and knees and searched under the fittings. He retrieved the pears, rubbed them over with his biodegradable rice bag and placed them carefully back onto the display. He then retrieved the apples. One was just out of reach, so he had to lie on the floor to make his fingertips reach the edge of it. He struggled to tickle it into a position where he could grab it. 'You, absolute bastard piece of shit!' Finally, he flicked it against the back wall under the fixtures, and it bounced back far enough for him to take hold of it.

He slid back on the polished floor and stood up, holding his prize. He examined it. He noticed the bruising on the apple's skin. He went to the apple display and placed it into the array of fresh apples with the bruised side hidden.

He put the bag back on the pay station and went to leave.

This is NanoSecurityFilm™, a trademark of Sattva Systems™. You appear to have forgotten to pay for your goods and services. Please return to the Pay Station to complete your purchase. This is the third helpful message. If you have changed your mind, then please return all goods to their original place of sale, and ensure they are in the same condition as when you selected them. You need to pay for one damaged apple. Please deposit One File at the Pay Station. Consideration of other customers is paramount to us here at your friendly and local GreenGrocers™.

Brady screamed, 'Aaargh!' He remembered his One Green File, and he marched to the Pay Station. He put the File into the slot. The Pay Station said, in a male voice this time.

This is your NanoPayStation™, a trademark of Sattva Systems™. Your biological readings suggest you are at an elevated stress level and might be under pressure to deposit your File. This is a polite customer notice. Please be aware that one biodegradable bag has been removed and not paid for. Please return when you are willingly able to deposit your payments. Thank you for shopping with GreenGrocers™.

Brady knew it wouldn't work, but he was blazing. He charged toward the door, wondering if his power and bulk would punch a hole in the film. It didn't work. The NanoSecurityFilm™ enwrapped him, it even made him stand up straight and pushed his arms down his side and held him there, like a human statue.

This is NanoSecurityFilm™, a trademark of Sattva Systems™. You appear to have not understood our helpful messages intended to help you improve your shopping experience. Please wait until one of our representatives comes to assist you. Your custom is always our highest priority with your friendly and local GreenGrocers™.

4.ON DISPLAY

Brady had to endure the strange looks of other customers as they came and went. Some avoided looking at him. A father and young daughter were the first to openly discuss the Brady exhibit. The girl, a precocious child of about eight years old, asked her Daddy, 'Why is that man standing there?'

'That's what happens when you do bad things,' he said, 'He was probably stealing the food.'

'Shouldn't somebody call the police? I mean, he looks scary.'

'Don't worry, sweetheart. He can't hurt you. We shouldn't need the police anymore. Not here. This is a place of hearts and minds.'

The girl teased her Daddy, 'You used a binary term of endearment. You said, sweetheart. The teachers say we shouldn't use them anymore. Will you be trapped like the naughty man?'

He ruffled her hair and laughed, 'I think that wouldn't register on any level of criminality, but you're right, us older folks have still got a lot to learn. Now come on, let's pick up the food.'

Brady wondered which was worse, the public shaming or having to listen to, over and over again, the Pay Station thanking every shopper for their custom, followed by the doors thanking them for their honesty and wishing them a nice day.

A couple of bored teenagers, a boy and a girl, toyed with him for a while. As she stroked Brady's frame, the girl informed her male friend, 'He's quite a specimen - look at that physique. Are you sure he can't hear or see me?'

'He's in stasis. It happened to the Crow when he tried to burn down the school. He was stuck like that for hours until the caretaker found him. He still had the petrol can in his hand. And the NanoSecurityFilm™ had even sealed the petrol that had spilt from his can.'

'I heard about an attempted arson. What happened to him?'

'He was expelled from the community and sent to some members of his Trad Family on the outside. Apparently, if they didn't take him, then he would have to fend for himself. No second chances.'

Brady couldn't feel the girl stroking his arm. 'Look, his tattoos are fading.' This news alarmed Brady, but he couldn't move his eyes enough to look down. The boy moved in closer, 'But not all of them.'

'Why is that do you think?'

'I think it's cleaning out the synthetic materials.' He jabbed his fingers into Brady's arm, 'These look like traditional tatts - they are probably made with natural plant dyes.'

'Do you think he can feel me touching him?'

The youth traced his hands up through Brady's inner thigh, but then a voice announced:

This is NanoRespect™, a trademark of Sattva Systems™. A sexual act without the permission of the potential survivor has been detected. Please refrain. This is your first warning. The welfare of our consumers is our highest priority.

She laughed, 'You might get a File Note and fine for that.'

Brady had enough lateral vision to watch them leave the store hurriedly but laughing together. He fretted about his fading tattoos. *I paid a fucking fortune for them. It's part of who I am. They've no right to remove them from me.* He was then left again with the shoppers and the Sattva Systems™ announcements.

He caught snippets of conversations, an elderly couple complaining about machines talking to them, instead of being served by humans. He whole-heartedly agreed with that sentiment. He also heard a large group of eco-warrior types complaining about why they need technology of any description anymore until they listened to the warning of increased stress levels detected, asking them *if they were feeling ok*, followed by a *thank you for being a part of our Green Journey*. They hushed to whispers and completed their shopping, but he could tell, as they passed him on the way out, they weren't as happy about the situation as they should have been.

No pleasing some - they got the whole damn world, and it's still not enough. Spoilt fucking brats.

He wondered whether the Nano-Fucking-Whatevers would be picking up his own stress levels. He guessed he'd been here for about four hours. *I should be tiring, but I don't feel it*. He checked himself over, in his mind, wandering over every inch of his body. *I think, if anything, I'm feeling better than before*. He remembered the bit about the travellers and the planes and the disputed health benefits. *If I ever see Pops again, then I'll tell him about this.* However, this thought embarrassed him. *Getting caught in a heist is manly and something to be proud of - a badge of honour. This is pathetic - caught stealing groceries.*

Suddenly he heard a lot of noise from outside of the shop. He couldn't see, but he could hear it from further down the High Street. He heard slamming vehicle doors, and then it sounded like a riot had broken out. He couldn't make out clearly what they were shouting. There wasn't any coherent chanting like there would be at a demonstration. This was more like a round-up. He picked up snippets of angry voices. 'Fucking get your hands off me. You've no right...I live here, you sonofabitch...You can't make me leave...' The only responses from the Green side he could pick up on was the mention of, 'A Green Adjudication Panel will assess your claim...You are not Green...It is not a family membership deal...' He wondered why the clingfilm wasn't working on them. *Maybe I'm special.*

There was more slamming of van doors, and then Brady picked up on the demonstrators pounding from within the vehicle. This went on for about an hour before calm and then eerie silence descended - apart from the incessant robotic shop announcements. Brady began to wonder if he'd been forgotten about amid all the drama.

Brady was held in suspended animation for six hours when at last, somebody turned up and started talking to him as if she might free him from his GreenGrocers™ nightmare. She was a petite slender black woman, in her early twenties, he guessed. *I'll break her in half like a twig if I must.* Then he thought better of it. *If they have this level of security for a fucking bruised apple...*

'Hi there. I'm Lizzie. I'll Unfilm you, but you'll have to be assessed by the Disciple. I'm not convinced you are one of us, but we don't judge people on their appearances. The Disciple will decide if you are eligible to stay here or whether you belong in the Trad world.'

Brady tried to answer but couldn't move.

'All you need to do now is bring your anger and stress levels under control, and the Film will leave you and return for recycling.'

She waited patiently. Brady was still dwelling on the lost investment of his tattoos. The Pay Station and the Exit were making their Sattva Systems™ announcements for the hundredth time. It was not conducive to bringing Brady to a calm state. A dog caught his eye, a mangy old mutt to most people, but Brady thought it might help him calm his fraught emotional state if he imagined sketching it. He pictured a fresh sheet of paper and a stick of charcoal, and he began to draw, starting with the eyes. Within a minute, he noticed the weight being retaken by his feet as he was placed back on the ground. He wondered at the strength of the SecurityFilm™ - as he now assessed that he had been held a few inches above the ground the whole time. He had a tingling sensation as he sensed the Film was leaving his body. He couldn't explain how he knew, but he intuited that it departed from within him, and not just layers on his skin.

Lizzie smiled, 'Much better. Welcome back.'

'Am I under arrest?'

'No. We haven't got a suitable or humane place to detain you. Only people who want to be here, in the spirit of saving Her, can stay. Those who don't - simply have to go and make their way in the old world.'

'Great. Then I'll be off then. I don't want to be here a minute longer than necessary. Bye.'

He went to walk out of the exit when he was stopped - again.

This is NanoSecurityFilm™, a trademark of Sattva Systems™. Your shopping indiscretions have not been rescinded by the Disciple of your community. The NanoMarkers™ in your system need to be assessed before you can travel freely within the Green Community. Have a happy and Green Day.

Lizzie smiled, 'We won't hurt you. We haven't harmed you - have we? We just need to follow the protocol. Please, walk with me. This won't take long, and then you can go on your way.'

Brady felt like he was with a parole officer. *There must be some way to fool that SecurityFilm™ stuff.* 'I suppose if I had been in a vehicle or a confined space then that thing couldn't have got to me. Is it just a shop security system?'

She knew he was pumping her for information, and he wasn't particularly subtle about it. 'The Film is made up of the finest, tiniest NanoBots™ imaginable. If you were in a vehicle, they would secure the entire vehicle - if you were driving. On the other hand, if you were a passenger threatening the driver, they would seep into the vehicle almost instantaneously and secure you - the Security Protocols™ would track the vehicle. There is no escape because there is nothing small enough to prevent the Security Protocols™ from entering and securing the transgressor.'

Brady knew she was right. *There's no escaping these Security Protocols™ Machines.* He related it to being in jail, and the period after exploring all means of escape - and concluding that there weren't any - and then the acceptance that followed. 'Ok, how did they know to attack me?'

'The Security Protocols™ didn't attack you. They don't spy on you. They are here for everybody's safety and mental wellbeing.' She looked at him and could see him attempting to work out the puzzle. She wasn't sure if he could understand scientific rationales but tried to enlighten him. If she could convince him, then he would be less of a problem to West McFarland in the long run, 'It detects signals in movements, signals given off in the air, hormones and pheromones. After millions of experimental trials and decades of research, they can spot signals that the human body emits. If you even thought about harming someone, even an animal, the Security Protocols™ would pick up the signal before you even had the time to act on this impulse.'

Brady considered Lizzie's explanation and what it meant to his predicament as they walked.

He knew they were heading south. It brought back a lot of memories. They passed the High School, where he learned how to be a gang member. As they ventured further southwards he looked, with a mixture of pride and regret, at the places where he graduated, the Central Valley Modified Community Correctional Facility and the Golden State Correctional Facilities. He laughed when he thought about them completing a new build, just for him to live in later, the Ridgecrest Supermax Prison.

Lizzie watched him chuckle to himself as he passed the Correctional Facilities.

He pointed at the buildings. 'What did you do with the inmates?'

'We let them go.'

'Surely, they created mayhem before they left?'

'We gave them a demonstration of our SecurityFilm™ and said if they left the city limits immediately, then we wouldn't come looking for them. They chose freedom.'

'And the Supermax?'

'The prison officers had their own ideas about what should happen to hardened criminals. They acted before we could - unfortunately.'

'This SecurityFilm™. Is it well known, y'know, what it can do?'

'Sattva Systems™ and the GreenRevs, have been preparing for the Revolution for decades - some developments were held back until the Glorious Green Day arrived. They thought we were conspiracy theorists and a cult, but we had trillions of dollars backing our cause. Sattva Systems™ had to play their games - to look like any other greedy Corp - even we had doubts, but Bodhi's love for Her was beyond doubt, and now that love has been realised. We are the Green Revolution, the GreenRevs, and the hundred-year plan has begun.'

He rolled his eyes. 'Good luck with that.'

She ignored his sarcasm. 'We are nearly there.' He saw a modern structure - he didn't have to guess that it would be environmentally friendly, and eco this and that. They entered the compound, and banners lined the pathway: *Welcome to your New Green Town Hall.*

A man in a robe left the hall and came out to meet them. He had crystal clear green eyes, his bare feet glided across the dusty path, and the Sun seemed to glow around him. *Fuck. This guy has really got the Jesus look nailed down.* He laughed at his own unintended pun. *I see how this is gonna go. He's going to try and sell me his magic potions. I've seen these con artists do their tricks a thousand times already. Well, Brady Mahone ain't goin' to fall for this crock of shit.*

The Jesus figure gasped at the sight of Brady. He inspected his tattoos. 'My God.'

'Cain - what is it?' Cain flashed Lizzie a look which she took to mean as *later*. He called out, 'Hey, Siddha.' A slender Asian man came over. Brady looked around. He hadn't noticed before that all the people here seemed to be of slim build. *Must be all the vegan shit they eat that makes 'em all so scrawny.*

'Siddha, I want you to look after our guest for a short while. Get him food, drink or whatever else he needs.'

Siddha turned and said sarcastically, 'And what do you require, sir?'

'The name's Brady, no need for all the phony pleasantries. I need the bathroom.'

'Of course - Brady. If you'd care to follow me.'

Cain watched Brady follow Siddha and waited until he was inside the Town Hall. He whispered to Lizzie, 'What do we know about him? I notice he has a Satt™.'

'He shouldn't be here for starters. Mrs Wilson said that he saved her from some troublesome youths on the wrong side of the Shell™.'

'And why was she there?'

'They were throwing rocks at her car - she forgot that she was safe. She panicked and veered off the road - there is a lot of last-minute travel before the old vehicles stop working. They tried to attack her, but Brady intervened. The problem is that he managed to go through the SecurityFilm™ as if it wasn't there.'

'He must be Green, then?'

'I don't think so. He had no Green Credits. He attempted to steal from the GreenGrocers™ - but there, all the SecurityFilms™ and Protocols™ worked perfectly. Unless the NanoShell™ let him in because he saved Mrs Wilson?'

Cain thought for a moment, 'No. It isn't that. It doesn't work that way.'

'What do you think?'

'I'm going to contact Sissy or Bodhi with this. It's important. I just can't figure out why.'

Lizzie gasped, 'You know Bodhi!'

'I've had dealings through an intermediary for years, but I have never been in direct contact with him. Our business had to be conducted in the utmost secrecy.'

'But you are a Disciple; therefore, you must have been granted an audience for him to bestow the status upon you.'

'I didn't meet him individually. I was one of an audience of more than a thousand Initiates - and there were thousands of these Green Initiations. I am a Disciple, but that is not unusual. One day, we will all be Disciples. All I have that marks me out as different from the other townsfolk is that I receive the next version of NanoSuit™ ahead of you. I am Orange™, whereas you will all - very soon - be given a chance to buy the Red™. I am not a chosen one - I am simply an *early* one.'

Lizzie was a believer but still found his quasi-religious demeanour a little pompous at times. Still, he had access to the future plans of Sattva Systems™, which nobody else in McFarland had. *And what we have achieved already has been pretty fucking awesome.* 'So, you've seen Bodhi. What was he like, y'know, in the flesh, like?'

Cain looked at her with his crystal green eyes. 'He looked remarkably like this man who calls himself Brady.'

'It can't be him. This Brady creature is a Trad-Alpha-Male. He's exactly the kind of man we would have been afraid of - before the Green Revolution.'

'Bodhi did say we would be tested. There were always going to be anomalies in the implementation phase, and he said we would have to watch, learn and report back.'

'Is that what you are going to do?'

'Yes. I want you to talk with Brady and find out more about what he wants from me - us. Bring him along to the Town Hall meeting later this evening. In the meantime, I'll Satt™ someone at Sattva Systems™ about this development. You never know - even Bodhi himself might want to discuss this with me.'

'Wow, holy shit! Can you imagine? He's like the King of the World right now.'

'He is just one step ahead of the Disciples at the moment. He has developed and taken the Yellow™. He has promised that by the end of the one-hundred-year plan, Bodhi will have no more power or Green Credits than any other man, woman, or child. We will have saved Her, and we will live out our lives serving Her. He is only a guide.' He paused, 'Is there anything else I should know?'

'He says his full name is Brady Mahone, and there was another weird thing - his synthetic tattoos were erased exceptionally quickly. As you know, it usually takes weeks. He had natural tattoos which were completely unaffected.'

'You used to have tattoos. You are more of an expert on this than I am.'

'They are the sort which Readers - spiritual tattooists design. They read the receiver and then decide upon designs which will protect or guide the recipient.'

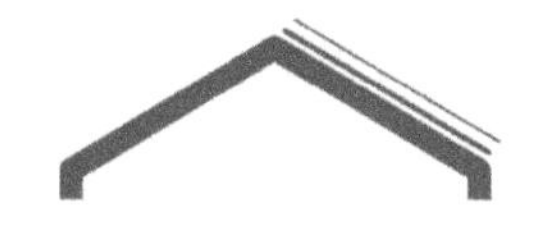

5.TOWN HALL MEETING

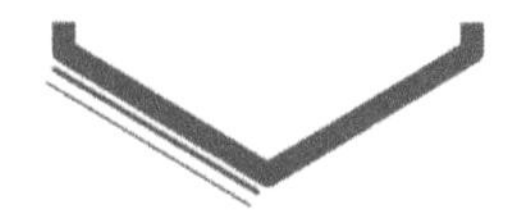

Brady made the most of Lizzie's hospitality during the afternoon. He ate a lot of fruit but gave the vegetables, beans, and rice a miss. 'I'm not into all this rabbit food nonsense,' he had informed her, as politely as he could muster under the circumstances. He enjoyed the ice-cream though, as long as he didn't ask what was in it. As they chatted, Brady assumed they knew everything about him, but still gave absolutely nothing away - he could spot a good-cop interrogation from a mile away.

He asked her about the meeting, as they watched the volunteers placing out the chairs. 'How many are coming tonight?'

'We are preparing for twelve thousand - should everyone decide to attend.'

'The population of McFarland is bigger than that, isn't it?'

'The West Side of Highway 99 took the Green Incentives in the fifties. Those who didn't like the culture slowly moved over to the Traditional East as the decades moved by. They thought they were wealthier because of their accumulation of material goods. It sped up the migration when in the last few years, the West Side began to reduce its reliance on the Internet. We operated on slow speeds to aid the withdrawal symptoms. That was tough, but worth it in the end. They had their chance to do it our way - now they can have the Wild West – or rather, East - they always pined for.'

But Brady had travelled West from Ridgecrest. He knew he shouldn't have been able to be here at all - if all Lizzie was saying was true.

She continued her spiel as though giving him a guided tour. 'This was the blueprint for most towns and cities across the globe. The powers that be saw communities that were impeccably behaved towns, which used up very little of the local resources, and were becoming less reliant on the Internet - as a curiosity but ultimately harmless. Better still, as this was happening all over the world, the problems created by climate change receded dramatically, saving them billions in the currencies. What's not to love?'

Brady didn't take the bait. He would let them complete their investigations on him, and only return when he had figured out a way to make it pay.

'Do you want to give them a hand with the chairs?' she said. 'It'll keep you busy.'

'What's the pay?'

'Nothing. Except for the warm glow of knowing that you helped our community.'

'Yeah, all the same darling - I think I'll pass.'

She thought for a moment. It wouldn't do any harm to test him out. 'There are a few broken wooden chairs where the legs have come out of their sockets. With a bit of brute force and natural glue, you could probably fix them.'

He looked disdainfully at the sad-looking chairs beyond the stage area, near the fire exit. *I could escape, I suppose - but I could gain some valuable intel if I stick around.*

'I could give you two Green Credits for your contribution to our community.'

'Ok. Deal.' *It won't hurt to have some currency, and two Greenbacks would have got me out of the shop bind.*

He wandered over to the broken chairs. He spotted the store cupboard and found some wood glue. He saw craft tools but decided against trying to steal any of them. He'd had enough excitement for one day. He sat cross-legged on the floor and put glue into the round holes. He did need a firm grip to generate enough force to jam the legs into the holes.

Just as he'd finished Lizzie returned. *This is no coincidence – she must have had me watched.* Still, he gave nothing away. 'All done. They should last for years.'

She examined them and nodded. She closed her right hand, then looked into his eyes. She then closed her eyes as if she had gone into a momentary trance. When she opened her eyes again, she opened her right hand and revealed a Two Green File chip, which Brady thought looked like one of those old-fashioned SD cards. She put it between her thumb and forefinger, and it glowed green. Brady took it off her, with his big fingers struggling to grasp the part of the File left showing. As he did, it glowed once more.

'I give this *freely* to you, for a job well done.' She smiled mischievously. 'This can only be given or redeemed by another Green Community Member - it has no value to Trads or outsiders, but you already know that - don't you?'

'Of course,' he lied. 'Everybody knows that.' He made his ignorance evident to her when he asked, 'It doesn't have to be used in this community though - does it?'

'No. It can be used in any Green Community - anywhere on Mother Earth.'

Brady put his Two Greenbacks in his pocket. 'Here, I'll get you a Distor™,' Lizzie said, wanting to laugh at his incomprehension. 'It stands for Dispenser and Storage. It will keep your Green Credits from being damaged. It keeps a tally for you.' She added, jokingly, 'Don't worry, they are free of charge.' She briefly went into the storage cupboard and returned with a small tube and handed it to

Brady. 'Don't be concerned about its small size. You can transfer small change to larger File amounts as you attain more.'

He held it and then dropped his Files into it. 'Hold the top of the tube with your thumb and forefinger,' she said. When he did, a luminous green display stated: TWO GREEN CREDITS. *They put the fucking Green word on everything. It's fucking brainwashing, that's what this is.*

'Great. Thanks. I'll have fun spending them.'

She laughed and took his hand. 'The Meeting will be starting soon. I'll show you to your seat. You'll be at the back, as you seem a little unsure of how things work around here. Plus, we want our audience to be as relaxed as possible, and you are a bit intimidating - if you don't mind me saying...'

'Fine with me. What happens afterwards?'

'Cain wants to have a chat with you. He wants to know more about you. I'm going to organise a place for you to stay overnight, and tomorrow, you can do whatever you want to do.'

'You mean I can leave if I want?'

'Of course. But if you want to stay, I think you might need help assimilating into our way of life.'

Fuck that, he thought. *This isn't how I want to live my life. I'm not changing one prison for another.*

She showed him to his seat and then rushed off as though she had a lot to do - or organise. Brady sat back, putting his feet on the back of the chair in front of him. *It's not like there's anybody sittin' there yet.* He looked around at the very ordinary-looking people slowly filling the hall. There were no reservations, so it was hardly surprising that no-one sat anywhere near Brady. For something to do, he checked off in his mind the odd person he recognised in the crowds. The old man, Gus, smiled at him, but mostly, anyone who had seen Brady earlier pretended not to notice him. Siddha beamed at him beatifically, and Brady smiled back at him sarcastically. *I know a snitch when I see one.*

The lights dimmed a little, and a few test shots lit up the big screen and the few smaller screens that surrounded the audience. They were followed by a few sound tests, as each individual set of speakers were checked. *They obviously want everybody to get the message.* Then the lights went back up. It was 7:50 pm. Brady looked in the direction of the projectionist. *I know him. I did time with him at Juvie.* He unhooked his legs from the chair in front and pulled himself to his full imposing height and walked over to the scrawny white guy who operated the projector. Brady stuck out his big hand. 'Hey man, I'm Brady - remember me?'

The fear in his eyes told Brady that he did, even before he could answer. 'Yeah,' he said, extending a nervous hand in return. 'Vance. Uhhh, look. I've been going straight for five years now. I don't want no trouble, and the movie will be starting soon. So, you can see I'm...'

'Hey, calm down, man. I just want to ask you a few things.' Brady didn't want to make friends with this low-life – a mugger, if he remembered right - and he was aware he would have to get to the point. 'What do people want around here that the regime doesn't allow them?'

'It's early days sir...err, Mister...too soon to tell.'

He moved in menacingly. 'Well, give me an idea.'

'If you stress me out, I might not be allowed to operate the projector - you must know how the SecurityFilm™ works.'

Brady did, all too well. He backed off - a little. 'Look, Vance, quit acting like a baby and just help a brother out here.'

Vance looked around, to see if anyone was watching, but the crowds had their eyes trained onto the stage area - waiting for the show to begin. 'I only know what I deal with.'

Brady picked up a blank black file and examined it.

Vance gulped and said, 'People are already missing the pre-crash stuff - the kind of things that will be banned here. Things that could be put on those, the Information Files.' He looked at the clock. He couldn't be late, and he had his final checks to carry out. 'Sattva made these files in the last few years. The general public wasn't that interested because everything was streamed. I now know, of course, that Sattva had transferred millions of acceptable items from the Internet to use in this environment.'

'Like what, exactly?'

'Stuff for educating the kids. Lots of scientific things and approved entertainments.'

'And it's all boring, and some of these whining Greens still want a drop of the good stuff - ain't that right.'

'Yes - yes. They are worried that the kids will get bored once the novelty of the Revolution wears off...'

'And you can supply them?'

'Not from in here. They should have old machines on the outside for manufacturing the Bootleg Files. I'm an Inner, you see. If you have a non-approved criminal record, but have proved your Green credentials, then you can remain, but I'm not allowed to come and go out of the Community Perimeter.'

'What's an approved criminal record?'

'Political activism - arrested at demonstrations, hacking for the cause...'

'Ok. Let's cut to the chase. If I could get this stuff, would it be worth my while?'

'Yes. People here would give a lot of Green Credits for high-quality Bootlegs. I could be your middleman,' he added, weakly.

'Yeah, sure - so you could rip me off. You'd buy them from me, and re-sell them for a fortune, or maybe you'd pirate them and start your own business – right?'

'No. Not at all. The Green Credit system won't allow it. It works on a system of give and receive. A purchased Black File turns to Green when the transaction is completed between you and your buyer. The newly formed File can only be used by the person who bought it from you. The only Files allowed to be replicated and passed on are the Green Community Information Films.'

'So, what's in it for you?'

'I thought you could pay me in stock. Y'know, you could give me a spare copy for my own use. I love old movies, that's why I've taken this role to earn my own Green Credits. It's that or farm labouring, working on the Highways or Operation Clean-up - this is a dream job compared to that.'

Brady frowned, 'I've had that SecurityFilm™ attack me. Is this legal enough for me to get away with this kind of activity?'

'Yes. As a culture, our community was generally against manufacturing. I say, generally, because there was a lot of things that they took a pragmatic approach with. There were pockets of physical software around - very little, to be fair - but it did enable people to trade, and there was no blowback from the Security Protocols™. It didn't even issue any warnings.'

Brady placed a big hand on Vance's shoulder and smiled, though there was still a hint of a threat in his eyes. 'Write down your address - and if I track down some of this stuff, I'll come find you.'

Vance wrote his address in his notebook and ripped the page out and gave it to Brady. 'It's a warzone out there – I mean, so I've been told - and only the conspiracy freaks were into this stuff. It was old-fashioned tech, but some wanted to keep their stuff off-grid - especially the more disturbing entertainments, shall we say. They'll be hard to track down and they won't trust you - they're paranoid.'

'That's my problem, not yours.' *It's one thing getting to be a Green Credit millionaire,* he thought, *but what the fuck have they got here to spend it on?*

'Hey man. If ya don't mind me asking? How did you get in here?'

'Just lucky, I guess.' Brady looked up and spotted Siddha coming toward them. He said, 'Is everything ok, Vance?'

'Yes, Siddha. Everything's workin' just fine.'

Siddha looked at both of them, and asked, 'Do you two know each other?'

Brady smiled broadly. 'I was just checking out his equipment. I was getting a bit bored, sitting all on my lonesome.'

Vance held out his hand and offered Brady a Blank File. 'Here, take this as a souvenir.'

Siddha watched closely as Brady took it. It didn't turn green. 'It's not a Green File,' Vance said. 'It isn't part of the system, until it's activated. You're going to need a lot of these.'

'Can old used or pre-recorded Files be overwritten?'

'Not here, but they should be in the Trad world.'

'Thanks, man.'

Brady returned to a seat. Other people had taken his, and the ones nearby. He didn't need to check, but he knew Siddha would be keeping a close eye on him from now on. He wasn't happy. He felt hemmed in by the people around him, and his seat was too small for his frame. He shuffled and fidgeted. He knew he was annoying the people around him, but also knew they wouldn't have the nerve to challenge him.

The lights went down, and the Jesus-like figure of Cain glided across to the centre of the stage. A spotlight picked him out, and he spoke gently into the tiny microphone affixed to his white robe.

'Welcome - all of you. Welcome to the Green Community of McFarland, California in the United States of America, and now a member of the Green World Alliance. Over the next few days, there will be meetings, just like this, to introduce the New Green Deal for Mother Earth. Our goal is to repair the damage to the planet caused by toxic humanity over more than two hundred years in the false name of progress. We are not a backwards-looking society. We are a future-forward society - and this is just the beginning.'

The front rows of the audience stood up and clapped and cheered. Brady guessed these were the activists of the GreenRevs. Brady observed the audience he could see in the semi-darkness. *I notice the liberal lefties aren't quite as enthusiastic. They just want to know what's in it for them - same as it ever was.*

Cain continued with his quiet but authoritative speech. He was preaching from the pulpit to his Green believers. 'We will be implementing the cutting-edge technologies which have been available for the last fifty years but weren't utilised because governments took the bribes of the dirty businesses and corporations to suppress the Green developments. They left us no choice but to ruin them and do things our way. The right way.'

Brady wondered whether everybody here knew they were going to lose everything they owned. He could tell by the clothes they were wearing that they weren't poor. *They musta really believed in this shit - and fair-play to them, they backed the winners. I could do with finding out what made them so sure to bet that big.*

'We are going to show you a movie from our partners at Sattva Systems™,' Cain announced, 'and afterwards we will have a Q & A.' He nodded toward Vance, and the lights went down. The screens in front of, and around, the audience flickered into life. Brady spotted Vance load the Black File into the side of the old-tech projector.

'Sattva Systems™ have always dedicated ourselves to leading-edge...' Brady showed some interest in the action sequences at the start of the movie. There were scenes from all over the world - of governments using every kind of military, chemical and biological interventions, to try and rid themselves of the GreenRevs, but they were impervious to all attacks. *I thought the guy on the TV had been hit in the face by a bullet,* he thought. *But he didn't even seem to notice.* The audience only gasped when one government started to threaten to kill the children they had put in place as human shields - and there were tears when that threat was carried out - but it didn't deter the GreenRevs. There was a map of the world, showing all the countries changing from the pink and blues - to Green.

The film lost Brady, though, when they began the tour of the labs at Sattva Systems™. He didn't often sleep, but if there was one thing that could do it, it was being sent back to school.

The NanoTech™ Division pioneered the purification and filtration systems which could prevent and protect any attacks on the water delivery into your Green Communities...Exotic properties...vaccine delivery...Diamonoid shell...

Brady began to doze off while the jargon fell into white noise at the edge of his senses. Nanoscopic level...quantum effects...analyse electrons with colliding photons...frequency of light.

He had leaned back in his chair, and he awoke with a start as it was just about to tip over. The people he could see around him looked like they were in a trance. *I can't say I find this particularly fascinating,* he thought. 'Einstein's photo-electron effect where direction, speed and energy...' Brady mocked the narrator out loud in a whiny voice. 'Einstein's photo-electron effect where direction, speed and...' He heard a woman shush at him. 'Fuck you, Lady Know-it-all.'

Still, Brady did quieten down. Typically, somebody would laugh with him, if he had said something like this in a cinema - but not here. *I also don't want any more of that fucking SecurityFilm™ on me,* he thought. *I suppose that means that Brady gotta be good and stay out of trouble.*

He endured more of the Sattva Systems™ propaganda. Superconducting cube levitation...magnetic train...target individual cells...self-replicating cells...life enhancement.

Brady missed the movie ending, his mind having wandered. He noticed the audience around him, clapping politely, and the cheering from the distant front-of stage dwellers. And then the lights went up. Cain returned to the stage to take questions. There were a number of fear-based questions. What if they try to attack our communities? What if they try to steal our Green Credits? What do we do if we get sick? Cain reassured them - they had thought of everything. He repeatedly referred his questioners back to a portion of the movie, to explain in technical detail, how the NanoTech worked to protect them.

A girl of about nine-years-old asked 'Will the animals in Africa be protected?'

Cain beamed. 'What a marvellous question. I'll tell you the truth. Our NanoShells™, like the one which protects our community of McFarland, have been activated around Nature Reserves and National parks all over the world and especially in Africa. Our GreenRev explorers installed them - it took twelve years to complete. There is a short-term issue, and that is with the poachers who are still inside the perimeter. This means, some animals will die, but as the poachers leave the perimeter then they won't be able to get back in. Only those with the Green Credentials and Green Credits will ever be allowed to go into this land.' He looked up from the girl to address the whole audience. 'This thinking is at the heart of everything we do.'

An old woman asked cynically, 'Who out of all of us here will benefit most from this revolution? You look like you are doing ok from this - being our self-appointed leader and all.'

'You raise a valid point - and one in which I will answer fully.'

This I gotta hear, Brady thought.

'We are progressing through the Nanowear™ Colours. I will always be one colour ahead of you, but at the end of the process, we will all - each and every one of you - will all be on the same highest level, and all at the same time. We will all be equal.'

'That's all well and good,' the old woman said. 'But how long before this dream comes true? I haven't got long left in this world. Not that I'm ungrateful. I've lived to see this day - but what about my children and grandchildren?'

'Gloria – is it Gloria?' She nodded. 'Even your InfraRedPrimer™ NanoWear™ will give you some limited life-preserving and life-enhancing properties. Could I be so bold as to enquire about your age? It is so hard to tell with the effects of NanoWear™?'

'I am eighty-four.'

I woulda guessed around sixty, Brady thought.

'You should comfortably go beyond one-hundred years old,' Cain said, 'but you might only attain the Orange™ by that time - which is where Bodhi Sattva is now. Put another way, you could reach the levels of the Leader of Sattva Systems™ within twenty years. Bodhi only experiments with new developments on his own body first. He does not agree with animal or human trials. He considers this deeply unethical. When he is satisfied that the latest developments are safe, and working as they should be, then he moves all the Disciples up to his previous level, and then you all will move up a level.'

He peered intently into Gloria's eyes. 'Alas, you may not see the end - but after many more years of a healthy and active life, I'm hoping you will see just how wonderful the future will look for your family.'

An audience member shouted, 'What will we need to do? How much will the next level cost?'

'You are InfraRed™, and I am Red™,' Cain laughed. 'What I have is the NanoArmour™ you saw in the movie. All the activists received this, like so many of my comrades down in the front rows.' Again, more cheers. 'You will all have to earn one-hundred Green Credits. You earn these with your environmental good works - this helps Mother Earth. Some of you good people have already acquired this amount from before today, but you cannot buy the RedNanoWear™ early. We don't want a society of haves and have-nots. You all have to have the Green Credits earned and then use them. When you have the Red™, you will be safe to travel anywhere, even in the lands left to the Trads. They will be unable to harm you.'

Now, I know what to get those Green Credits for, Brady thought. *I gotta have me one of those Suits™.*

'And after, you can all save up for the Orange™. I can't give you the details but trust me - you are all going to want that. It's amazing.'

6.CLOSE CALL

After the meeting had finished, Brady searched out Lizzie. He needed some action and thought he might be able to persuade her to join him for the evening. When he found her, he started helping the nearby volunteers to stack away the thousands of chairs. He didn't need to know why they were doing this or what they were going to use the space for. *This will impress Lizzie – women like her like a strong, helpful guy*. He looked her up and down, watching the way she moved. *She keeps herself in good shape - I like that*. Lizzie sensed Brady was watching her, but her job was to keep an eye on him, so she wasn't overly concerned.

After showing off his power and strength - compared to the other volunteers - and not too subtly - he made his move. 'Interesting movie tonight.'

She smiled. 'I'm glad you thought so. I hope you learned a few things.' *Even though you looked half-asleep through most of it - you're not exactly the brightest star in the sky*, She thought.

I hope I don't have to pass a fucking exam to get in her pants, he thought. 'Yes, I did. This Nano stuff is everywhere. Is it watching us twenty-four-seven?'

'Of course not. We would need streaming for that, and that doesn't work anymore.'

He carried on stacking chairs, and Lizzie did the same next to him. He noticed that it seemed easy for her. 'So, how does it happen to be around at exactly the right time?'

'It monitors the physiology of all living things. It reacts if there are heightened negative stress markers. There will come a time when it will work internally - this will be a leap in medical advancement. But it can already work, externally.'

'Like repairing sunburn.'

He does know something then, she thought. *I was beginning to wonder.*

'Somebody mentioned a place for me to stay tonight?' he said.

She knew where this was going. 'I believe Siddha is arranging your accommodation.'

'Couldn't I stay at yours?'

'Well, you don't waste any time.' *I'll string him along first and see if he has anything interesting to offer*, she thought. *It could be a good opportunity for intel.* 'You can walk back with me when we've finished here. I live in the same house as Siddha and Cain. We'll see how we get along, first.'

As they walked back, Brady tried to be as charming as he could, although he let her do the talking. *These liberal-lefty girls love the sound of their own voices, which is fine by me, as I don't have a lot to say - and they are tricky, all too easy to say the wrong thing*, he thought, zoning out. *Keep nodding and smiling Brady-boy. She'll think you're one of those good listeners. Don't lose her now - she's wriggling on the line.*

'Nearly there now,' she said. 'Just a few hundred yards to go.'

He struggled to keep his self-control, but there was a question bothering him – and he needed an answer. 'Why are you living with Siddha and Cain? Don't you get your own place here?'

'In the Green Communities,' she said, 'there is no more property ownership. Technically, in the Trad areas, there shouldn't be, as all the electronic deeds have been wiped.'

'I know plenty of people that won't give up their homes that easily.'

'We're not concerned with them. They can fight over their petty possessions if they want to.'

They'll fight to the death over them, he thought. *But maybe that's the plan.* He knew he'd hinder his romantic prospects if he opened up the debate, so he asked, as calmly as he could, 'So, who owned the place you're staying in before...y'know?'

'It was Siddha's. We are happy for people to stay in their original homes because they are emotionally attached and connected to them, but now, they have to let others move in where they have spare bedrooms. It's environmentally sound, and they pick up extra Green Credits for their generosity.'

'Why would they willingly agree to do that? It just doesn't seem very... American.'

'Risk and reward. If the NanoWear™ develops as hoped - then the life expectancy of every Green Community dweller could double, or even triple - especially for today's and tomorrow's children.'

Brady never wanted kids, so this was an abstract concept for him, but he could understand the price to pay for decades more life was worth it.

When they arrived, the front door wasn't locked. He could see Siddha, Cain and about a dozen others in deep but seemingly informal conversation in the lounge as Lizzie led up the stairs. *Straight to the bedroom is an excellent sign*, he thought, *and I don't have to talk to the weirdos first.*

As soon as the bedroom door closed, he grabbed her, and kissed her and then they tumbled onto her bed. He half-expected to be covered in SecurityFilm™, but he wasn't. *I'm good to go.*

She began to hurriedly undress. Brady was hungry for her. She watched him take his T-shirt off. *This should be interesting*, she thought. *Fucking an alpha-male Trad. At least he's in good shape.*

'I haven't got any - y'know – protection,' Brady whispered.

She smiled. 'That's ok. I'm Filmed, and I'm Red™.'

'Will I notice it?'

'Only one way to find out.' She kissed him, and then they made love.

Later that evening, they made love again. Afterwards, Brady felt more tired than he could remember. He yawned. 'Sorry babe. I don't usually fall asleep.'

'I've heard that one before.'

'No, really. I hardly sleep at all, but since I've been in this place...'

'Lack of stress. You've probably spent your whole life looking over your shoulder for the next threat - but here, there aren't any.'

He didn't need to give this much thought. 'It's true - you're right. It's just a bit boring.'

'You're saying I'm boring?' she teased. She grabbed his cock, and it responded. 'I think you're answering in your own way.'

He flung her over and entered her hard. He had been reasonably restrained, out of something like politeness, before - but he might not see her again after tomorrow. *I'm going to take what I need*, he thought. *I'm going to have you the way I want. I'm going to fucking enjoy this.* He fucked her as hard as he possibly could, and he held her in a bear hug, squeezing her to the point of hurting her.

But she didn't struggle or even seemed to notice his power. He looked at her face. Her eyes were closed, and she was panting softly, gently moaning. She opened her eyes slowly and smiled, then closed them again. As he powered into her, his arms squeezed her with such force that any average woman would snap. He squeezed her until he was exhausted, and he climaxed for the last time that night.

He fell away from her, breathing hard. She kissed him on the cheek. 'I'm going to sleep now,' she said.

Within minutes, Brady fell into a deep sleep, too.

At around 3am, Brady stirred. He could hear noises. There was a ringing sound in the room, and in the distance, he could hear gunfire. In his sleepy state, he was confused. Lizzie woke up. 'It's your Satt™ phone,' she said, rubbing sleep from her eyes.

Brady hadn't received a call on it - Lucian had looked after the set-up. He retrieved it from within the pile of discarded clothes. It kept ringing until he figured out how to answer it. 'Hello - who is it?'

'It's me - Lucky. The Hodgson Boys are attacking us. Archie's holding 'em off with the old machine gun, but they've split up. We can't hold out for long - even with a weapon.'

'How many are them?' Brady heard Lucian shouting over the machine gun noise to Archie.

'Archie said there are the two boys. Their Daddy is disabled and can't get out of the house without their help - and one of them's got a wife and baby.'

'Ok. Hold them off. I'm coming over.'

'What is it?' Lizzie said.

'You could say it's Trad problems. I don't want that fucking SecurityFilm™ to stop me going to help my Foster Daddy. I'm finding it fucking hard to keep my stress levels down.'

'Get dressed, stay calm. I'll go and get Cain. He's the appointed one and can stop the NanoTriggers™ if he is with you.'

Brady took a deep breath and dressed calmly. *I guess stealing knives from here is out of the question,* he thought. *I'll have to pick them up at the ranch.*

Cain stood in the doorway looking like a vision from the Bible, with his robe, beard and crystal green eyes.

'Thank you, Cain,' Brady said. 'I owe you one - we gotta hurry.'

'Where are we going?'

'The Mahone Ranch.'

Cain climbed into a bland, cream-coloured, ceramic FusionPowered™ vehicle, and Brady squeezed in beside him. He noticed Cain inserting a Green File which glowed green as the car whispered into life. 'The Mahone Ranch,' he said, 'with urgency.'

Brady watched him drive in conjunction with the car. *I wonder if the Satnav systems have been unaffected. It was as if they were working together*. 'If it's in emergency mode,' Cain said, 'it can sense my intentions with regard to cornering and braking.'

They quickly reached the point on the road where Brady had first entered the town. *These are clever bastards I'm dealing with,* he thought. *This could be some kind of ruse to get me to leave.* But Brady was beyond caring. He leapt out of the car, and Cain effortlessly kept pace with him. The unmistakable sound of Old Marvin the Machine Gun grew ever louder - the bullets pulsing, presumably every time some movement caught Archie's eyes.

Brady hadn't noticed that Cain had split away from him. *Fuck him*, he thought. *He probably wants to negotiate with the Hodgson Boys - ain't no point in that.* He could see Archie now, with Lucian behind him, peering into the darkness. 'Hey Lucky,' Brady hissed, between shots. 'It's me, Brady.'

Lucian looked around, picking him out in the gloom. 'Hey, man. Good to see you. We need help.' Brady noticed Lucian whispering to Archie, and then he patted Archie on the shoulder and left him nursing Old Marvin. Lucian made his way over nervously to Brady. 'One of those boys is trying to distract us by making movements near that fallen tree about a couple a hundred yards away. I think the other one has made it to the little wood on our right.

'I'm gonna grab a hunting knife and see if I can find him,' Brady said. 'You two concentrate on keeping the one in front of you nailed down.'

Brady went into the ranch and grabbed one of Archie's old hunting knives and circled back around the house toward the wooded area. He knew every square inch of this place, as he used to play there every day when he was a boy. For a hulk of a man, he was exceptionally light on his feet, unlike Gary Hodgson, who crunched his way along the narrow path between the trees. Brady crept up behind him.

Gary stopped, as if some instinct was trying to warn him, but it was too late. Brady grabbed Gary and slashed his throat so hard that it almost removed his head. Brady dropped the body on the floor and set off to locate Alan Hodgson. As he approached the edge of the treeline, he heard another round of machine gunfire. For a moment, he wondered if Archie had spotted his movement and mistaken him for one of the Hodgson Boys, but then he heard Archie cry out in anguish, 'Jesus Christ - I've gone and shot Jesus Christ!'

If he had shot Cain - and he could hardly have missed him with that many bullets from close range - then Cain didn't seem to notice, as he strolled toward the fallen tree where Alan might have been hiding. Archie cried out again, 'Did you see that? Ya did see what I saw, didn't ya? That was one of those bona fide fucking miracles, that's what that was.'

Brady knew this would make it much easier for him now. If Alan saw it, then he would be utterly distracted. He ran around the area to the back of the fallen tree. He could see Alan, and he watched Cain approach him with his arms open wide, his white robe glowing in the darkness. Alan stood and looked into Cain's crystal-clear green eyes, ready to receive his forgiveness. 'I come in peace,' Cain said, in a soft voice.

But then, he spotted Brady creeping up behind Alan. 'No!' he shouted. He wasn't too late, as such, as Brady would never have let this lifetime threat to his Foster Daddy live. But Cain was appalled as he watched Brady hack his victim to pieces.

'It's over Pops,' Brady shouted in Archie's direction. 'Hold your fire.'

The three remaining Hodgsons left their home to come and make sense of the slaughter and the image of Christ before them. A grizzly old man led the way in his wheelchair, and a young woman, with her baby in a pushchair, trailed behind him. 'You ain't gonna get away with this boy,' the old man growled. 'There's laws about killing my boys - you know that.' He pointed at Cain. 'And you...'

An axe plunged through the old man's skull, cutting him off mid-sentence. 'I prayed for this day - you sick fucks,' the young woman screamed, dropping the axe and wiping the blood from her face. 'You answered my prayers.' She fell to her knees. 'Every day they raped me, used me as their slave, they did.' Amid her tears she pointed at the old man, slumped and oozing blood. 'And that old bastard used to get off on watching them do that to me – so you have to forgive me.'

Cain was horrified at what he saw and wondered if scenes like this were playing out all over the world. She then noticed her blood-spattered baby. She picked her daughter up and hugged her tightly. 'Oh, my poor baby. Mommy had to do it, or you would have replaced me when I got old. You must forgive Mommy.'

She made her anguished plea to Cain. 'Tell me that you forgive me - please.' He didn't answer - he couldn't. He was still digesting the horror of the scene before him until Brady nudged him. 'Won't hurt to tell her - will it? The baby's too young to remember. All it takes is a few words. Even if it's a lie - it's a good lie.'

Cain was reeling. He thought about the government forces killing the people they used as human shields in the name of preserving their way of life. *Have I become one of those people?* He also looked at Brady and considered the awful test that Bodhi - the great Bodhi - might be putting him through. He then looked at the young woman and her child, and her words. The hell she must have gone through. He knew that she would never be allowed into his world, the Green Communities, as they were now sealed to newcomers. *The future holds little in the way of comfort for those like her.* He looked again at Brady, who nodded in a way that suggested that Cain should just get on with it. *If all it takes is a few simple words from me to give her comfort,* Cain thought, *then who am I to deny her?*

'What is your name?' he said.

'Mary-Lou, my Lord,' she sobbed.

He transfixed her with his green eyes. 'Mary-Lou. Your God forgives you.'

'Thank you. Thank you.' She picked up her daughter. 'My poor Amie. Mommy will clean you up and make everything better - I promise.'

Cain turned away, appalled at the enormous falsehood he had committed. He was close to tears. Brady put his muscle-bound arm around Cain. 'I think you'll feel better back in your own place. Thanks for your help. I'll walk ya back to your car.'

As they ambled back to the New Road, both Cain and Brady seemed eager to grab some nuggets of information from the other. 'What's going on here, with my Pop's place?' Brady said. 'Is he trapped here?'

'When the NanoShells™ were activated, everyone was sealed into the boundaries they were in at that moment.'

'I think I saw that yesterday morning. It was like one of those aurora things they teach you about at school.'

'You must have been mistaken - you cannot see NanoTech - it's too small.'

'I got good eyes. I saw the Green goo rolling on down the road, and you can't say I didn't.'

Cain laughed. 'Green goo. Good God, is that what they call it now?'

'My Pops calls it that. I hadn't heard of it before.'

'It's a corruption of the ancient conspiracy theory from the dawn of the Millennium - they called it Grey goo back then. Supposedly, it was going to destroy the human race, instead of saving the world.'

'Sounds like one of my Pop's theories - except you haven't involved extra-terrestrials - yet.' Brady laughed heartily, and Cain relaxed.

'Like all good conspiracy theories, it starts with a few facts and then twists them out of shape. There was a massive oil spill, and Sattva Systems™ cleaned it up by applying NanoTechnology™ to break down the carbons in the oil. It was a huge success. Everybody was happy except for the lunatics...' Cain could see that offending Brady's Father wasn't helpful – so he changed his angle. 'The conspiracy theorists, however, put it all over the Internet that this was in fact, a trial run, to exterminate, all carbon-based life forms. Unfortunately, these theories spread like wildfire, and yes, even alien invasions were involved.'

Brady still wanted an answer to his earlier question. 'I watched this Green goo move around the boundaries of these two adjoining ranches - my Pop's and the Hodgsons - does that mean we are trapped in?'

Cain looked uncomfortable. He knew Brady couldn't harm him. It was that he was supposed to be the giver of good news to his people. 'No, they will never be able to leave this place.' He tried to soften the blow, and justify the decisions. 'But they are lucky. They have a green space to work and plant. It's much harder for those in the cities. And if there hadn't been anyone living there, the NanoShell™ would have claimed their land as well. It's programmed to take all unoccupied natural land - the fields, the farms, as it protects Mother Nature. The City Trad dwellers will not be allowed to gain access to plunder Her, anymore.'

'So, you'll let them starve.'

'I don't think it will come to that - do you? We know the kind of men and women that are left. They are avaricious and cunning - they'll think of something. You would think of something, wouldn't you?'

Damn right, I would, he thought. *I would take or persuade your goody-two-shoes people to give me what I need - you self-centred pious bastards.*

Cain went on. 'From what I've witnessed here tonight, there will no doubt be violence, lawlessness - it will be a survival-of-the-fittest situation. I'm glad that our communities won't be a part of it.'

'What about the Government, the army, police - the President?'

'Anybody still loyal to the President has lost everything and will not be paid. They won't stick around for long - especially those with families, who may be in grave danger. The President will hide in his bunker, but when he decides to venture outside, he will never be able to leave the White House grounds. He will be in the same fortunate position as your Pops. He will have some green spaces to plant crops, although his stores should have enough food and drink to last him for years - possibly.'

Fuck - it's going to be hell in these so-called Trad areas, Brady thought. Still, he tried not to let his reservations show. 'But I can still get me one of those RedSuits™?'

'It would appear so. If you were to come up with the required one hundred Green Credits, then I would be duty-bound to apply it to you.'

They reached Cain's blandly designed car. 'I want to put my mind at rest before I leave. I hope you won't feel insulted. It's not my intention.'

Brady was intrigued. 'What do you want?'

'I want to see for myself whether you can still enter the Green Zone.'

I could do with checking this out myself before I make any further plans, Brady thought.

'Sure thing.' He crossed the New Road - as Brady had christened it. Dawn was lighting up the horizon. He slowed, as though he expected to walk into the invisible barrier - but if it was there, he didn't feel a thing. He walked a further fifty yards into the Green's territory and then wandered back to Cain, who didn't look entirely happy at the result.

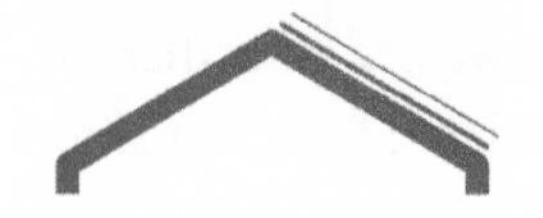

7.NEW DAY - SMALL WORLD

Once Brady had returned to the ranch, everybody relaxed - a little. Brady didn't need sleep, but he knew all this late-night drama wouldn't be good for his Pop's health, so he encouraged Archie and Lucian, to head off to bed for some shut eye. *I'll give them the bad news later in the morning*, he thought, though the sun was already rising before they went to bed. Still, he hoped they would sleep. *Poor old Lucky, he goes and breaks out of one jail, and now I gotta tell him he's ended straight up in another one.*

He looked over to the Hodgson homestead in the distance and wondered about Mary-Lou and her baby. *Someone gonna have to tell her, as well. Ain't gonna be easy, the girl is already at her wit's end.*

He waited for them to wake up naturally. Lucian was first to arise. *He's still adjusting to the time outside of prison*, Brady realised. While Lucian poured himself some cereal, Brady made them both coffees. Brady wanted to speak to them together about what he had discovered the previous night, so he left the significant issues alone, for the time being.

'How ya feeling Buddy?'

'Still sleepy. It was quite a night.'

'Feels like the world's gone crazy - we were only inside for ten years, weren't we?'

Lucian laughed. 'For you, it was ten, for me, it was five - remember?'

Brady knocked back his first hot, black coffee, 'Seems like a lifetime ago, already. What do you want to do today?'

'It'd be nice to just chill the fuck out, y'know? Catch my breath and all.'

'Amen to that.'

Archie must have woken up and smelled the coffee, as he shuffled in to join them. He hadn't bothered to dress; he had slung his old and worn-out dressing-gown on. 'Pour the old man a coffee, would you, son.' He paused. 'I wasn't dreaming last night. I saw Jesus.'

'Was that before or after you raked him with Old Marvin?' Brady roared, and they all laughed. 'He's one of the Green's Disciples - as they call themselves,' he said, once they'd calmed down.

'Well, I know I hit him,' Archie said.

'He was wearing what they call a RedArmour™ NanoSuit™. It's how those GreenRevs deposed the governments. They claim it's worldwide.'

'Well, it won't be for long. The good ol' boys will soon regroup and kick their Green asses back to where they belong.'

'I don't think so, Pops. Looks like they've got it pretty sewn up to me.'

'We'll soon see about that - once the Internet is back up and running, we'll organise. That's if it ain't one big hoax - some kinda publicity stunt.'

Brady paused and looked at Lucian, then his Pops. 'In the meantime, you've got something closer to home to worry about.'

'What, man?' Lucian asked, nervously.

'You're fenced in. You can get as far as the edges of the roads which surround yours and the Hodgson's ranches, and that's it.'

'For how long?'

'Cain seems to think forever. He also made out that if you weren't here at the time of this *Green Takeover*, then you would already have lost this land already - to them.'

'Fuck them!' Archie spluttered. 'They can't do that - this is the fucking United States of America - the Land of the Free. Me and Old Marvin will soon sort them out.'

'Like you did with Cain last night? I've seen first-hand what their NanoTech™ can do, and it's pretty damn scary.'

'But we can't just sit here and wait to die, and then hand over my land. We have to do something.'

'Brady, you're the one for plans,' Lucian said. 'Is there anything we can do about this? I mean, this is better than prison and all, but...'

'I've got nothing. They've won. We might just have to count our blessings for now. Pops has got his bunker, with supplies to last a hundred years.' He turned to his Pops. 'Gotta say it. You were right, old man. You always said there'd come a time when other folks would have wished they'd have prepared like you.'

'Can't say it's bringing me a great deal a comfort, boy. I was hoping to pass the ranch on to you when it was time to meet my maker.'

'Sorry Pops. I didn't want to be the bearer of bad news.'

'Not your doing, son.'

'What are your plans, Brady?' Lucian asked. 'From what you're sayin' you can come and go as you please.'

'It would appear so. Those Green weirdos are none-too pleased about it - they treat me as if I'm some kinda freak.'

'You see?' Archie said. 'Already things aren't going to their plan. There might be others like you, and then you could band together, and fuck 'em up big time.'

'You never know, but for now, I think we need to concentrate on our survival and immediate needs.'

'Such as, boy?'

'I was thinking about earning some of their Green Credits to help buy you fresh food. Your stores are basic and designed for surviving - not living.'

'Fuck boy, I'd rather see you die like a man than do these environmentalist's bidding for a few lousy pieces of their fake currency.'

'It's the only money in play, now - but it's not just that. I want a hundred Green Credits to get myself some of that RedArmour™. It makes you pretty damn indestructible.'

'I don't know, boy. That's how the aliens infect you. They give you something they think you want, and then you end up volunteering for their tests and probes voluntarily. They'll put those Nano things inside you, and then they'll take you over from the inside out. You mark my words.'

Brady slumped in his seat. 'Fuck. You know what, Pops, I think you could be right. They did seem awful determined to get everyone to buy into it. You were spot on about the bunker - still not sure about the aliens though...' He smiled, but he wasn't mocking Archie. *He has got a point*, he thought. *I should steer clear of those Suits™ until I've seen what happens to the others. This does feel more like End of Days, rather than the New Beginning these Greens are selling us on.*

Brady noticed that Lucian seemed distracted, he was gazing in the distance, in the general direction of the Hodgson Place.

'We still need extra supplies and other stuff to make life more bearable here. I had picked up an idea, but I'm not sure about how I can put it into action.' Brady pulled the Black Blank File from out of his pocket. 'Are you familiar with these things?'

Archie took it from him. 'Sure. Blank Files. A few of my buddies - not many, mind - used them to store away some of their more personal pleasures - ancient tech - antiques, truth be told.'

'I know it's a long-shot, without the Internet, but do you know where I could find some of these old buddies of yours?'

Archie smiled weakly. 'You'll have to accompany me to my control room - down in the bunker.'

'Are some of your electronics back up and working?'

'I wish, boy. I'm going to have to resort to ancient methods of my own.'

'Are you coming, Lucky?'

'Nah, I'll rest my head, and look out over my new home, if ya don't mind?'

'Sure thing.'

Archie had already opened up the entrance to his bunker. Brady caught him up and followed his Pops down the stairs. Brady hadn't been down here since he was a kid, and those damp cellar smells brought the memory of those happy days immediately back to him. They were only about twenty feet under the ground, but he could remember the younger Archie, and his wife telling her all about the place, excitedly. It could withstand a nuclear blast...three-inch-thick steel...encased in a foot of concrete. He remembered his Pops getting into computers at this point, and then down the rabbit holes of his conspiracy theories and secret organisations. He was shaken out of his reverie when he spotted the table-tennis table. His old bats were still near the net, next to an old ping-pong ball.

'Come on, boy,' Archie said.

'Pops, you still got the old table-tennis gear? Remember when we used to play down here for hours in the winter?'

'Sure do. I used to keep you entertained when your Foster Moms used to complain that you were becoming a real handful. You recall how boisterous ya used to be back then?'

I never thought about it before - I was always on the go, he thought. *Didn't sleep much back then, either.* 'Yes, Foster Moms was a fine woman. I really should've appreciated her more while she was still with us.'

'She loved you like her own son - that I do know.'

Brady noticed the climbing wall. I used to love playing there – though it seemed so small to him, now. He went past the small bedrooms and living quarters, to the back of the bunker to Pop's inner sanctum. There was a wall full of electrical equipment of all the twenty-first-century vintages. Most of them were switched on and blinking away. Brady thought of a taunt he used to use on the slower kids at school, and he smiled, ruefully. *The lights are on but there ain't nobody home*. 'Any activity, Pops?'

'No. Not a peep.'

Archie used a screwdriver to open a ventilation grill. He reached inside and pulled out a black leather notebook. 'Things like this you couldn't put on the web - not in one place.' He handed it to Brady.

Brady scanned through the passwords to his accounts and secret groups. *No Internet - not much use to anybody now*. He turned the pages until he came to the A-Z tabs. These revealed names, addresses, mobile numbers, web-addresses, handles and other notes.

'Some of the folks in there are still alive, I think - I hope,' Archie said. 'Goes back years, my little black book does.'

Most of the physical addresses were all over the world. 'I don't think I'll be able to travel far. I got the impression that most of the infrastructure has been compromised.'

'That'd be the plan of it. We used to debate this kind of stuff all the time, we did - about destroying the systems which held the countries together at source. Come to think about it, there were some environmental activists on these online forums...'

'What do you mean, Pops, when you say, at source?'

'Don't nobble an airplane, destroy the airport - better still, sabotage the fuel. You could do the same for motor-vehicles, power-stations, even the fuel for generators... Thank God I got my reserve fuels years ago. Otherwise, I couldn't even keep my bunker going.'

'And you think they've thought about all this?'

'Fuck, I remember we even talked about fucking-up the economy. When the whole cashless society came in, we joked at how easy it could be.' He clicked his fingers. 'Bingo, hello!'

'What is it, Pops?'

'Sattva Systems™ overtook mASSIVE as the biggest company in the world about ten years ago. They were worth fucking trillions already, but you know what they did next, boy?'

'What?'

'They borrowed trillions more. Everyone was like - what the actual fuck? Why would they need to do that? But it's obvious now...'

Everything's always obvious when Pop gets on board his conspiracy train.

'...We have fucking funded this take-over of the world - they gone and did it... I kinda admire them, in a strange way. They got us to pay for our own takeover, and they don't have to pay the money back - because all their loans have been written off.'

Brady thought he understood - but he wanted to be sure. 'So, you're saying that Sattva Systems™ and the GreenRevs got together years ago to plan for a time when they guessed the Internet would crash, and in that time, they went around the whole planet, planting their NanoBots...'

'I think they did more than guess... The viruses and the solar storms were real, and we all knew it would cause massive disruption. In the Twenties, we had the Fave Wave virus, and the Thirties, the Doom Trilogy - China Virus, combined with another solar flare, and a mercifully small, but still significant asteroid hit. We were all paranoid, this time around - we were primed - but the GreenRevs were laser-focused. It's gotta be, boy.'

Brady shook his head. 'Well, it's too late now. I've gotta focus on what's in front of me. Can you pick out a couple of local-ish leads in your book who might be able to help me?'

'What you are looking for, exactly?'

'I'm thinking about making Black Files, with stuff I can sell in these Green Communities. They have strict content rules of what they can view - y'know, worthy stuff, science, education, authorised musical and film content.'

'You think there's a black-market demand?'

'Yeah. So I need to trade for a bulk load of blank Black Files, then find old mediums of storage, if any exist still.'

'You mean tapes, discs, physical formats? You'd need working hardware from back in the day.'

'That type of thing, yeah. I'd also need to know what our people would want from the Green Communities in return. You can't steal from them because their security systems are impenetrable - so, I would have to buy from the Greens, and get it back to my dealers.'

Archie thought it over. Brady could see he was troubled, torn over whether to tell him or not. 'Come on, Pops. I need this. The world has changed. Even your old friends are going to be looking after their own needs now.'

Archie winced, and then sighed. 'There are one or two possibilities reasonably close to here, and lots in the wider California area. - there's a guy in Bakersfield who fits the bill. He's a creep - he used to deal in kiddie porn - he specialised in off-line mediums.'

'I ain't dealing with nonces - I'd rather crush him with my bare hands.'

Archie frowned. 'You ain't gonna get the luxury of choosing. The other guy has been off-line for so long that he must either be dead or in prison. I would use his resources first, and then crush him,' Archie said, laughing uncomfortably.

'Is there a phone number? Maybe a landline or whatever - something might still be working. You could call him, and at least let him know I'm coming - and check if he's still around.'

'He don't deal with phones, not even Satts™ - especially not Satts™. Paranoia kinda comes with the territory, y'know.'

Brady shrugged. 'What's this guy's name?'

'Small Hand Don - on account of his withered left hand.' He opened the notebook to P for Don Pickerstaff. 'He won't trust you. You'll have to say that the Arrow sent you and quote the code in the book. Be careful, boy. He has a thing for Chloroform.'

'What the...? Honestly Pops, you worry me with the people you know.'

'If ya want to find dirt, sometimes ya gotta get dirty.'

'Why Arrow?'

'Easy for me to remember, and it sounded kinda cool... Archie... Archer... Arrow.'

'Let's hope he can get me what I want,' Brady said, darkly, 'but I'd rather die in hell than deal with child porn. It ain't me, Pops...'

'Don't think that... I never done anything like that. I won't lie, a lot of the people on these forums were into collecting it - there were women as well as men. I know you might find it hard to believe. But I don't want you to think worse of me. I wouldn't have wanted you to know anything about this, but you'd struggle to find...'

'I know Pops. They would never have let you look after me when I was a kid - they would have run their checks...' He paused. 'I love you Pops.'

Archie was embarrassed, Brady could tell. He changed the subject. 'Thank for this, Pops - better get back and check-in on Lucky.'

'I'll just stay down here for a bit longer. If you don't mind.'

Brady left the bunker alone and went over to the porch. It would be a beautiful day if the world hadn't gone to hell in a handcart. Lucian was staring into space.

'How are ya feeling? There's a lot to process - gotta admit it's been one helluva fucked up couple of days.'

Lucian had never felt so small as he did today. He was more than a foot shorter than Brady and probably half his weight. *If Brady is a bear,* he thought, *then I'm a rat.*

He had been catching a few rays of the early afternoon sun, as he sat back in his chair on the decking. He sat up, he pushed back his lank, greasy black hair, and then brushed his thin black moustache down with the edge of his index finger. 'If I'm going to be locked up, there are worse places than here, I suppose. Are you planning on leaving soon?'

'I don't know whether it's better to try to go into the towns early before the looters have picked the place clean or to wait until all the carnage has calmed down. One thing I do know is the ones who get organised the quickest will be the ones who prosper.'

Lucian brooded. He didn't want to see his friend leave - he might not return. *Even Brady might not survive out there,* he thought. *Not that we've got any evidence - even the Free News channel wasn't working on Archie's TV. It might have calmed down already - for all I know.* He felt guilty, though - because there was another part of him that wanted Brady to leave before it was too late. 'What are you planning to do if you do go?'

'I might have to break into some places and look for old-style entertainments - hard copies. It's likely to be old folks' places - maybe a thrift stores.'

'It's a shame that I can't come with you - even if I could, I suppose I'm still on the run, technically.'

'Ancient history, now. Seems odd that no-one is coming looking for us.'

Lucian laughed. 'Yeah, we're the world's most unwanted criminals.' But then, he stopped laughing - abruptly. Mary-Lou had appeared outside the Hodgson Homestead, she was hanging out the washing. *She's probably trying to wash out the bloodstains,* he thought. *That was the dress she had on before.*

'What is it, brother?' Brady said. 'What's troubling you?'

Lucian sighed heavily and closed his eyes. 'If it's true - that we ain't never gonna leave this place - then she is the only woman left in the world. And I likes her, but she ain't never gonna choose me over you.'

Brady glanced at Lucian, and then looked over at Mary-Lou. She seemed to spot them watching her, and she hurried back inside the house. 'Hey, I haven't even been thinking that far ahead, yet.'

'That's because you got all kind of exciting things to look forward to. You can go where you please and have other women out there. I ain't got nothing.'

'It ain't my fault, man.'

'I know. I know.'

Brady thought about the situation. *I don't want Lucky to be a problem, and I owe him. Pops ain't gonna be happy if he gets stuck with the boy, especially if he's gonna be moping about the place.*

'If you're planning to get it on with Mary-Lou, then you're gonna have to come on all sensitive, like.'

'You mean you won't try and get in there first?'

'I won't try and get in there at all. She ain't my type,' he lied. 'Remember, she's probably traumatised, and she's killed, now. It's always easier, the second time,' he added, 'only half-joking. Just in case you're thinking of just rushing in and taking her.'

'I ain't no rapist,' Lucian snapped.

Brady raised his palms. 'I'm kiddin', man. But she probably hasn't figured out she's trapped here yet. That's a bit of information someone needs to tell her... Sensitively.'

Lucian sighed, looking resigned. 'Thing is, I've never had much luck with women. What would you do? Y'know, if you were me?'

I'd probably do something to make Brady Mahone look bad and Lucky look real good. 'Well, there's three bodies to bury.' *And I don't want to be the one to bury them,* Brady thought, suppressing a laugh.

'Should I go over there, and offer our help?'

'*Your* help. Don't bring me into this. Anyways, it'll be better, if you just do it - otherwise, it will look like you are doing a deal with her - y'know, you saying and all - if I buries your kin, then maybe you can...'

'But that will take hours of back-breaking labour - that's worse than fucking prison, man.'

'Do you want to win the girl, or not?'

'Like you said, I could just take her.'

'You could, but don't blame me if ya wake up one morning with a splitting headache.'

Lucian stood up sharply. 'That ain't funny at all - that just ain't fucking funny.'

'Calm down, come on, I was just joshing with ya. Y'know I love you, man. Just think it through. She will see you, working hard, doing something for her, and she didn't even need to ask - and if she looks at me, she will see a lazy, arrogant and selfish son of a bitch. She'll think the Lord has sent her a real good man to take the place of the Hodgson Boys. You gotta play it cute.'

Lucian thought it over. *It sounds like a lot of hard fucking work, but Brady is stepping aside,* he thought. *I better be grateful, or he might change his mind.* 'You're right. I can see how that might work. I've got to win her over.' He tried to change the subject. 'What's the deal with these old-style entertainments?'

'The Greens are going to be starved of unauthorised movies and stuff. I'm going into bootlegging. My plan is to find old-formatted items, then arrange to have them converted onto the Black Files by dealers in the Trad districts. Like this one.' He pulled out his blank Black File and passed it to Lucian. 'And then I'm going to trade them for Green Files - I can then use these to buy anything we need or want, from the Green communities.'

'What sort of things do we need?'

'It's early days, I don't really know yet. All I know, from years of listening to Pops, is that things that were worthless in one time can become super valuable in another and vice versa. He used to talk about olden times when men travelled the world hunting for spices, sugar and even tea. All I gotta do is figure it out, what the next big things might be.' He looked at Lucian, 'I owe you, man - anything I do, I will do it for you, Archie...and Mary-Lou. Y'know I'm nothing, if not loyal.'

Lucian laughed. 'Look after yourself, man. I don't want to lose you.'

'Thanks. Now go get that girl.'

8.THE HIGHWAY

Brady left the ranch. He had decided to travel light. He had his jeans, white T-shirt, and black leather jacket - a plastic bottle of water poking out of a pocket, and Archie's contact book in one inside jacket pocket. In the other, he had his Satt™ - it bulged out, ruining the cut of his jacket. *That was one thing about the older tech – at least it was small.* He had a large hunting knife in a leather sheath which hung from his belt adorned with a skull and crossbones silver buckle. He couldn't see why he would need a wallet, but he'd borrowed one from his Pops, complete with an old credit card and Driver's ID. The only other item he had was the car keys for his stolen Mustang.

As he came to the New Road, the first thing he noticed was that he had wandered into the Green Zone without a problem. *I still got it - whatever it is.* The second thing he noticed was that his Mustang had moved. Moved wasn't the right word – been dumped was more appropriate. The Mustang appeared to have been picked up and dropped near Lucian's Mini. The bumpers of the two cars were entangled.

Won't be a problem to get it free, he thought. *Just need to rev it up and blast it into reverse.* He got into the Mustang and turned the key. The car spluttered and then let out a loud bang before dying on him. He saw a cloud of blue smoke in the rear-view. *Fucking great, must be thirty miles to Bakersfield. Just as well I'm not in a hurry. I won't get there until nightfall now*. The Mustang gave a strange odour, and

Brady wondered if it might be toxic, so he jumped out of the car - sharpish.

The New Road seemed eerily quiet as he marched along looking for the signs for Highway 99. *If all the cars are fucked like Pops guessed, then I'll walk as the crow flies.*

As he approached the junction to the Highway, he heard the roar of vehicles in the distance, but it didn't sound like regular traffic. He walked onto the Highway, and the road was empty, clear of obstructions - but off to the sides of the Highway, the hard shoulders were littered with abandoned cars and trucks. *I'm starting to get the hang of this fucked up world,* he realised. *I bet they triggered something in the fuel to stop the traffic in its tracks.* He also noticed the Highway looked... Clean. He passed a pothole which looked newly repaired, and the inside lane had white bicycle signs painted on the tarmac.

The Greens have commandeered the Highways. I'll bet they've taken the airports around here as well. He remembered his first night of freedom when he had watched the FusionPlanes™ and HeavyLoaders™ flying through the Green Glow. *If those lanes are marked for bikes, then the other lanes must still be used for vehicles. I'll walk down there for now.*

Brady noticed that some of the vehicles had broken up, having failed to withstand the fall after whatever it was had dropped them at the roadside. He glanced through some of the scattered possessions but didn't want to be weighed down on his travels. One truck had split open, and there were hundreds of taped up packages that must have fallen through the floor of the truck. *That sure is one big haul of cocaine, heroin - or something like that,* he thought. *I suppose it could be worth a lot of dough to somebody.* He then tried to work out if it was worthwhile taking this instead of messing around with his bootlegging plan. *If it was valuable, then they woulda come back for it...* He saw another painted bicycle sign. *Or the workers would've retrieved it.*

He marched along at a good pace for a few miles. The exercise was doing him good, giving him time to think. As he approached Famoso, the industrial noises grew in intensity, and in the near distance, he understood what had happened to his Mustang, though he wasn't without regret. *I liked that car; it was going to be my trademark - something to impress the ladies with.* Still, he watched in quiet awe as two ceramic looking vehicles used giant magnets to lift the abandoned cars up, and then drop them unceremoniously on the hard shoulder. The second vehicle was much larger, with a crane to remove the lorries and tankers. Upturned domes sprung out from the opposite side to the hard shoulder and acted like suckers onto the Highway, to give it stability. *Pops would have loved this,* he thought. *They really do look like aliens.*

He watched the vehicles for a while. They fascinated him. He used to love the Demolition Derbies and the Monster Truck events when he was a kid. A couple of trucks passed him. He noticed them giving him the eye, suggesting he shouldn't be here. *Maybe, the road is closed while this work is being done.*

They stopped a few hundred yards in front of him, behind the other working vehicles. One group of people jumped out and fixed up the potholes with a substance which seemed to set exceptionally quickly, while the other team painted their bicycle templates on the chosen lane. He heard laughter from them, they seemed happy and motivated. *They ain't messin' about,* he thought. *They're really goin' for it.*

As he closed in on the workers, one left the group to come and check out Brady. He was a big guy, too, dressed in moss-green overalls - not unlike military garb. On his cream-coloured ceramic looking hard hat, the words seemed to proudly proclaim that he worked for Sattva Systems™.

He reached out his hand and shook Brady's, firmly. 'What are you doing out here, buddy? It's not safe until we've done the full clean up - unless you are already Red™?'

'No, I'm not Red™ yet - gotta save up.'

The big guy looked him over. 'I could see if I could get you on the team. We could always use big strong guys like yourself.'

'What's the pay?'

'Five Green Credits per day. I'll soon have enough to feed and keep my family, and to save up for the RedSuits™ for all of us. After that, gotta start saving for the Orange™. I'm hearing they could cost a thousand apiece - but still, talk about affordable Healthcare.'

Five Green Credits for a day's back-breaking work. It didn't seem a fair deal to Brady. 'Thanks for the offer, but I think I'll pass this time.'

'Suit yourself, buddy. Where are ya heading?'

'I've got an old uncle in Bakersfield. I just wanna check he's ok.'

'If he's in the non-Green area, that could be tricky. It's gone fucking mental in there.' He looked at Brady, closely. 'There's a couple of things that are troubling me. Do you mind if I check out a couple of things with you?'

'Sure. Knock yourself out.'

'I'm assuming you are Green. Otherwise, you wouldn't be here - but you didn't know to keep away from the Highway this week - it was well publicised, everyone shoulda known. Also, there were supposed to be Town Meetings today, to warn people to stay out of the cities until further notice, unless you were Red™ - which only the GreenRevs and the Disciples are.'

Brady felt his Amazon rainforest story would be a bit weak for this guy. 'I'm checking things out, as an independent. Then reporting back to Sattva - another pair of eyes kinda thing.'

'And who do you report to?'

'Do you know Cain and Lizzie from McFarland?'

'Ah man, you should have said so in the first place. I love Cain. Is there anything I can do to help?'

'I've been in some remote areas for the past few years - securing borders.' *I'm sure there was a question from a kid about animals and parks.* 'Anyways, I'm a bit out of the loop with what's been happening closer to home, so Cain said to just ask any Green friend I came across.'

'Of course – shoot.'

'What's the deal with the vehicles at the roadside?'

The big guy looked over toward the hard shoulder. 'They'll remain there for a few weeks – to give the Trad folks a chance to recover any belongings from them – seems only fair.'

Only fair? Brady thought. *You've wrecked their vehicles - in the grand scheme of things...I suppose.*

'There's a no-mans-land corridor,' the big guy went on. 'Beyond the hard shoulders, which will remain open for a while.'

'And why's that?'

'To give the Trads a chance to get to their vehicles for a short while - kinda goes without saying - and there's likely to be an exodus as families attempt to reunite from different areas. It'll only be temporary, mind you. Once the vehicles have been collected for recycling or decontamination, then the hard shoulders will become Green Zones, and then the no-mans-lands will revert to us.'

'We are going to keep the roads then? Y'know, you'd think they would be the first things to go, if you care about the environment, and all that.'

'I hear where you are coming from, buddy, but once we are done, the road networks are going to be sprayed with NanoRepair™ and NanoProtect™, so that means they will be designed to last forever, even after the buildings have gone. They've clearly got plans for them... But I'm not privy to them, not at my level.' He wondered about the flimsiness of Brady's story, but he was Green, and he knew

Cain, so he put it down as a test of some sort. He decided to give as many correct answers as he could.

Brady heard something which sounded like coaches turning into the Highway from the direction of Famoso. They pulled up to a gap between the abandoned vehicles. He watched as families were forcibly removed off the buses and marched beyond the hard shoulder of the Highway. The Greens returned to the coaches, as though they were busy - and had many more trips to do. The families tried to return to the road but couldn't break through the invisible wall. They were distressed and agitated, and obviously yelling, but the wall shut out the sound of them.

'What's going on?' Brady asked.

'It's another strand of Operation Clean-Up. Those folks didn't qualify to remain in the Green Zones. They may have been hanging out with friends or even other qualified family members. You can't go feeling sorry for them, though. They had plenty of opportunities to lead a more sustainable lifestyle, but they chose to keep on exhausting Mother Earth's precious resources. They made a choice. We are sending them to live out days in the hell they created - the Trad ways. Good luck, and good riddance to them.'

Brady recognised one of the teenagers who teased him when he was strung up at the GreenGrocers™ in McFarland.

He saw the figure of Siddha alighting the coach and heading his way. Brady braced himself for capture - he knew he couldn't land a blow on a RedSuit™. *I wonder if I could restrain him - a bear hug, perhaps?* He then followed his thought through. *I just can't see what good it would do me.*

Siddha glanced at Brady, suspiciously – but spoke to the big guy beside him. 'Hi Bill. Any trouble here?'

'I was just chatting to Cain's friend here. Sorry buddy, I didn't catch your name.'

'Brady. Brady Mahone.'

'Brady told me that Cain okayed us filling him in on what's happening here – he's been doing good things for the Green cause in some pretty remote places.' He sensed the tension between Siddha and Brady. 'I haven't done anything untoward, have I?'

'No, my friend,' Siddha smiled. 'You have done a superb job on the Highway. Thank you. I'm sure Brady won't hold you up any longer.'

'Cheers buddy. I'll get back to the crew.'

As Bill strode away, Siddha hissed: 'If it was up to me, I'd wrap you up in Film and dump you in a ditch, but Cain seems to have plans - or orders to follow - with regards to you.'

'And you know better than Cain? Are you jealous of him? Do you want to play at being a leader?'

Siddha refused to engage. Brady should have known the plan was to have no leaders - eventually. 'Where are you heading?'

'Bakersfield. I'm going to visit my uncle - check he's ok.'

Siddha wanted Brady far away, and fast – so he smiled in a phoney attempt at cordiality. 'At the old Police layby - a few hundred yards past the Green Highways Team - you'll find some GreenBicycles™. You could use one of those.'

Brady scoffed. 'I ain't ridden a pushbike since middle grade.'

More evidence of his ignorance, Siddha thought. 'They are protected by GreenShells™ - meaning if you were riding through Trad areas, then nobody could harm you - not as foolproof as a RedSuit™, but still very useful. Also, only a Green could use it. It's a rental - if you leave it, then it's available to others to ride.'

Brady thought of the fountain and tried to disguise his sarcasm. 'I suppose I get to earn some Green Credits?'

Siddha smiled, falsely. 'Yes. If you ride it for more than ten miles in one day, then you get to earn a One Green Credit File, for your use of sustainable transport, and the commitment to your physical fitness, and mental wellbeing.'

I suppose it would be quicker, he thought, *even if I'll look like a fucking dork*. 'Well, consider me sold.'

'Better be on your way then, but there is one more thing.'

'And what's that?'

'I don't trust you, and if you return to McFarland, I'll be keeping a close eye on you. Am I making myself clear?'

'Crystal.'

9.GRAND TOUR

Brady strode passed the Highways Team, and Bill gave him a wave. *Seems like a nice enough fella,* he thought. *Not like that Siddha creep.* He examined a few of the stranded vehicles at the roadside. Brady liked his cars but had become a little out of touch with the latest designs since his time inside. *Some of these are electrics and hybrids. I don't get the problem they would have with these babies.* He even wolf whistled as he came across a top of the range supercar. He peered inside, for old times' sake. The glove box was open. *I bet he took his gun with him,* he thought - *assuming it was a him, of course.*

He took a swig of water. It was hot in the desert-like sunshine.

A hundred yards further on, he came to the Police Patrol Car layby. There was an abandoned Police vehicle here, as well. He spotted the racking containing the GreenBicycles™. *They must be new - there was no reason to have bikes next to the Highway, before.* He pulled one out - it was feather-light. He didn't feel confident about it carrying his weight. He carried it down to the Highway and then started to ride it. Brady wasn't a natural cyclist, but the bike seemed to keep itself upright - as if it had invisible training wheels. He began to move more quickly, and a digital display appeared across the handlebars, which showed his speed, distance covered, and his progress toward earning a Green Credit.

After five miles, he came up against a traffic jam. The hard shoulder was relatively unobstructed, because the Highways Team hadn't reached this part of Highway 99, yet. He weaved, slowly, around the cars that had slid off onto the hard shoulder, and into the bulk of the stationary traffic. All the vehicles were deserted. There were no dead bodies – or at least, none that he saw. He noticed the silverish sheen to the road, and he could make out footprints, and small-wheeled tracks.

I guess these tracks could be made by suitcases or pushchairs, he thought. *Make way boys, Inspector Mahone is on the case.* He hopped off his bike, the vehicles increasingly close together as he approached the front of the queue. He carried his bike, grateful that it was light. There were a lot of heavy vehicles obscuring his view into the distance. Looking down, he noticed the silver sheen was everywhere. Whatever had happened had happened to every vehicle, not just selected ones.

After slowly making his way through a further mile of traffic, he came to the head of this traffic jam. There were jack-knifed articulated lorries, which had been slammed into by many other vehicles. *I'm guessing the momentum carried them forward even if the engines cut out.* Brady did find some dead bodies in this carnage – though they didn't shock him. He'd seen plenty before. He entertained himself by imagining cops picking through the wreckage – solving the puzzle, piece by piece.

Looks like after the engines cut out, then the car filled up with something which smelled like poisonous gas. This made the occupants flee the scene. 'And then what happened Inspector Mahone?'

I'm glad you asked me that. My deduction would be that they fled the scene, taking the things they could grab real quick with them.

'Oh, Inspector Mahone, you are so clever.'

Yes, I am, but that's not all I deduced - my sexy sidekick babe. You see, I'm guessing they ran into the no man's land, maybe there was smoke on the Highway, and then they walked southbound to Bakersfield, or wherever because they were heading that way in the first place. Having said that, I suppose some might have headed back - if home was that way.

'That's amazing, I love the way you think.'

I know, I have got excellent powers of deduction...I also, have tremendous powers of seduction.

'Oh, Inspector Mahone, I have to make love to you right now.'

He laughed. *I'm already talking to myself,* he thought. *Clearly this fucked-up world is gonna take some getting used to.*

There were a few hundred yards of clear road ahead before the next set of traffic chaos awaited him. The same scenes were playing out across the median strip. An accident had crossed the divide, affecting both sides. He wondered if the median strip had a GreenShell™, and if not, had people been able to cross the Highway on foot to either side.

He hopped on and off his bike, depending on the obstacles before him. His handlebar display flashed at the ten-mile point to alert him to his Green Credit award. He stopped. *I may as well take it. Lord knows I needed it in that bastard GreenGrocer™ shop.* The end of the right-hand-side handlebar glowed green, and a Green File emerged, encouraging him to use his thumb and index finger to retrieve it. He took it out and placed it in his Distor™, the display informed Brady that he was now the proud owner of three Green File Credits.

10.BAKERSFIELD

Brady rechecked the details in Archie's notebook. *I know roughly where to find Lakeside County Road,* he thought. *It's near a Lagoon, but that ain't in Bakersfield, that's in Castaic. I think Pops musta got that wrong.*

It still troubled Brady that he would be in contact with a lowlife like this Don Pickerstaff. He reflected upon his time as a small boy when he was taken in for fostering. He could remember being scared because the woman who handed him over seemed to have utter contempt for the Mahones. *Looking back, I would've expected them to tell me how fortunate I was that a wholesome family would want to take me in.*

His Foster Daddy did most of his day-to-day upbringing, while his Foster Ma drank herself to death. *But I always felt loved by Pops - he didn't do anything that wasn't right by me.* He racked his brain for any signs of abuse he may have suffered. *In those early months, Pops spent an awful long time down in his bunker.* He thought about what those kiddy porn perverts were in to. He had overheard plenty of disgusting conversations from in jail - the things they did to them. He also remembered the justifications that it was out of love. Mostly, it was about the movies, photos, and the sharing of information. *Pops isn't like that. He's not one of them.*

He also tried hard to remember if there was anything suspicious about Pop's use of the camera or the family camcorder. *I can't say I recall anything inappropriate, just the usual birthday pictures, and movies about the festive season, and the fireworks for the Fourth of July celebrations.* He knew he was going to have to remain calm and controlled with this Small Hand Don and give his Pops the benefit of the doubt. *He always says to me, 'Treat people as they treat you.' And Pops has always treated me real good.* He thought again on his Pops friendship with this man. *It could be that Pops didn't know at first about what this guy was into. Knowing Pops, he just met him on a group that was discussing UFOs.*

As he arrived at the outskirts of Bakersfield, Brady tried to shake off his reflective mood. Even in prison, he hadn't spent this much time alone with his thoughts. Now, once again, he needed to be sharp. He knew he was wandering into a highly volatile situation. It wasn't long before he noticed the looted shops, but it seemed relatively quiet in the early evening sunshine. He guessed that the oncoming night would bring out the hardened troublemakers.

The more defensively minded people seemed to be struggling to form into groups - for support and protection. They congregated around their churches and other meeting places. Over in a nearby park, there was a speaker with a megaphone imploring a crowd to take back control of the neighbourhoods. The one thing they had in common, from Brady's perspective, was that they all looked at him with a mixture of distrust and apprehension - this aggressive looking hulk of a man, pushing his GreenBike™. Was he a Green? Was he indestructible like them? Or, if he was one of us, then how did he manage to steal one of their bikes?

All the roads were littered with broken-down vehicles as he made it to the heart of Bakersfield. A half-hearted attempt had been made by someone to break into an old-fashioned bookshop. Brady finished the job, ramming his shoulder into the door. He succeeded in knocking the door off its hinges.

Brady realised that there weren't any alarms sounding anywhere. There wasn't any power or lighting here. *Come to think of it,* he realised, *I haven't noticed any traffic signals.* He remembered the advertisements on TV for the new Green Communities, extolling local, sustainable power. He remembered the pathetic tagline: *Sure, it's more expensive than oil and gas, but what would you pay to help save the planet?*

The press ridiculed them - labelled them as a regressive cult. The reporters mocked these *environmental headcases* volunteering to live in areas where power was more expensive, and broadband was deliberately slowed down to the point of being practically useless.

They never saw it coming.

He took his bike with him into the shop and went straight to the Travel section. He grabbed a local atlas and went through the index. He was right, there wasn't a Lakeside Canyon Road in Bakersfield, but there was one in Castaic. That meant another day's riding and walking. He wondered about the prospect of sleeping rough in the freezing night to come. *Desert nights could be fun*, he remembered, *but they were always cold*. He ripped out a few pages, folded them up and pocketed them. He didn't want the whole atlas, as he didn't want to be marked out as a stranger in a strange land when he got there. Looking like a tourist could mark him out as a potential victim - even though trying him would be a very unwise move on their part.

When he found a camping store, he realised he wasn't the first to plan ahead. It had been picked clean of tents and sleeping bags. He spotted the locked storeroom. He looked around for a suitable chunk of metal to prise the door open. The looters were content for some instant gratification and didn't want to work too hard for their booty – but he wasn't afraid of a little fight.

It wasn't easy, but he managed to break in, and he went through the racks until he found a sleeping bag big enough for him, but also designed to be easily carried. He might not sleep much, but he'd welcome a little warmth while he rested.

He decided to push beyond the south of Bakersfield before finding a place to rest.

He came to Alameda. Usually, he wouldn't have given the place a second thought, but the lights were on. He guessed this was another Green place, like McFarland. He left the Highway and ventured a few hundred yards across some farmland until he found a disused barn. He figured that he was protected by the GreenShell™ surrounding the town. He propped his bike up, shook out his sleeping bag, undressed and slipped inside.

But he couldn't sleep. There was too much for his mind to process. He wondered whether the Greens had left the whole of Bakersfield to its own devices. He guessed they would take the Highways and the Airports, but it seemed unlikely they'd want the University. *Those layabout hippies are no goddamn use to anybody*. He wondered about the rest of the world for a moment, but Brady had never lived or moved outside California, so he soon gave up on that. His education began with the things he learned from his Pops and ended in the finishing schools of various correctional facilities - but that didn't mean he wasn't intelligent. He knew what made him - and the people like him, tick.

He pondered on how McFarland split into two sections. He guessed that a lot of folks would move away if their neighbourhood was invaded by undesirables, but most wouldn't want to go too far from the town they considered home. He remembered how the prices of real estate soared on the East Side but fell on the Green side of the Highway.

Brady wondered about Pops but guessed he would be holding up ok. He'd spent his whole life preparing for days such as these. And he laughed as he imagined Lucian digging those three graves. *That'll be the hardest damned work he'll have done in his whole life*. He hoped Lucian would find a way to make it work with Mary-Lou and the baby. Before he drifted off to sleep, he vowed to provide for them – somehow.

He was awoken at dawn by the sound of footsteps and conversation. He slipped out of his sleeping bag and snuck out the barn, dressed only in his underwear to check the situation. He watched an old couple walking their dog and chatting about their simple plans for the day as if they hadn't a care in the world.

After they had gone, he heard the sound of water from nearby. It was a fast-flowing creek, but the water looked fresh and inviting. He took off his underwear and went down the bank and immersed himself into the freezing cold water. He was invigorated and repeatedly dunked his head under the water.

He went back to the barn and got dressed. He packed away his things, and Brady felt refreshed and ready for the challenges ahead in this new world.

He made good progress down the Highway on his GreenBicycle™. The opposite carriageway was clogged with abandoned vehicles, but there were relatively few on the southbound side. He couldn't be bothered to try and figure out why that would be the case. That morning, he'd decided not to overthink things, and just deal with whatever lay in front of him.

Brady rode past those weird ceramic-like Road-Clearers - as Brady had christened them - and then climbed off his bike again, picking his way through miles more of littered vehicles of all shapes and sizes.

It had been slow going, but he finally made it to Castaic in the evening. There were familiar scenes of looted properties, and the loose associations of people trying to work out how they were going to make things work for their mutual benefit and survival.

Castaic was a small town compared to Bakersfield, but as far as Brady could see, it was a day further on in its evolution. Gangs had formed and begun hanging out menacingly on their chosen turfs.

The atmosphere was just like entering a new prison as an inmate for the first time.

Brady picked up his bike, effortlessly, exuding power and potential violence. He strode down the streets, confidently. He knew someone would be goaded into challenging the big guy, the new guy. It was how the system worked. And so, he wasn't so much as irritated when a brash young white guy, with jet-black crew cut hair, stepped into his path. Brady watched the assorted pack of youths and teenagers gather behind him. *Some of them look like they could be handy, but most are just a bunch of scared kids.*

Brady smiled a broad, self-assured smile. 'Hi, buddy. I'm Brady. Brady Mahone - and you are?'

'Vincent Cesare, my family, runs this neighbourhood - I assume you know who we are.'

I could say I haven't, just to fuck with them, he thought – but decided it wasn't worth the trouble. 'Yeah, I know the name. I hung out with a couple of your crew when I was in Ridgecrest. I just got out, a couple of days ago.' He laughed. He didn't know why - it just sounded funny.

'What were you in for?' He paused. 'Or were you a screw?'

'Armed robbery. I'd served ten of my thirty-five. Is this some kinda interview?'

'You think you're funny. I'll show you funny.'

Brady already had his hunting knife to hand. This guy wouldn't be a problem for him, but he had to be prepared for the next one, so he had to choose carefully. There was a fearsome man with a face full of tattoos. Brady decided that he would be next - this would send the others fleeing for their lives, with a bit of luck.

An older man came out from the shadows. He was stocky and wore an immaculate Italian suit. He moved in close to Brady, but Brady didn't move. *I've seen this move before.* 'I'm Abramo - what were their names?'

Brady was being tested. He answered, 'Luca and Georgio.'

'And how come they haven't returned home?'

He thought it wise to leave Lucian out of this story. 'I was the only one who survived the massacre.'

There was a sense of shock among the gang. Abramo looked to Vincent, who Brady assumed must be his son, before returning his attention to Brady. 'How did it happen?'

'A couple of the guards didn't think it was a fair and equitable solution to let the cons have a quiet and peaceful death by, say, leaving us to starve. They had other ideas.'

'What other ideas?'

'They had an antique Tommy Gun and pistol, and they shot the place up. They killed everybody, including Luca and Georgio. Apparently, antique weapons didn't have the whatchamacallit...I'm a bit out of touch...Kill Stream switch, is that right?'

He could see Abramo trying to figure out where he might find these old weapons. He didn't say this, of course. 'So, how come you escaped?' he asked, after a moment.

'I hid.' There was mocking laughter from Vincent which triggered a wave of sniggering from the rest of the crew. Abramo wasn't laughing. 'But then I killed both guards and left.'

'And what brings you here?'

'Nothing. I'm just passing through - putting some miles between me and Ridgecrest. I wouldn't be here - I'd be somewhere else if you hadn't gotten in my way.'

Abramo smiled. He liked the way Brady handled himself. He wasn't remotely intimidated, he appeared calm, and in control. 'Come inside, and we'll talk some more.'

'The thought of going inside - anywhere - doesn't exactly appeal to me. I'm sure you understand.'

'I just want to talk, learn a few things, and then, maybe you could continue on your journey. We could eat, I'm sure you could do with a hot meal?'

Italians and their hospitality, he thought. *But a hot meal would be nice, I guess.* 'Sure. Why not.'

He entered into the dark house, which was dimly lit by candles. *Add that to his shopping list for his boys - more candles, to go with the Tommy Guns.* Abramo invited Brady to sit at the dining table. He then barked out orders for food and drink. Brady watched the bald-headed chef, struggle to cook with a couple of camping stoves. 'When did the power go out?'

'Last night.'

'I don't think it's going to ever come back on. Do you?'

Abramo shrugged.

I wonder if the power at Pop's house has gone, he thought. *I best not stay away too long. He might need me to help to figure something out. I'll give him a call when I get out of here.*

They chatted for about an hour, as Brady gave a detailed account of everything he had seen and done since his escape while he was travelling down Highway 99. He described the machines, the traffic carnage, the Highways Teams, and the eviction of the non-greens from the villages. He didn't mention anything to do with his time in the Green Community in McFarland. *I don't know whether there are lots of people who can pass through the Green's SecurityFilm™ or if I'm the only one*, he thought. *I don't want to give these guys another reason to think I'm useful to them.* He ensured he mentioned the packets of drugs he'd seen. That would definitely distract Abramo, while at the same time demonstrating his own lack of interest in this area of crime. He wouldn't be seen as a threat if they weren't in competition.

'We are in the middle of the biggest turf war in history,' Abramo said. 'I could use someone like you.'

'You wouldn't want me,' Brady lied. 'I've got issues.'

'What kind of issues?'

'I breakdown a lot. It's in my head. It makes me unreliable.'

Abramo believed him because of the detail of his account of his time from Ridgecrest to here. Still, he wanted to use him as a sounding board before deciding whether he would let him leave or not. 'How do you think this turf war is going to pan out?'

'I can only go on what happens in prison.'

Abramo was intrigued. 'Please, go on.'

'We have our enemies - the rival gangs, and we spend a lot of time, energy and blood, in fighting them. Trouble is - the real enemy is the system which keeps us locked up. We should have joined together and taken on the guards and the governors.'

'And who are the guards and the governors now? Is it me - should the people take on me - is that what you're saying?' Abramo said, contempt creeping into his tone.

'It's the Greens. They'll march in and take anything they want. Even armies couldn't defeat them.'

'I don't believe you. They're hiding away, enjoying their victory, with their lentils and soup.'

'You think that, and you might be right. But if I were you, I'd be spreading rumours about what those Green bastards are planning next. Make them come to you for protection - it's what you do best. The alternative is to fight your war. Sure, you'll kill a hundred, for the loss of every one of your gang, but there are hundreds of thousands of people out there. Who knows - maybe the Greens want a turf war between y'all?'

Abramo considered this. 'So, you're saying I should be going on a recruitment drive?'

'If you don't, some politician will, and when people are scared, they head to the biggest flock. It's one of those safety in numbers deals.'

'And what will I get out of it?'

'Anything you are going to need in this new era - skills, services... I don't know what's going to be valuable anymore.' *I'm getting the Green's market*, he thought. *I might just have that all to myself. This Trad business is going to be absolute chaos.*

Abramo reached out his hand, and Brady shook it confidently. 'Thank you, friend. You've been excellent company. I'll let you go on your way. Pop in and see me if you're passing this way again - it will be good to catch up.' He called for Vincent to show Brady out. 'Escort my friend out of the area and ensure our people know that no harm must come to him.' Vincent nodded, though it was clear he wasn't happy about it.

They left the candlelit hallway and headed out into the cold night. Vincent's friends were attempting to use Brady's bike, but they couldn't get near it. It stood, immovable, where Brady had left it, leaning against a wall. They were throwing rocks at it and using knives to attempt to stab and slice their way through the invisible fence, but it was impenetrable.

I need to think quick.

'You must be one of those Greens,' Vincent said. He slashed a blade at Brady, and it grazed his forearm, beginning to bleed.

'You couldn't draw blood from a Green,' he said, his palms raised.

'He's right,' one of Vincent's crew called out.

'How come you can ride their bikes then?'

'I jumped a Green exactly at the same time he touched the bike. He fell off, and I stayed on. I must have fooled it into thinking I was the Green. Since then, it's been mine. You should try it - it might work for you.'

'Vincent!' Abramo barked, 'What did I say?'

Brady pointed to the wound on his arm. 'You got anything for this?' Vincent nodded, and one of his crew came forward with some cloth and tied it around the cut, to stop the bleeding. Brady knew it would soon heal - his wounds always did.

11.SMALL HAND DON

Brady pocketed the pages from the street atlas and stood looking at the three-story house on Lakeside Canyon Road. The bright sunlight sparkled off the vehicles from the car park to the right, forcing him to raise his hand above his eyes. He knocked lightly on the door. He didn't want him to think it could be the authorities.

From across the road, he heard someone shout, 'Fucking paedo!' Brady turned, and saw a middle-aged man on a pushbike, with a trailer attached behind it, probably carrying all his worldly goods. *He's accusing me of being a child-molester*, he realised. The middle-aged man knew he had committed a life-threatening error when he saw Brady turn to confront him. The pushbike man tried to peddle, but his bike moved slowly as it was dragged down by the trailer. Brady made as if he was going to chase him, and the man finally got the bike moving. Brady laughed - it looked like the guy on the bike was close to having a heart attack. He let him escape. He looked up and noticed the twitching of a curtain from the second-floor window.

He knew that Small Hand Don was at home. He listened at the door. He heard heavy footsteps coming down two flights of stairs, and then he heard the padding of bare feet until Don stopped at the other side of the door. A soft male voice answered, though the door remained closed. 'Who is it?'

Brady pulled out Archie's black leather notebook from inside his jacket - marked at P for Don Pickerstaff. 'The Arrow sent me.' He then spelt out the code *A F T 729*.

There was a pause before Don replied. 'What do you want?'

'Archie's my Foster Daddy. He reckons you are the man to help me locate some old tech.'

The door opened. They looked at each other, suspiciously. Don was checking out the apparent threat of this hulk of a man in front of him. Brady let his muscles loosen in an attempt to look relaxed - his shoulders dropped, his hands open. Don's round and flabby body was only covered by a garish blue silk robe with large flowers embroidered on it. He looked like he had stepped out of a bath, but he was dry. Out of curiosity, Brady looked for the deformed hand, but it was hidden within the flapping sleeve.

'Come on in. Make yourself at home.'

'Do you mind if I park my bike in your hallway?' Brady said. 'Nothing's safe anymore.'

'Of course. Follow me.'

'What does the code stand for?'

'Didn't Archie tell you?' Don said. 'Well, I don't suppose it matters anymore. It's *All Friends Together* - member seven-hundred and twenty-nine.'

He led Brady to the lounge, through the hallway adorned with signed framed photographs of famous children's TV presenters from the distant and recent past. The lounge was full of soft furnishings, but Brady instantly clocked the large display of children's toys near the TV. He tried to not make it obvious that he was checking the place out.

'So, you're Brady, if I'm not mistaken. I haven't been in touch with Archie for...' He was trying to work it out. 'Well, it must have been more than thirty years ago. Would you like a coffee? I'm having to use a camping stove. They're hot property - no pun intended.'

'Yeah - a coffee would be great.' Brady watched Don head off to the kitchen. He listened to him padding down the hallway, gauging where the kitchen was – and he heard a key turn in a lock before the padding continued. *It's no surprise that he's securing his secrets while a stranger is in his home,* he thought. *But I want to know what it is before I leave.*

As he listened to the sound of coffee being made, he turned to his immediate problem with his business plan. *I can't create files without power. The Greens have a power supply. I could make them in McFarland, but that's going to get complicated. I probably should have picked up those free drugs at the roadside.* He then returned to his original reasoning. *They would have been too heavy.* He didn't have any knowledge of dealing drugs, and he knew the narcotics industry required certain skillsets he wasn't sure he possessed. He also knew he would have had a hard time getting beyond the Cesares with a load of dope on him. They wouldn't have taken kindly to a drug dealer encroaching on their turf.

Don returned with the coffee. 'You're deep in thought for one so muscular,' he said. 'What's perplexing you?'

Brady stuck with his last thoughts, hoping it would come across as truthful, and establish trust. He knew he didn't want to bring up the subject of child pornography – and certainly didn't want to explore his Pop's relationship with this toad. 'I was wondering what would happen to the drug market, now.'

Don's tone was superior, overly intellectual. 'The drug market is flooded. In my line of business...' He paused. Brady knew he should ask, but he didn't. He acted like he wasn't concerned. Don went on. 'I deal with the major players - you could say our specialities cross.' He leaned in as though he were letting Brady into a secret. Brady could smell the man's body spray and aftershave, and he tried not to show his discomfort as Don's dressing gown slipped off his leg, exposing the absence of underwear. 'They tell me the Greens are dumping huge quantities of smuggled drugs from abandoned vehicles on our side of their invisible walls.'

Brady remained composed, despite feeling strangely intimidated. 'Why would the Greens do that?'

'It's been done before.'

Brady put aside the knowledge that Don was a predatory paedophile - and if he was a friend of Pops, then he was more than likely an obsessive conspiracy theorist. He felt more comfortable dealing with this version of the perfumed man in front of him. And sometimes Pops was right with his predictions.

He sat back in a deliberately relaxed pose and drank some coffee. Don mirrored his guest's posture - it was a well-practised move. Brady encouraged Don to continue.

'Over a hundred years ago, the government feared an uprising from the Black civil rights movement, but instead of sending in the military, they sent in the drug dealers.'

'I don't follow.'

'They flooded the area with ample supplies of super-cheap heroin. They sent the opposition into a drug-induced haze.'

Brady weighed up - as he always did - stories like these before he came to his conclusion. 'I can see how that would apply to our current situation.'

'While the dealers, were fixated on the loss of their cash, cars and rushing off to secure their substantial properties in the suburbs - the addicts were swarming at the kerbsides like flies on roadkill. They've got more than enough to take themselves and all their friends to oblivion.'

'The dealers are saying that?'

'Yes. Also, they don't know what to ask for payment if they did still hold the poor unfortunates in their grasp. There's no money, nothing seems to have any value at all - except for the pleasures of the flesh.'

Brady knew there was no point in being coy with this man. 'And how is your business?'

'Like everybody else in this current catastrophe, it has slowed, somewhat. It didn't help with the fucking Internet crashing, never mind the loss of power. I've lost my contacts list - they were all in encrypted files online.'

'Why does that matter?'

'In a business which relies on the utmost discretion - we would discuss our more tactile, shall we say, arrangements and trades in secrecy.'

Brady didn't want to help Don with his business venture - but he did have Archie's contact book. Don shuffled in his chair, straightening his robe. Brady saw Don's withered hand for the first time, before he tucked it back into the silk sleeve of his dressing gown.

Brady considered the usefulness of Archie's contact book to Small Hand Don. *It's more than thirty-years-old*, he thought, *and surely most of them have either moved on or died in that time.* He considered Don and his Pops. *But they haven't moved. Pops has his secret bunker. Don's got his area which required locking before he let me in. The nonces in Ridgecrest, all had secret places in their houses for porn stashes and even hostages. I wouldn't know if they were still at these addresses, but Don would. He's active, and even if only half of them were still valid, that could still be valuable to him.*

Brady needed to find out if his Plan A was still a viable option. 'Don, I value your opinion. Do you think they'll ever get the power back on? I'm thinking that it's fucked, forever this time.'

'I never underestimate the endeavours of the human species to triumph over adversity. However, considering the comprehensiveness of the destruction of the infrastructure on our side of the fence. I would say your succinct conclusion is appropriate - it's completely and utterly fucked - forever.' He paused. 'Normally, you could tap into somebody else's power supply, but the only people who have that are the Greens, and they live beyond walls of indestructibility.'

Not for me, they're not. 'Is tapping into power supplies an easy thing to do?'

'Well, not for me - I mean, could you imagine me scrambling up to a power line?'

Brady did not want to imagine Don, in his bathrobe, climbing anywhere.

'Not a problem for Archie the Arrow in his younger days, though,' Don added.

This information gave Brady some hope, but also, fear. He hoped Pops wasn't going to try to climb trees or pylons to attempt to sort out an electrical supply. He didn't know how high they've built these Green Fences – he was almost certain they were entirely enclosed, but Pops might not believe that.

He changed his story a little, looking for a new angle to deal with Don. 'I promised my Foster Daddy that I'd bring home some old tech. It seemed important to him, as he's... He's been unwell even before all this. But now, with the loss of the power supply and all, I can't see how useful it would be to him. The thing is, I made a promise. Who knows, it could be his dying wish.'

Don looked at Brady closely, and Brady wondered whether this man could tell he was lying. Still, he went on. 'And if the power has gone forever - like you say - you might not need it. Of course, I wouldn't expect you to give it away - I would have to offer you something in return.'

Don slavered and looked Brady over. He could barely disguise his desire. 'What are you looking for? I don't believe for one minute that you haven't got a plan for how to get it working. But let's assume that the only value it might have for me is what it's worth to you.'

Brady finished his coffee, then relaxed back in his chair. He needed to play his part in this game. He thought this was the right moment to bring Archie into the deal. Brady believed he had Archie all wrong, but Don saw Archie's motivation through his own prism. 'We need machines to overwrite Black Files with music and movies, and maybe even games. We're looking for the ones who didn't use the Internet.' He watched Don thinking over the proposition. Brady licked his lips as Don studied him. 'We also need a large supply of Blank Files to make copies with.'

'I have the tools to satisfy your requirements. I don't believe you have the benefits in kind to satisfy all of mine.'

'I don't know... You haven't seen what I have to offer.'

'And what's that?' Don reached over and clasped Brady's knee. He wanted confirmation. He stroked Brady's thigh. Brady reached down and gently moved Don's hand away.

'How about, I'll show you mine if you show me yours,' Brady whispered.

'You want to see my equipment first?' Don said, teasingly.

'Yes, and if you do... I'll give you something to satisfy your desires for the rest of your life.'

Don was wary, but intrigued. 'You'll have to accompany me to the second floor.' He reached out his hand, offering to help Brady out of the chair. 'When did your Foster Daddy first love you?'

In normal circumstances, the inference of a question like that, and in the way that Don put it, would have seen him dead already. 'I can't remember, I was only five when they took me in.'

'Yes - so young. I wish I could remember the first time my Daddy loved me.'

Brady had heard these conversations before. In Ridgecrest, they were heavily protected for services rendered by some of the more psychotic inmates. Some used these topics to wind the other inmates up, while others were wishing for an understanding of their motivations. Ridgecrest inmates weren't known for their empathy. *I can't remember that far back,* Brady thought, *but Archie has only shown me the love and support of a good father. Surely, I would remember something like that happening.*

Don unlocked the second-floor room. It was a familiar scene that greeted him - almost a home from home, except here it was in a second-floor room in Castaic, and at home, it was in a bunker in McFarland. All the expensive computer equipment covered a whole wall - and all of it was dead. Don opened a walk-in wardrobe, which had been converted into a storeroom. Everything was neatly stored, from the old-fashioned CDs, DVDs, computer games, SD cards and files. Other boxes contained an array of every kind of old-fashioned cables. He also noted there were items which were of no use to him, like old hi-fi equipment and vinyl records. More chillingly, there were young children's toys, dolls and teddy bears.

Don adjusted his dressing gown and brushed back his mousy-brown hair to cover a bald patch. 'I've shown you mine.'

Brady reached into his jacket pocket and pulled out his Archie's contact book. 'This is my Pops' contact book. It's how I found you. It has hundreds of other names, and codenames - and lots of other details. Will this do for payment?'

Don tried to grab it from Brady, but Brady whipped it away. 'Ah, ah, ah - you can look, but you can't touch.'

'Ok. Let me see.'

Now it was Brady's turn to tease. He opened the pages, slowly, at random. 'If you package up what I need, and with a thousand Blank Files, then... Will you consider our trade complete?'

'Only if you have dinner with me tonight. I'm starving for company. I'll have everything ready for you by the morning.'

He's playing for time, Brady thought. *He's up to something*. Brady considered the practicalities of his situation. He might need more of

Don's stuff in the future, and he could only carry with him a bike full of gear at a time. He remembered the guy on the bike with the trailer.

'The guy who heckled me,' Brady said, 'the one with the bike. I know you saw him - is he from around here?'

'He's a small-time crook. I had the misfortune to deal with him, once. He lives at number 483. He's set himself up as a courier.' He changed the subject, eager to obtain an answer to his more pressing question. 'So, are you staying for a little sleepover?'

'I can do that. But just so we're clear - I'm sleeping alone.'

It was freezing cold in the dead of night. With a working power supply, Brady wouldn't have noticed the desert-climate temperature drop, but without power, Brady felt he was trying to get some shut-eye in a stone-cold mausoleum. He pulled his sleeping bag around him, but he didn't get inside it. He didn't want to restrict his movements.

Earlier, he had heard Don creeping down the stairs, and padding around softly in the hallway. He half-expected Don to come into the lounge to try his luck seducing him, but instead, he heard the sound of a key unlocking a door, followed by the sound of it locking again behind him. A couple of hours later, the reverse happened. Brady wondered if he had a bunker underground like his Pops had, back home.

Next came the sound of Don moving up and down the stairs. Brady got up to investigate. He didn't want to engage Don in conversation, so he peered through a crack in the door which looked out into the hallway. He watched as Don dutifully brought down another cardboard box of equipment and accessories, to add to the two he had brought down earlier. A few minutes later, Don brought the fourth box down - and then, it went quiet.

Brady went into the hallway, feeling like a kid at Christmas having a peek at the presents before the big day. Don had kept his side of the bargain. There were neatly tied cables to keep them from entangling, along with the hardware secured in bubble wrap, and a tray of blank Black Files complete with batches of sticky labels for them.

Brady was delighted with the result of his negotiation, but he knew his dilemma. He had his criminal code of - a deal is a deal, but this was his Pop's property he was offering up as his stake. Also, there was the guilt about enabling his paedophile host, to re-establish his ring. *The world is shot to shit anyways,* he thought. *Why is one more fucked up situation my concern?* But his inner voice couldn't quell his disquiet. *Just because the world has changed shouldn't mean I have to change with it. What kind of man would I be if I helped scumbags like Small Hand Don out? I mean, I steal stuff, but I ain't never put kids in harm's way. I'll string him along, but he ain't getting his slippery hands on Pop's book. End of.*

He reasoned that he should try and at least get a couple of hours shut eye - he wanted to put in the miles on his journey back to McFarland. Still freezing, he wrapped his sleeping bag around him, and finally managed to drift off into an uneasy sleep.

An hour later, in the darkness of the lounge, he heard something – something in the room. He listened intently. There was no sound at all. He closed his eyes again but still listened. He heard the sound of breathing coming up behind him, and then an arm snapped tight around him, and he smelled something chemical, his eyes adjusted to the darkness in time to make out Don's withered left hand bringing a white cloth to his face.

Brady jerked his head from side to side to avoid the cloth, but Don was stronger than he looked. Don managed to press the cloth on his face, but Brady inched away enough to bite down hard on Don's withered hand. Don squealed as the cloth fell to the floor. Brady was light-headed. The chloroform made him feel like he was fighting in a dream - but he was still much stronger than Don. He flung himself to the floor, taking Don down with him. He managed to get on top of Don, holding his hands around Don's throat until the life was squeezed out of him.

Brady lay next to Don's dead body for long minutes, as the effects of the chloroform began to clear from his brain. He wasn't thinking straight, obsessing about Don's secret room. He needed to know what was down there before he left. He wasn't the kind of idiotic criminal who would take the small prize and leave a jackpot in the cellar for someone else to have.

He noticed Don was fully clothed, he felt around trying to locate pockets, but everything he touched felt rubbery. *He obviously had plans to dispose of my body*, he realised. *I guess that's why he's dressed in fisherman's waders. He was going to dump my dead body in the Lagoon.* He removed Don's waders and checked his jeans. He found a wallet, with a Driver's ID and some now useless credit cards - but he didn't find keys. *Fuck it,* he thought. *Who needs keys anyway?*

He found the locked door. He tapped on it, to check its construction - he wasn't going to bust a shoulder trying to break it down if it was reinforced. But it was wooden. He took a couple of steps back and launched into the door. Then, he kicked out at the lock area of the door, and the door came off its hinges, clattering down the concrete steps.

Brady walked down the steps and entered Don's bunker. It wasn't like his Pop's. There was a bed in the centre of a room, with an en-suite shower, toilet and washbasin. He noticed the filming and lighting equipment around it. He could guess what this room was used for. There were four locked doors. He undid the bolts, rattled the locks, but the doors didn't budge. He looked around for the keys. He went to a medicine cabinet above the washbasin and found four keys hanging up, above the shelves of condoms and assorted lubrications.

He heard a voice. 'Take me. Leave the young ones alone, please, I beg you. Have you killed Mr Jell-O? Is that why you've broken in? Please Mister, let the young ones go. You can take me, instead.'

Brady followed the voice to the fourth room. He fumbled with the keys until he found the right one. He opened it, and a girl of about fourteen stood before him. He expected her to be bedraggled, but she was clean and wearing silk pyjamas. She was slim and pretty with her long blonde hair. He noticed the teen magazines on a bedside table, but even he could tell they were decades out of date. 'Are you the police?' she said, nervously.

Brady laughed, 'No, but you are free to go. What's your name?'

'I can't remember my real name, but... He calls me Angelique. I was kidnapped when I was five.'

Brady felt awkward as a hulk of a man comforting a young girl after all she had gone through, and he was concerned his attempts at sympathy might be misunderstood. He put a respectful arm on her shoulder. 'You're in safe hands now. I ain't gonna hurt ya.' He smiled. 'I'll let the other ones out.'

'They will be scared. I'll do it - they trust me.'

Brady handed her the keys but said, 'Don't get their hopes up. The world has changed since you've been in here. You'll never find yours or their parents. Unless you live very close to here.'

She began to cry, and Brady put his big arm around her, but she moved around and sobbed heavily into his chest, as years of bravery and resolve dissolved into a pool of tears. Brady held her close, knowing that a hug was all he had to give her. Eventually, she pulled away from him, wiped her tears away and put on as happy a face as she could muster, before freeing the other captives. Brady stood back and watched as two boys were released - Brady guessed they looked about eight to ten years old, and then a girl of about seven completed the freed hostages. Angelique hugged them all, whispering softly to comfort them all as best as she could. He looked into each of their rooms and saw the same set up as Angelique's - but in place of the magazines there were assorted toys, games and children's storybooks.

Brady couldn't - or didn't want to - take them under his wing. All he could do is offer words of advice about possible next steps. He justified his lack of chivalry. *I can't stay because my Pops needs me*, he told himself. *I can't take them with me because they can't travel through the Green Walls - and in any case, I'm no good with kids.*

'Hey, Angelique,' he said, finally.

She went over to him. 'Yes, Mister.'

Brady was happy with Mister - he didn't want his name associated with a place like this. 'I know this is a big ask but... Keep the kids down here for about an hour. I've got to get rid of the dead body of your Mr Jell-O.'

'Will you come back?'

'Yes, but only for a little while. I'll think over your situation, and what you can do next. Maybe you could do the same. Maybe get the kids involved – it might give them something positive to think about.'

'We're free - what could be more positive than that?'

Brady smiled, though a dark thought crossed his mind: *You haven't seen the fucked-up hell hole of a world you are about to re-join.*

Brady returned to the body of Don. He slipped Don out of his waders and put them on himself. He picked the body up in a fireman's lift and carried him outside. There was no point disguising the fact he was disposing of a body – there wasn't any law enforcement left, anyway.

As he walked a few hundred yards to the Lagoon, he noticed the odd curtain twitching. One old woman smiled from across the street, and she had some children in tow. 'Now, now. Stop crying, we'll soon be at St Stephen's, and you'll be safe and warm there. It's not far...' The woman had a pink sash around her with *Save The*

Children emblazoned on it. She seemed disinterested in Brady and whatever he was up to. When they had gone, he guessed she feigned this, so as not to attract attention from a man like him, with a drunk or worse on his shoulders.

Brady splashed into the Lagoon, and as soon as he found the deeper waters, pushed the body of Don in, watching him float away. As he emerged from the Lagoon, he removed his waders. The thought of being this close to Don Pickerstaff's slimy, rubbery clothes made his skin crawl. He dumped them on the bank.

Before heading back to the children, he decided to complete another errand.

He wandered up the road until he came to number 483. He rapped on the door. 'Police! Open up.' He stepped away from the peephole and as the door opened slightly, he was delighted to see the same guy who had called him a paedophile earlier in the day. Brady pinned him up against the wall, roughly, and the guy cried out in pain. 'I need the trolley from your bike, and you're going to give it to me.'

'But what if I haven't got it anymore?'

'Then I'll take your life instead. So, what's it going to be fuck-head?'

'It's out the back, but it's got my stuff in it.'

'Show me.' He rammed his arm up his back - close to the point of dislocating his shoulder.

Outside, he used the quick release on the trailer. He looked inside and saw tinned food, toilet rolls and pasta. Brady tipped it up, sending the contents scattering. 'You can keep this. And stay away from that house. The nonce that lived there is dead, and it's a Mob House now. Am I making myself clear?'

'Yes.'

'Repeat it back.'

'It's a Mob House, and I've got to stay away from it.'

Brady wheeled his trailer back to Don's home and went to check-in with the kids.

'It's ok,' he called into the cellar. 'You can come up now.'

Angelique led the kids up, and they huddled behind her nervously. Brady had already started to load his trailer, with his files and electrical equipment. 'What are you going to do?'

'We want to find our parents. Will you help us?'

Brady frowned before answering quickly, he didn't want to offer them false hope. 'No. I've got things to do, and where I'm going, you wouldn't be allowed to enter.' He thought about their plan, he guessed they would have an overwhelming desire to go home. 'The only people I can think of to help you would be the church.' They looked at him, hopefully. 'I think there's a place nearby, where they could help you better than me.' He looked at them all, they were scared. The youngest were putting on a brave face. 'Ok, wait here. I'll see if I can find help.'

Angelique stood up straight, as though she were preparing herself for hard times ahead, but with a sense of purpose. 'Ok, that's what we'll do. We need to get home. Our parents will be worried sick.'

Assuming they're still alive, he thought. 'There is another option. The owner of this place is dead. You can have it. It will be safe for a while, even if it's just while you get fed and watered.'

'No. No,' one of the young boys cried out. 'Please don't make me stay here.'

Angelique turned around and cuddled him. 'We are only a few steps away from escaping our nightmare - our hell. Surely, you can understand that, Mister?'

Brady knew exactly how that felt. 'Of course.' He sighed. 'I'm packing up my things. I'll keep guard, while you get ready and gather up anything you might need. It's going to be cold at night, so make sure you've got plenty of warm clothes and blankets - and grab stuff to eat and drink.'

Angelique smiled a *thank you* for the advice, and then led the children to the kitchen. Brady continued to load his tech into the trailer. He'd already raided the kitchen for food and drink for the journey - anything left over he would give to his Pops. He grabbed some bags that the children could carry, and he went back to his trailer to fill them up with the sort of things the kids would like to eat and drink. Small Hand Don had plenty of supplies with these kind of guests in mind.

He used the elasticated straps attached to it to secure his chosen items securely into place. When he had finished, the children had returned, loaded up with little toys and teddies. He wondered if they had been sensible and practical in their selections, but guessed, if what they had chosen had made them feel better, then that would have to do.

Angelique stood up on tiptoes and kissed Brady on the cheek. 'Thank you for rescuing us - you saved our lives.' He was surprised and thought she should have feared him, but if she was afraid, she didn't show it.

They left the house. Brady pushed his bike and trailer with the kids in tow. It didn't take long to find St Stephen's Church. Even though Brady had brought the children to their door, they eyed him suspiciously as if he was dumping his own children or rounding others up in the hope of a reward. Brady wasn't interested in obtaining gratitude or approval. The women took the bags off the children and ushered them inside the church, and then closed the door to keep them safe from the monsters outside.

12.LIZZIE

Lizzie welcomed her pupils to class on the Third Green Day - as the third day after the Green Revolution would come to be known. The pupils sat at their desks, each inlaid with a Sattva Systems™ Green File computer. The launch of the SattvaGreen™, as it was abbreviated to, was a much-ridiculed machine. Its' primary benefit was its exceptionally low energy usage. However, it had the slowest Internet processing speed of any comparison model - almost to the point of being useless. It also used a backwards-looking slot for work with the defunct Black File Chips. They were ridiculed for being a so-called Green Company who manufactured physical files. Their devotees, however, bought them with old money and were allocated Green Files to add to their collection as a reward. They sold well in the revisionist new Green Towns and districts.

The Greens, in these places, drew the kind of quiet disdain that used to be reserved for communities such as the Amish - but they weren't hurting anybody.

Lizzie's Junior Ecology class today was for the eight to ten-year-olds. Every child was expected to learn at their own pace, and certainly not to be in competition with each other.

'Now children, please put in your Files marked New Day.'

The children put in their files, and the screens lit up with a picture of a verdant green tree with the sparkling rays of dawn splintering between the leaves.

'To celebrate the beginning of the saving of all Mother Earth's vegetation and animals - we will be giving you a Green Credit to take home at the end of each school day to your family. Your families will be so proud of you.'

An excited murmuring of children filled the room.

'In your second slot, place a blank Green Credit with your thumb and index finger.' There were slots on both the right and left sides of the screens, so as not to appear to discriminate against those who were left-handed. Lizzie helped a disabled girl with her File. All the Files glowed green.

'I will authorise them at the end of class when I put my Group Award File in.' She held it up for the class to see.

The children enjoyed the lesson, which focused on the animals that might now be saved from the ravages of mankind. Much was made of the ringfencing of the rainforests, national parks and any other significant green spaces.

Her final class for the day was Senior Humanities. She knew this would be challenging, and the offer of a Green Credit wouldn't stifle the expected more incisive questioning. She asked for their attention during the lesson, with the promise that she would answer any questions they had for her at the end, to the best of her ability.

She gave the class a potted history of the last hundred years - not because they were unaware of it, but to try and remind them of the context, and how they had made it to this point. 'Decade after decade, we warned them of the consequences of Climate Change, but they never took it seriously,' she said, closing the lesson. 'Even when all hell was breaking out around them, with the mega-storms of the late thirties and early forties... We tried to communicate in a civilised manner, but the people who held the levers of power wouldn't listen, or would pretend to listen if the voters and consumers could be won over. This is why it had to come to this.

They left us no choice but to save Mother Earth and bypass the Traditional Cultures.' She smiled. 'Does anyone have any questions?'

A hand went up, and she laughed. 'Daryl. I thought you'd have something to say.' The class chuckled.

'You indicated that they wouldn't use the technology invented by Sattva Systems™, and yet they ended up being the largest tech conglomerate in the world. That doesn't make sense to me.'

'When Sattva brought a product to market which had no competition, like the Human NanoBubble™ in the Twenties, which solved the public transport issues after the third great pandemic of the decade. It made financial sense for governments to let it freely come to market. But when Sattva developed FusionPower™, the dirty energy producers were threatened, and they used their lobby powers to encourage governments to impose punitive tariffs on its supply. The same happened when Sattva introduced Intense Recyclable Energy. So, yes, Sattva made trillions of dollars, but it was forced into the niche markets in Energy and Transport.'

'Niche markets?'

'Yes. The tariffs made FusionPower™ energy supplies and vehicles expensive. Only the Green Communities, who were prepared to sacrifice other material possessions were prepared to live in them.'

'But my parents were poor.'

'Your parents were good people, and hard-working, and they collected lots of Green Credits for their assistance on projects to help the environment. The Green Credits had no value to the Traditional Cultures, then, but they collected them as a matter of faith. This is what helped them to become part of our McFarland Green Community.'

Another hand went up. 'Dawson - what would you like to ask me?'

'I disagree with the way we are treating the Trads. I know they were mean to the Greens, but I worry about the people I used to know. We all have extended families out there, and I think it's cruel to take away their basic needs.'

The rest of the class murmured their support for Dawson's question. Lizzie had been dreading this - but she knew it needed to be addressed. 'For over a hundred years we have warned about Climate Change. We have made suggestions, offered to help them, and with Sattva, we even offered solutions. They always promised much but delivered little. It might have carried on that way if it wasn't for the irrefutable evidence that the Earth was entering into the Runaway Greenhouse Phase.'

Dawson slumped. 'I kinda know all that, but surely I should have been able to take my family, and my girlfriend, in. I should have tried to save them - or at least have been allowed to try.'

Girlfriend, she thought. *That's the crux of his angst.* 'I'm sorry Dawson, I know this is upsetting. I, too, have had to leave old family and friends behind. But here's the deal: the planet was going to die, and eight billion people and every other living thing were going to perish. The GreenRevs, working alongside Sattva Systems™, have saved more than nine hundred million people across the globe, and they will live in low energy and sustainable communities. We are preserving all of Mother Nature's creatures. But we had no choice. A line had to be drawn over who to save, and who to leave behind.'

'But couldn't we have made exceptions?'

'No. If they weren't Green, then they would soon start up the old ways to hoard material possessions. And we haven't attacked anybody,' she added. 'We could have developed the technology to do it, but our ethos is not to deliberately harm or hurt anybody. The Traditional Cultures are cunning and inventive and will soon learn to forge new societies and new ways of living - and that's absolutely fine. But we will put our time and effort into healing Mother Earth.'

She looked to the only hand left raised. It was Martina, whose cheery and constructive disposition was always a relief to Lizzie. 'Yes. Martina.'

'My parents always told me that the thought of returning to pseudo-feudalism was an unattractive proposition but were enthralled with the prospect of saving the planet with cutting edge technology. Do you have any insight about what the future might have in store for us?'

Thank heavens, she thought. 'At the moment, you are confined to the community for your own safety. There is a lot of turmoil beyond the NanoShell™. However, when you attain the Red™, you will be completely protected. That will be the point you could visit your old friends and family.' *By then, though*, she kept to herself, *you'll be heavily dissuaded from dealing with any Trads, but we can cross that bridge later.*

'But after that? What then?'

'The Orange™ is an exciting prospect. It will enable NanoBots™ to patrol your body, working in conjunction with your antibodies to target sources of illness. You could be cured before even becoming aware that you were ill. Also, this will vastly improve your quality of life as you grow older. I know that doesn't seem important now, while you're young and healthy, but trust me - it will matter a lot when you approach middle age and beyond.'

The class eagerly asked for more, their questions crowding into each other. 'Well,' she said, 'this is just at the early planning stages, and there's no guarantee that the clever people at Sattva Systems™ could pull it off, but a little bird told me they're trying to get rid of the need for the textile industry, due to its heavy use of the environment's resources...'

'We are all going to get naked in our Red™ see-through suits,' Daryl called out. 'You won't need clothes with those on.' The class burst into riotous laughter.

'Technically, that's true,' Lizzie replied, 'but I'm not going to start strolling around naked.'

'Shame!'

'Daryl - that's enough. You know what happens if you stray close to verbal sexual assault?'

Daryl knew about the SecurityFilm™. They all did. 'Sorry, Miss.'

'You can still call me Lizzie.' She smiled. 'As I was saying, the Yellow™ upgrade might make the RedSuits™ take on any appearance you would wish to adopt, literally, second by second. For instance, if you were to go to the Trad areas, you could have your appearance set to blend to make you or your old friends feel more at ease. Another application might be simply allowing you to appear in what makes you feel good or how you feel at that moment - though I'm not sure I'm looking forward to those classes,' she added, playfully.

The bell rang for the end of the day's lessons, and her class departed. Some were discussing the YellowSuits™, but one or two of the class were patting Dawson on the back.

As she made her way back to her communal home, she reflected upon the day's lessons, feeling contented - she had done a satisfactory job.

The smell of cooking from the kitchen greeted her as she entered the lounge area, where Mollie was chatting with Cain. They looked remarkably relaxed considering the tumultuous events taking place in the world, and on their proverbial doorstep. Siddha called out from the kitchen. 'Hi Lizzie. We're having Fried Wontons followed by Thai Basil Eggplant - is that ok with you?'

'Sounds wonderful - can't wait. I'll just go and get changed.' She smiled as she mused on the sharing of her insights on the YellowSuits™ with her class. Getting changed might become a thing of the past - but how stressful might it be to have an infinite choice of clothes. She changed into her jeans and a flowery blouse. *I should have mentioned that people wouldn't be able to class themselves by how expensive or desirable their clothes were anymore*, she thought. *They would have appreciated that - I'll have to remember to mention that in the other Senior Humanities Group*.

Back in the living room, she slumped into the armchair. 'How's your day been?'

'Good,' Cain said. 'Though I thought there would be more drama.'

Mollie nudged him. 'Tell Lizzie about your phone call with Bodhi. I still cannot believe you've actually spoken to him.'

'I know. It's like getting through to God - and he wants me to call him once a month.'

'Oh, wow!' Lizzie gasped. 'How did that come about?'

'Well, I put a message through about this Brady character, and he phoned me back, personally.'

'What did he say?'

'He said that we should monitor him if he returns - and he's certain he will, after I told him about his family situation on the farm just off the New Green Road.' Cain omitted to tell Mollie and Lizzie about the carnage on that night at the farm, but he had informed Bodhi of every detail - Bodhi had insisted on it. 'He wants him monitored, but not prevented from doing anything he wants that doesn't break the SecurityFilm™ Protocols™. He informed me that he has told other districts to do likewise. He thanked me for help and promised that I might be one of the first to take the Orange™.'

'That's wonderful news,' Lizzie said. 'I'm thrilled for you.'

'You had a close encounter with this Brady,' Mollie teased. 'I heard you two together - you know - intimately. What was he like?'

Lizzie laughed, a blush appearing on her cheeks. 'He was ok.'

'Only, ok?'

'Yes. That's an accurate appraisal of his skills. He's a bit one-dimensional - typical alpha-male Trad, all force and strength, but lacking finesse. Still, a pleasant enough experience.'

Cain changed the subject, without trying to conceal it. 'Siddha said he spotted Brady on his way down Highway 99 en route to Bakersfield. He apparently, had no trouble crossing through the Green Zones there, either.'

'He's quite the anomaly,' Mollie said. 'But Bodhi believes he is the only one.'

'I get the impression that Bodhi knows he is the only one, but still, Bodhi might want us to think that way, so it doesn't spread any panic.' He fixed Lizzie and Mollie with his crystal green eyes. 'After dinner, I've asked Mrs Wilson over for a chat. I want you to lead the conversation, Lizzie, as I might be a little intimidating for her.'

'No problem, Cain. What do you want to find out?'

'The precise details of how she came into contact with Brady and how he came to go through the NanoShell™ with her.'

After dinner, Cain cleared the dishes and washed up. It was how things were organised - there were as few hierarchical structures as possible, while still maintaining a chain of command for communication purposes. He brought in herbal teas. As he passed a cup to Siddha, he said, 'Are the Hodgson and Mahone Ranches without power?'

'Of course.'

'I want you to restore the supply - off our grid.'

Siddha frowned. 'Why would we possibly want to do that?'

'Bodhi's instructions. He said Brady would, in all likelihood, try to tap our power lines. He doesn't want him to even try. He said it would be dangerous to us.'

'When do you want it done by?'

'As soon as possible. Could you do it while we are dealing with Mrs Wilson?'

'It'll be dark by the time the FusionPower™ team have eaten with their families, but I'll do it. It wouldn't do to disappoint Bodhi,' Siddha added, smiling.

They heard a knock at the door. Lizzie answered and ushered Mrs Wilson in. Cain offered her tea, but Mrs Wilson seemed too overawed to agree. Still, Cain insisted that it would be his pleasure, so she asked for a Peppermint tea.

Siddha smiled at Mrs Wilson as he passed her on his way out.

As Cain headed back to the kitchen, Lizzie took over. 'Am I in trouble - for letting that man come into the village?' Mrs Wilson asked.

'No, not at all. We just want to ascertain exactly how he managed to breach the Shell™. It may be that he has the right to be here.' Mrs Wilson was about to answer, but Lizzie invited her to sit down on the sofa. Cain brought in the tea, and Mollie and Cain left the room together, though remaining within earshot of the conversation. Lizzie sat beside Mrs Wilson, twisting around in her seat to face her.

'Would you mind if I called you Margaret instead of addressing you as Mrs Wilson?'

'Maggie. You can call me Maggie.'

Lizzie smiled. 'Now Maggie - exactly what happened on the day you met Brady?'

'I was driving over to visit my sister - it was a low powered electric car...'

'Honestly Maggie, we know you are an honourable member of the Green Community of McFarland. We are only interested in this Brady character. Please, be at ease.'

She sighed. 'I was distracted by some boys who were throwing rocks at me - I know I shouldn't have been concerned, but it was the first day of the NanoShell™ being activated, and it was just instinct to swerve away from the rocks... And I lost control of the car. I was terrified, I thought I was going to die when the car left the road. Then those boys came over, and I could tell they had bad intentions.'

'And did you see Brady at this point? Was he with these boys?'

'No, I don't think so.'

'Then what happened?'

'Wait - I just remembered something. When I lost control of the car - I nearly ran somebody over - it might have been the man you're calling Brady - I saw a figure for a split second.'

'Was this on or off the New Green Road?'

'It was definitely off the road.' Maggie sipped at her Peppermint tea, and Lizzie mirrored her – one of the many interview techniques she had learned. Maggie went on. 'I was shocked, but Brady came over to see if I was ok. I think I was rude to him - all I could think of was getting back to the safety of the Shell™.'

'What did Brady do?'

'He was chivalrous. Actually, he shielded me from those animals – though those two give animals a bad name. They came at him with knives, but he protected me. He edged backwards toward the road, with me behind him. These thugs moved in for the kill when they realised that I might reach the safety of the road, and that's when we both fell. As we did, we nearly got run over. I didn't wish to be ungrateful, but while Brady was distracted by the oncoming cars, and looking back at the thugs, I crossed the road and left him behind. He might have saved me, but I still thought he looked terrifying.'

Lizzie placed her hand upon Maggie's. 'That's completely understandable. Now, I want you to think carefully before answering. When you both fell through the shield, did you fall first? You said he was in front of you - or did you fall through at the same time?'

Maggie thought hard, her lips pursed tightly together, and she pulled up her right hand to her chin. 'We stumbled. I remember thinking he was going to fall into me, and he was a big man, but he swerved at the last second as he was falling...' She pulled her hand away from her chin and looked straight into Lizzie's eyes. She seemed pleased to be able to give her the definitive answer she desired. 'We both fell through the Shell™ at the same time. We were very close together. I'm sure that's how it happened.'

'Thank you, Maggie, you've been very helpful.'

Maggie was embarrassed to ask her next question, but she knew this would be her only chance. 'I lost my car. I don't know if it's recoverable, now that it has left the Shell™... I don't suppose...?'

'I'll have a word with Cain. I'm sure he will be able to help you out.'

When they had finished their tea, Lizzie showed Maggie out, Mollie volunteering to drive her home. Lizzie returned to the lounge to discuss the situation with Cain.

'We cannot rule out the possibility that he somehow acquired a free pass through the Shell™ by saving her,' she said.

'I don't believe that, but it can't be ruled out,' Cain replied, 'The opacity of the Shell™ has always been a tricky thing. If it had been opaque, then Maggie wouldn't have seen the Hodgson Boys, and they wouldn't have been able to see the road. But it would have made the Community feel claustrophobic, and that wouldn't have helped their mental health. It's not like this transition period isn't already tough enough for our people to get their heads around.'

'What about the semi-opaque version of the Shell™?'

'When I saw that, my first thought was how my younger children would view it. I have to say the visions of blurred out people seemed quite nightmarish. I think the only option was to go for the Clear View, it gives the impression of having nothing to hide - and natural light is always the healthiest option. You mustn't blame yourself.'

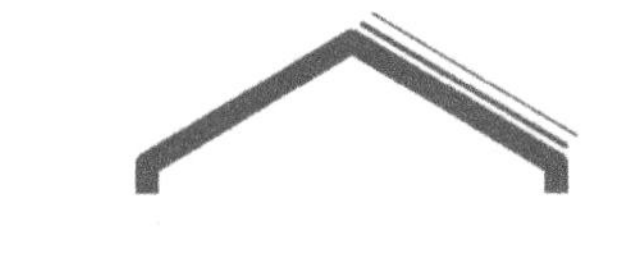

13.GREEN BEACONS

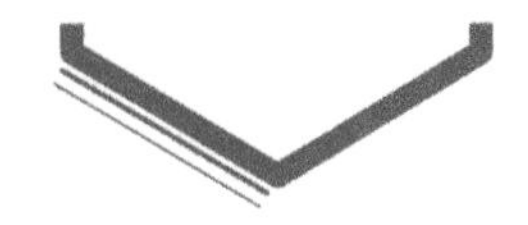

Brady locked up Don Pickerstaff's home and kept the key. There might be other resources he could plunder from here in the future. *Although*, he thought, *next time I hope I have some kinda vehicle instead of a bike to travel back and forth.* While it was out of his way, by heading southwards at first, he wouldn't have to pass through the Cesare's territory. He had a loaded trailer on the back of his bike, and knowing criminals, even if the contents were of no value to them, they would confiscate them anyway - just in case they were missing something that he had thought of.

There were other advantages to going this way. The land to the left of him was barren, so carried little in the form of hidden threats. He hadn't thought to check out if this was under a GreenNanoShell™, but also, he would soon reach Highway Five, which he knew was Green Protected.

In standard times - like just a few days ago - he wouldn't be able to access Highway Five, as this road ended up as a bridge that went over it. Now, though, he could scramble down the bank, carefully picking out a path that would accommodate his bike and trailer and cross the almost deserted road to pick up the northbound carriageway.

The newly painted cycle lane was smooth and easy to travel on, even with a heavily loaded trailer, and Brady was beginning to enjoy his newfound hobby of cycling. He made good progress through the early evening, and it struck him that the sound of the world had changed. He was on Highway 5, soon to hit the busy intersection to join Highway 99, but all he could hear was birdsong and the sound of cicadas. Even the nearby urban areas seemed quiet. He noted the lack of police sirens and wondered if the Police Department still existed. Brady chuckled at the thought.

Later, deep into the night, he stopped for a while, to gaze in wonder at the glittering stars in the heavens. Around him, the power-cut areas were enshrouded in darkness, but in the distance, he could see the ethereally lighted green domes encasing towns, districts and other protected areas. He watched in awe as he saw one small dome merge into another. *I guess that's another Trad area being reclaimed by the Greens*, he thought. It also increased his concern for his Pops.

After a couple of hours, he suddenly heard the sound of rumbling and popping in the distance. He could just about make out a couple of creamy, ceramic looking flying vehicles cruising at an almost impossibly low altitude, one travelling south, and another crawling up behind him travelling north, both very close to the sides of the Highway. He quickly moved his bike and trailer to the central reservation, as this felt like the safest place to be. He hadn't seen a car pass him by for hours.

These planes seemed to be shaped like petrol tankers - except about four times longer. As they gradually moved closer, he noticed they were suspended in the air by giant drone-type propellors. They were about a hundred yards away from the edges of the Highway, but they had stiff hoses pointing in the direction of the road. *Looks like a whale with a hard-on*, he thought.

As they passed near him, and he could see that they were spraying the vehicles which were placed at the sides of the Highways by the road crews a couple of days ago. When they were travelling away from him, in their diverging directions, he went over to the abandoned off-road vehicles to investigate. He spotted movement as people scurried away into the nearby trees and undergrowth. Brady guessed they had been going through the vehicles and picking them clean for anything useful.

The silver-ish goo covering the vehicles wasn't wet, like he guessed it would be. Instead, it was a dry illuminated Film. After a minute or two, he began to notice tiny holes appearing in the vehicles, and even on the tyres. Then he heard the popping and banging of bursting tyres all around him. He instinctively lay on the ground for cover, until he realised what was happening. He saw the tyres' shrapnel bouncing off the GreenShell™ and, encouraged to take another look, he saw the vehicles slowly crumbling away.

Reassured, he mounted his bike and continued his journey back to McFarland. He whooped and hollered every time another tyre exploded. He figured the further he travelled northward, the longer ago the vehicles were doused in what he guessed was some kind of Nano Technology. *All I've heard from those Greens is Nano-this and Nano-that,* he thought. *They probably take Nano-shits, too.*

He didn't mind the noise. It took his mind off the pedalling, and he barely noticed the miles he was clocking up. He appreciated the work out his leg muscles were getting. *Feel the burn man, feel that fucking burn.* There was the sound of creaking metal, as if it was collapsing under its own weight - and then came the enormous bangs of lorry tyres exploding all around him. *Woohoo! Hell yes!* And then there was an explosion the size of which Brady had only ever dreamed of witnessing, as an oil tanker blew up. As the flames rose hundreds of feet into the air, Brady watched the NanoShell™ rise up with it, as if it was magnetised to the flame; then the NanoShell™ formed an archway over the Highway to block the debris from falling onto the road. *Wow! This is like a hundred Fourth of July's rolled into one.* He watched in awe as the silver goo completed its tango with the jet-black smoke. *Oh, my fucking God - it's eating the smoke - it's eating the fucking smoke. This is amazing!*

The oil tanker explosion seemed to trigger a chain reaction in the other vehicles as one-by-one they all blew up. Brady road the bike with no hands, he stretched out his arms to welcome the fiery devastation. He felt like a God as he bellowed, 'Sattva Systems™ - You fucking raaaaaawwwkkk! Woohoo! Yeah!' Then, up ahead, where the northbound plane had overtaken him, the scene played out again, and Brady pedalled quickly to make sure he was in place for the encore performance. *You couldn't have a show as good as this for all the money in the old world.*

Eventually, the explosions only went off intermittently, and the fires and smoke were doused as if God Almighty had a heavenly fire extinguisher. It was mid-morning, and the sun was getting hot. Brady's legs were sore and painful from the build-up of lactic acid, so he decided to rest up for a while. He did some stretches and some cool-down exercises, and then strolled along the edge of the carriageway. He saw the slow but unmistakable signs of the cars and trucks dissolving away, and more disturbing, he spotted the same thing happening to the occasional dead body – some of which, he realised, were children. He thought about what might have happened to Angelique and her brood of broken kids. *It seems I'm having a mental cool down as well,* he thought. *Poor little bastards.*

He had stopped at a bend in the road. He worked out where the sun was likely to be in the next couple of hours and checked the position of the trees at the side of the road. The goo hasn't affected the trees, bushes, and grass at all. He listened to the sound of birds for a moment. *This will do to get my head down,* he thought. *There'll be shade for the next few hours.* Even the sound of far-off explosions couldn't prevent Brady from falling into a deep sleep. He dreamed of all the explosions he had witnessed the night before, and it was the best dream he had ever had.

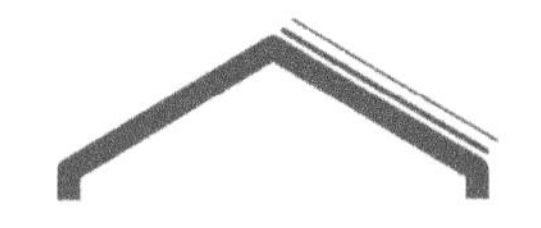

14.HOME ON THE RANCH

It was night, and Brady left Highway 99 and picked up the New Road to McFarland. The lights from West McFarland were aglow, but the Eastside had disappeared in the darkness. He was alarmed to see the unmistakable signs of a power supply from the Hodgson and Mahone Ranches. He pedalled quickly - he needed to know that nothing untoward had happened.

A few hundred yards from the homestead, he saw three graves marked with simple wooden crosses. Brady called out, 'Hey, Pops. It's me, Brady. I don't want to be mistaken and get myself mown down by Old Marvin.'

He was relieved to hear Lucian reply. 'Hey man - did ya have a good trip?'

Brady walked his bike up to the homestead and hugged his buddy, slapping him on the back a couple of times. 'Oh man - I wish you could have seen what I've seen, but that can wait. How have y'all been?'

'It's all good, man. Your Pops is sleeping. He's even insisting that I call him Pops as well. That's if you don't mind, of course. I don't want to look like I'm getting my feet under the table.'

Brady smiled. 'You're stuck here, man. Don't you worry. You're like a brother to me now.'

Lucian beamed. 'Come on in. You want coffee or something to eat?'

'Coffee would be good, but give me a hand bringing the stuff in from the trailer first, would ya?'

'Sure thing.' Lucian helped unload the trailer, making quips about it looking like the worst antique heist in history as he examined the hardware and cables.

'You've still got a power supply,' Brady said.

'Yeah. It went off for a day, and we all thought - oh shit, here we go. Your Pops, I mean, Pops was trying to show me how to try and tap into the neighbour's supply - but they've got this - I dunno - an invisible wall of some kind. Anyway, we were trying to come up with another plan when - hey presto! The power just up and came back on.'

'Well, that will save us a lot of trouble.'

Lucian yawned, the long night's watch showing on his face. 'Hey,' Brady said, 'I slept in the day, I ain't tired. I'll take over the watch. I'm used to it.'

'If you're sure - I am beat.'

'No problem, we can catch up in the morning.'

Lucian smiled, yawning again. 'Maybe we could all get together and plan what we're going to do over a meal tomorrow night. I could invite Mary-Lou...'

'Sure. Why not?'

Brady had reason to take his time in the shower. He had just returned from his gruelling few days of travelling on foot and by bicycle. Lucian, however, seemed to take forever, readying himself as though he were attending a wedding. Archie took care of the meal arrangements, with enough frozen meat in his bunker to last for decades, he had been panicking about his freezer supplies when the power went off, as his generator had broken as well.

The evening air was fresh and cool, and the dining table was set for four adults. Archie had even scrubbed up an old highchair -

which had been abandoned in the barn, along with other junk that Archie couldn't part with - for the baby.

There was a light tapping at the door. 'Hey, Lucky,' Brady called out, 'you have a visitor.' Archie's laughter roared from the hot kitchen. Lucian brushed himself down and straightened himself up and went to the door. As he opened it, his jaw dropped. Mary-Lou had dressed up to the nines for the occasion. He held out his hand, and she took it. 'Welcome to the Mahone Ranch,' he said, formally. 'And you too, little Amie.' He looked at Mary-Lou. 'Do you mind if I take her?'

'No, sir.'

Lucian unstrapped Amie from her pushchair and held her close to him, before placing her carefully in the highchair. He pulled out a couple of toys - Archie had also retrieved them from the barn - which Amie promptly began to chew. 'She's teething,' Mary-Lou said, softly.

As they ate until they were bursting, they chatted enthusiastically about the events from the past few days. The only thing Brady didn't cover in detail was the line of business Small Hand Don dealt in. Brady talked about him as if he was a small-time antique dealer. He also didn't mention the freeing of the children – which didn't fit the narrative he had created.

Once the past few days had been thoroughly picked over, Archie broke out his once-famous moonshine, and they began to brainstorm their plans for the future in more detail.

Archie brought up the subject of securing the premises. Brady hadn't even thought about this. In his mind, they were trapped here forever - end of story. 'I'm saying, son,' Archie said, 'that if your business venture is successful, and they love your Files of movies and stuff - what's to stop those Green sons of bitches from just strolling on over here and stealing all your stock? After all - you make out like they are invincible. Even you and Old Marvin couldn't stop them. Ya see what I'm getting' at?'

'I never thought of that Pops. They seem so Goody Two Shoes - but you're right, that's what I'd do. What can we do to stop them - or at least make it more difficult?'

'I've got big strong fences surrounding most of the place, and the Hodgsons have got barbed-wire on top of theirs.' They all thought about it for a few moments. 'We could dig ditches, that'd slow 'em down.'

Lucian looked distraught at that idea. 'It took me a day to dig three graves, and I still got backache.'

'It won't stop 'em Pops,' Brady said. 'We might be ok. They might not be like that. They might be law-abiding, God-fearing folk.'

'Now come on, son, you ain't making sense with your own logic. You want them to buy your contraband, don't you? If so, you better hope that lots of them are exactly like us.'

Mary-Lou spoke up. 'Do you mind telling me what you are planning to sell to them?'

Lucian wanted to be the one to answer. 'Entertainment files. Brady figures they will get bored or just miss the stuff from the old days - y'know, the nostalgia market.'

'So, you would take the stuff over to them and let them pick out what they want?' Brady leaned in. He was curious, and Mary-Lou was obviously either shy, or her personality had been beaten out of her by the Hodgson boys. 'What's the point of barricading us in here, if you are going to carry your goods into West McFarland, anyway? It seems to me that your strength and demeanour is not much of an asset there.'

Brady wasn't used to having his manly power questioned. 'Don't get sarcastic with me,' he said. 'You ain't no more than a mere slip of a girl.'

'Brady, man,' Lucian interrupted, 'I don't think she meant you to take it like that. Mary-Lou is trying to help.' He turned to her. 'Ain't that right, Mary-Lou?'

She didn't answer. She withdrew, looking away in quiet defiance. Brady remembered the way she slammed down the axe into the old-man Hodgson's head. *I might be underestimating her,* he thought.

'I'm sorry, Mary-Lou,' he said. 'I'm not used to the sort of company that questions my plans.'

She looked around the table. 'I was concerned that you might get robbed.'

She paused, to see if Brady would object again. 'I know,' he said, softly.

'We've got the power back on, and I'm guessing you've got a printer - one that doesn't need the Internet or Wi-Fi?'

Archie laughed. 'Well, I've at least got that covered in my plans for End of Days.' They all laughed with him.

'Well, I could make a catalogue of your goods and services. My granny used to do that for a living. She would travel door-to-door, selling her wares. The customers would place an order, and then the company would deliver it later.'

'That's a damn fine idea, little lady,' Archie said.

'There are other advantages with doing it this way, too,' she added.

'Like what?' Brady said.

'You don't need to make any spare copies - you just make a copy at a time, when a customer orders it. You won't have to waste unsold stock.'

The men looked at each other and laughed. 'Welcome aboard Mary-Lou,' Brady said. 'You're the new Marketing Director here at Mahone Enterprises.' He raised his glass. 'I propose a toast to Mary-Lou.'

Mary-Lou had other ideas, too – she'd thought about making sample copies and trailers for Brady's wares, for instance - but she didn't want to impose any further. She was content for a happy mood to have been returned to the group. She saw too many similarities between Brady and the Hodgsons to ever feel that she could be truly comfortable with him. She feared his innate criminality. *I'm stuck with these men for the foreseeable future,* she thought, *and I have to survive for the sake of Amie.*

They all knocked back their moonshine, and Brady and Archie slammed down their glasses in celebration. Brady noticed that Lucian was deep in thought. He wondered if he was worried about his intentions toward Mary-Lou. 'Are you ok, buddy?'

'Yes. I'm still thinking of the original boundary problem.'

'I can see your mind whirring, I know you too well, my little friend.'

'I'm trying to look at our problem by putting myself in their shoes. From what you've told me, they're quiet, well-disciplined and, for want of a better word, good people - honest citizens at heart. You're hoping they might go for a little low-level criminal activity, like bootlegging, but nothing more serious than that, or they risk being expelled - and look how long they've sacrificed to get to this position. It shouldn't take much to put them off any bad intent they may have towards us.'

'I'm listening,' Brady said. They all were.

'We just need warning signs around the place.'

'You mean like: Trespassers Will Be Shot?' Archie said. 'We already got them, boy.'

'I was thinking something scarier - to them, anyway. I was thinking Sattva Says...' Lucian smiled and continued with his idea, 'I know how to build billboards. If I copy the Sattva Systems™ Logos, then I could put official warnings and consequences for encroaching on our land. They will think we are some kinda test facility for Sattva Systems™. It might work.'

Brady slapped him on the back. 'If you can do that, then it's worth a fucking try. We'll start tomorrow - but tonight, we celebrate.'

15.MAHONE ENTERPRISES

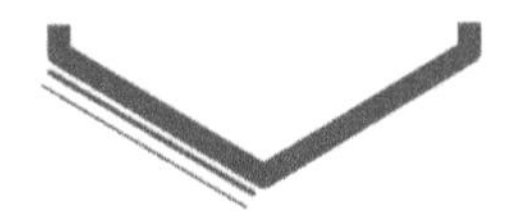

Over the next few weeks, the Mahone Family, of which Lucian, Mary-Lou and Amie were now honorary members, worked hard setting up their new business. Brady helped Lucian build and erect the fake Sattva Systems™ Billboards, placing them all around the Mahone and Hodgson Ranches - while Archie and Mary-Lou began work on putting the old electronics hardware together and testing it until they were confident in how to use it efficiently.

Archie had a few old CDs and DVDs from the early part of the century to use as test pieces, though certainly not enough to launch a business with. Mary-Lou practised putting snippets of his collection onto the Blank Black Files, then improved her skills to organise them into chapters, content groupings and overall indexing. Archie loved working with Mary-Lou, and his mood brightened with every passing day. It was beginning to feel, to him, like there was a future worth living for in their Brave New World.

Archie selected a couple of feasible computers and printers which had the potential to work off-line. They were basic models even back in the day, so they were brilliant for this technological scorched earth.

Once up and running, Mary-Lou began working on a catalogue design. At night, sometimes she would be alive with possibilities, potential layouts and designs buzzing around her head. Her initial fears of being trapped forever with such a collection of misfits changed to hopes for her - but she couldn't see what kind of life existed for her toddler Amie in the future, unless someone, someday could find a way of destroying the Green barriers that kept them boxed in. Sometimes her thoughts travelled into the outside world, worrying about the millions of people who were worse off than her.

Brady had become used to being on the ranch, but he felt he had become too comfortable there. Even he had begun to worry about venturing back out into the Trads territory. He didn't like that term until Lucian had said it was actually quite polite, in the circumstances - in keeping with the Liberal-Eco's branding. If some of the Nazi Fucks in Ridgecrest had have won, they would have called them all vermin or cockroaches.

Brady knew he had to go and find stock for his venture. He wasn't used to feeling this sense of responsibility. *I can't believe how much work they've put into making my idea work*, he thought. *I'm responsible for a team of people, and if I let them down...*

He thought about saving up for one of those RedSuits™, but his Pops' words still rang alarm bells within him. *That's how they get ya, son.* He took out his Distor™, which lit up with his three Green Credit Balance and put it back. *Still, a long way to go before I get to one hundred Green Credits, anyhows.*

He didn't want to return to Castaic just yet, as he didn't want to travel that far again - not yet, anyway. East McFarland was metaphorically on the doorstep, so it made sense to try and find the stock he needed there. He considered the old thrift stores, thinking they would be a good starting point. *I ain't no Robin Hood*, he told himself. *I'm going to be stealing from the poor to give to the rich fuckers on the west side. I suppose business has always been this way, and I'm a capitalist pig now.*

For a few days, he went into training. He needed to be prepared to fight - he didn't know how things were going to be organised over there. He planned to stay close to the Highway where it split the town from North to South. He could always head to the NanoShell™ for safety if he was outnumbered.

Brady was going through Archie's coats, when the old man asked, 'What are you looking for, boy?'

'I don't want to take the bike and trailer with me. They're too conspicuous and might slow me down. I was thinking of a coat with a lot of deep pockets.'

'I got a poachers jacket - one of those wax ones that's good for keeping out the rain. Except it don't rain here much, and it's too warm to wear in the sun.'

'Let's see it anyways.'

Archie opened a closet and retrieved the black wax jacket that was as long as a trench coat. He unrolled it - it hadn't even been hung up. 'It will do the job, and it will be warm at night,' he laughed, 'but you sure ain't gonna be inconspicuous wearing that during the daytime.'

Brady tried it on and explored it. It fitted him ok, and it seemed to have pockets on the inside and out. 'It's perfect Pops. Do you mind...?'

'Take it, boy, it's yours.'

Brady decided to head north to East McFarland later that evening. He figured that, in this coat, he wouldn't look too out of place on his first day there. He had a jemmy in one of his pockets, and Archie gave him a glass cutter, in case he needed a quieter way to break and enter. Then, there were the other objects he took around with him, his hunting knife and his Satt™. He wondered if he should bother taking the satellite phone with him, as he hardly needed it since he had it. He remembered being chided by ex-girlfriends in the past for never using the phone. *I just ain't big on conversation,* he thought. Still, he put it in a pocket, just in case.

He took a walk to the Highway, staying under the Shell's™ limits beneath West McFarland. He half-expected to be challenged, especially when he spotted Siddha looking up and down the Highway with binoculars, but even he acted like Brady had every right to be there.

He paused when he left Highway 99. He took a deep breath as he left the sanctuary of the NanoShell™ and headed over the Highway back onto East McFarland side of town. He could smell the remnants of barbecues in the air. *I suppose they've figured that out*. He wondered if the gas was still usable in the canisters or whether they had gone entirely back to basics. As soon as he passed the first houses, he heard a whistle, and then another. It made him feel uneasy - he was being watched by unknown assailants in the dark. He wandered north into the town centre, not surprised to see the looted supermarkets and the burned-out shells of other now unrecognisable buildings. In the centre of town, he noticed the whistles had become less frequent. He heard another whistle, and he looked up, almost able to make out a figure from a window in a block of apartments dart back into the shadows. Brady moved on, warily.

He noticed a pattern as he walked past the businesses. The chain stores were the ones which were wrecked, whereas the family businesses had been boarded up. He moved into the back streets, and the whistles continued to follow him. He looked up above the boarded-up panels, to the shop signs above the entrances, stopping outside a likely business: Old-Timey Marvels and Curios. He removed his jemmy and was about to go to work on the protective panels when the whistles merged to form an alarm. In the light of facing a faceless foe, Brady stopped, put away his jemmy and strolled on. The whistles only resumed as he began to glide past another set of buildings.

He sat on a bench in a deserted taxi rank, relieved, at least, to find the whistles had stopped. He considered other places he might find old stuff. He considered breaking into people's homes. *They couldn't stop me, they wouldn't dare.* But then, he guessed the whistles would start-up again. *The fucking Greens spent a fortune on that fucking NanoSecurityFilm™ or whatever the fuck it's called,* he thought, *and all they had to do was whistle.*

But then, he had an idea. He thought about the small industrial estate, near the Medium Correctional Facility of which he was once a dishonourable member. There were storage units - *and no fucking homes nearby.* It was back over the Highway on the opposite side to the Mahone Ranch. *It's worth a try - I'm guessing the Greens wouldn't have put their Shell™ over a prison. I wonder if there are prisoners still in there.*

He walked southbound down the Highway and wandered into the Bell & Sons Storage Facilities. It was dark, which meant it wasn't under the GreenShell™, and there was nobody around - no whistles. He jemmied his way through the outer door, and as there was no power - there were no alarms. It was a noisy process and breaking into the storage lockers would generate more noise, so he closed the door behind him.

He went to work on the doors, but the locks were more substantial than he anticipated. He went back outside and rummaged around the industrial complex. He found some metal bars, which looked like they would give him the required torque to break locks. He tried it out on the nearest lock-up - and it worked. He rooted through the various treasured possessions, which looked like junk to Brady's eyes. He tried another, and another, with similar results. All he was finding was clapped out gym equipment, old books, photograph albums, pathetic collections of knick-knacks - usually decorated with cartoon characters, or cutesy animals - and musty old clothes. Brady was sweating from his hard work, even in the cold desert-climate night.

Finally, he hit pay dirt. There were hundreds of CDs and DVDs - obviously a whole family's collection, adult titles mixed with children's music and movies. He remembered seeing a granny shopping trolley on wheels in one of the previous lockers, big enough to hold a lot of stuff. He went to retrieve it and loaded it neatly - he could get more in that way. He grabbed a cardboard box, filled it with more DVDs, and put it across the top of the shopping trolley on wheels.

He rolled his motherlode back to the highway - wishing the sound wasn't so loud from the little wheels rattling along on the concrete. Luckily, he wasn't disturbed, and he completed his first shipment by getting Archie off his night-time watch with Old Marvin to help him unload his haul into the barn.

'That's a great start boy, me and the young 'un, what's her face - ah yes, Mary-Lou - will work through them in the morning.'

'The night is young,' Brady said, 'so I'm going back to get the rest. The more choice we get, the better. We could make a fortune in those Green Credits - I just don't know what we'll spend them on.'

'I've prepared for this as best I can, but you can't really solve the problem of fresh food and water - for those Greens that's going to be their speciality. It won't come cheap, of that I'm certain.'

'That's all well and good, Pops, but I'm hoping they'll have some things that might be a little more fun - or at least useful. I've ridden on their pushbikes, and they got working vehicles, so I could do with earning enough for a car. Then I could go down to Castaic and get the rest of Small Hand Don's belongings.'

Archie shuffled, awkwardly. 'You never did say what happened with you and him.'

Brady frowned. He knew he was going to have to tell him everything that happened down there. 'He had four kids held hostage - either using them as sex slaves or pimping them.' He remembered the film studio set-up. 'Probably making kiddie porn movies as well.'

'So, you killed him?'

'Not before he tried to kill me first. He was desperate to get his hands on your little black book.' Brady still had it in his pocket. He handed back to Archie. 'Thanks, and all that - it did come in useful for the equipment and all - but I don't want to have anything more to do with your... Friends.'

'I'm sorry, boy. It's a long story, and I don't think you'd understand it. I gotta lot to answer for when I go to meet my maker - not least driving your Foster Moms to an early grave by drinking herself to death. It was on account of the shame of being married to someone like me, it was.'

Brady knew this was an admission, if not a confession. He didn't want the sordid details about other children, for now - all he could deal with was finding out about himself, and whether Archie had ever abused him. 'How come you ended up fostering me?'

'Your Moms wanted to foster children after she'd been refused permission to adopt. I tried to persuade her not to, but she went ahead and did it anyway. I knew they'd find out about my record - and when they did, they put a halt to the proceedings. And then, nearly a decade later, you were virtually delivered to us, without us even asking.'

'Did, they say where I came from? Who my real family was?'

Archie didn't want to admit that he wasn't interested at the time - all he was concerned about was how long they could keep him. 'They never said. I asked of course, but they just said that you'd had a troubled upbringing and that you were likely to be a challenge - a real handful, that's the term they used.' He squirmed. 'They told us not to spare the rod, and that we could do whatever we saw fit to make you shape up and fly right.'

'I don't get it, Pops. That sure don't sound like no carer type talk that I ever heard. Normally, it's all, love, nurture, educate and all those ten kinds of crap.'

'I know boy, but we wondered if we were picked because they believed we were unsuitable for nice children. Your Moms was deeply suspicious, and being the God-fearing woman she was, she thought you might be the Son of Satan.'

'What?'

'Well, after she found out about my past, she thought she was being punished. If it was one of those reverse psychology deals - ya know, the government is always up to all kinds of tricks - then I decided those bastards weren't going to fool me. So, I decided to show them that we could bring you up real good - and I did.'

Brady roared with laughter, but Archie knew his son's intent - there was warmth within it. 'I'm sure the authorities think you've done a grand old job with old Brady Mahone. I've been in and out of juvie and ended up in Ridgecrest Supermax.' He laughed again, and Archie laughed with him. 'And all for crimes I did actually commit...' Now they laughed uncontrollably. Every time one of them tried to control the laughter, it only made them laugh even more, until tears rolled down Archie's cheeks.

'You do know what I mean, boy?'

'I do. I love ya Pops, and I'm grateful to ya.' He put a big arm around Archie and then added, 'How come I stayed with you, for like, forever?'

'They never came back - and we never complained. I always suspected I was being secretly monitored by the Deep State and later by the Deep Cons, I got me a kinda antennae for that kind of activity.' He noticed Brady's eyes glazed over. *He doesn't need this right now*, he thought – more perceptive than Brady ever realised. 'Your Mom kinda came around - just a little, before her death. I think it surprised her how much you and me bonded. God rest her soul.'

16.JUDGE AND JURY

Over the next few nights, Brady completed his search and collections from the Bell & Sons Storage Facilities. He only found a handful of additional titles to add to his collection. On the last night, somebody connected to the owners - maybe even the owners themselves - came over with dogs to check out the damage which Brady had inflicted on their business.

He knew he had to try East McFarland again if he was to find enough to make his Green fortune. *First up - I'm gonna raid the Old-Timey Marvels and Curios shop,* he thought, *and I ain't gonna be a pussy about it. If they want to try and stop me with their scaredy-cat whistling, bring it on. I'll teach 'em not to mess with Brady Mahone.*

He cut a curious figure as he marched up Highway 99, with his long-waxed poachers coat - the trench coat-length version was fashionable back in the days of the Mega-Storms, all of forty or fifty years ago. The label suggested this one was an imported version from England. Here he was dressed like a Gamekeeper, pushing along a granny's shopping cart. He strode into East McFarland with purpose. He ignored the whistles, occasionally pausing to give them the finger.

He was just about to march into the street where the Old-Timey shop was located when a gang appeared and barred his way. This wasn't like any gang he had ever encountered before. There was a mishmash of ages - some of them were kids, there were different races, but there was no mistaking the self-appointed leader. He was huge and, Brady assumed, Mexican. He was dressed like a biker -

whereas his gang were not - and he carried a fireman's axe. He did notice that a lot of this guy's bulk wasn't muscle—the result of too many hours sitting on a bike and not getting enough proper exercise. He heard the whistles increase in intensity and regularity. The Mexican yelled, 'Shut the fuck up!' But the whistling continued. *The whistlers aren't with these guys - and girls.* He noticed.

Brady slowly reached into his pockets, and with his right hand, he fingered his jemmy. With his left, he secured his grip around his hunting knife. Brady was in no mood for negotiations with this fathead. He placed his feet, ready for action, and he revealed his weapons. He said, 'I just got out of Ridgecrest Supermax. I was serving life for murder,' he half-lied. 'You better be real sure you want to do this because if you don't get the fuck out of my way, then I kill you. I'm the real deal - I ain't no poser like you.'

He could see the fear spread through the gang, but the Mexican's plans for the future depended on showing his followers that he could deal with this. He said nothing - only swung his axe around, before lunging at Brady. Brady watched the motion and smartly eluded him. Brady continued to dodge as the biker kept coming at him. He only came at Brady with right-handed swings, and quickly, Brady could sense he was tiring. One of the gang members tried to creep up behind him, but Brady kicked him away, sending him tumbling to the ground, moaning. The biker tried to use the distraction to bring the axe downwards at Brady's head, but again he side-stepped him. The next attempt was the biker's last.

He swung from the right, trying to decapitate Brady, but he stepped inside the axe's arc and swung the jemmy's hooked ends into the biker's skull. In the instant that followed, he used the jemmy to pull the biker towards him and onto his hunting knife, which Brady thrust deeper and then sliced upwards.

He let the biker's dead body fall to the ground, but Brady wasn't finished. He knew from the first day he'd ever spent in prison that the performance - the show of power - was everything, when it came to getting the other inmates to stay out of his fucking way. He picked up the axe and forcefully chopped the head off his rival. The axe clanged into the concrete, and the head jumped as the jemmy buried in the skull bounced off the road before the dead biker's head went spinning across the street.

Some of the younger members of this nascent gang ran away into the shadows, but he also heard the sound of scuffles, as though they were being captured. He turned to the seemingly more brave or foolish ones with his axe still dripping with blood, and he roared, 'Who's next? Come on fuckers, if you want it, come and get it.' He took a quick step forwards and stamped his foot down, and the rest of the gang ran from the ghoulish figure with the dripping axe and the long dark coat.

Brady wiped his hunting knife on the clothes of the decapitated body. He retrieved his jemmy from the road. He was picking out the bits of skull, blood and brains from the hook ends when he realised he had been surrounded. He looked around, pretending not to see them. He inspected his jemmy and then returned it to its pocket.

He casually looked around and decided that if the gang were the prisoners, then these guys must be the guards. He recognised the black middle-aged woman who stood before him – they'd almost grown up together.

At every step of her judicial career in McFarland, from lawyer to District Attorney to Judge - Audre Jefferson was there to put Brady Mahone out of harm's way for the good folk of McFarland.

Brady said, 'Good evening Judge Jefferson. Is this one of those Kangaroo Courts I heard about? I can see you got people taking notes and all.' He stared menacingly into the eyes of the two women who were writing in their notebooks. *There may be a lot of them,* he thought, *but these are ordinary citizens, I could take half a dozen out before they've even thought of how they'd take me down.* He studied the crowd which amounted to about fifty people. There was an old Chinese man who was whispering in her ear. He had to be someone smart if the Judge was listening to him.

'Good evening, Mr. Mahone. I recall your defence lawyer asking for leniency as he claimed you were a thief but not a danger to society.' She looked at the decapitated body on the ground. 'I never rated him a good judge of character.'

'Just doing his job. I think circumstances have changed since then, don't you?'

'You are correct.' She stepped out from the crowd toward Brady, and the old Chinese man followed her. Brady thought, *I'll give them bonus points for bravery.* 'This is Professor Yuan Chu, he studied and later taught at Stanford University.'

Professor Chu stepped up to Brady to introduce himself. He reached out his hand. Meanwhile, Judge Jefferson had a discreet word with a couple of people in the crowd, and shortly afterwards, they brought over blankets to cover the body and the head of the deceased Mexican gang leader.

Brady thought. *I'm watching you.* Brady looked for somewhere to wipe the blood from his hands. He reached down and used the blanket covering the body, then stood back up to his full height, towering over the Professor. He shook hands with the old man, whose grip was feeble, and Brady assumed he didn't have long to live.

'We may be able to come to an arrangement,' Yuan said.

'We could have you detained,' Judge Jefferson said – though Brady noticed she didn't say *arrested.* 'But that would mean some of our community will be injured in the process - and they've gone through enough hurt, wouldn't you agree?'

'I suppose so.'

'And the resources we have are precious. We don't want to waste them on attending to prisoners.'

'So, what's this agreement?'

'We want you to stay out of East McFarland - for good.'

'Can't do it, Judge. I live here.'

The crowd murmured, but Judge Jefferson was undeterred. 'Don't play games with me Brady - you know exactly what I mean. Stay out of this area.' She looked at him and asked, politely, 'What are you looking for?'

'If I told you - the price would go up. Do you think because I'm a criminal that I don't know how deals work? You tell me what you want first, and then I'll tell you.'

'You've travelled, since the Green Revolution,' Yuan intervened. 'You have an ability that I cannot fathom. You are a source of valuable information for our community. All we want from you is your story, and for that, we would try to meet your price.'

Brady was intrigued - and flattered. He was talking to a professor from a world-renowned university, wanting to find out what Brady Mahone knew. He laughed. 'I think you picked the wrong guy, man. What did you study, anyhows?'

'I studied the use of Nano-Technology and its use with fertility treatments, particularly in the field of IVF.'

'Then what are you doing on this side of the fence? You should be with your Green friends.'

Yuan smiled. 'Many of my colleagues did indeed end up working for Sattva Systems™ and were handsomely rewarded for doing so - but my area of expertise was considered of little value to them.'

I hope I don't get a technical explanation for this, Brady thought. 'And why's that?'

'Because I was working on helping people have babies. Sattva Systems™ believed that the human race was already the biggest polluter on the planet. Adding more little humans didn't fit their overall goals.'

Brady's demeanour changed. He understood. 'What are your plans for East McFarland? This isn't like other places I've seen, so far. I ain't seen many, mind you.'

'We have a lot of different skills available to us. For instance, we're analysing what has happened to the old infrastructure - although the damage done seems to be substantial, down to a molecular level. This fits in with a Nano Technological attack. And we're experimenting with a mixture of old ways of generating what we need and maybe coming up with some brand-new solutions of our own. What we need is time and information. I don't think you are a man who wishes to harm us. The man you killed was the biggest threat to our community. We should thank you.'

Brady laughed, but it was suffused with warmth. 'The pleasure was all mine.' He added, 'I'll tell you what I know, but I can't see how it will be that useful.'

Professor Yuan Chu smiled and thought, *I'll be the judge of that.* 'Now, what was it you were searching for?'

Brady now wondered if he would appear foolish. 'Old entertainment, CDs and DVDs.'

'And how many of these - if we have them - would be enough to have you agree to leave us be?'

Brady thought about it carefully. 'One thousand. But all of them have to be different titles - I don't want lots of the same things. They'd be useless to me.'

Judge Jefferson addressed the crowd. 'Let's see some hands if you have any old CDs or DVDs at home. Come on, I can assure you, your assistance will be duly noted, and when we get back on our feet, your help with this matter will be subsequently rewarded.' More hands went up. The notetakers jotted down the names in their books. Brady wondered why they had more than one notetaker but didn't have enough interest to try and work it out.

'Well, Brady Mahone,' she said, 'it looks like we have a deal.'

Brady told them his story. 'There was a riot at Ridgecrest Supermax, but the guards started it, in a way. They put the TV on with them telling everyone was fucked. The place went up, but the guards shot and killed everyone with fucking antique weapons. I didn't kill the prisoners, your honour, but I did kill the guards - but they started it, it was a self-defence thing.'

'Duly noted. Carry on.'

'Well, then, I went home.' *I'll leave Lucky out of this in case they arrest him and claim they had a deal with me, but not with him,* he thought. *You can't trust these bastards.* 'To cut a long story short n'all, the Hodgson boys were throwing rocks at the cars, but they were hitting an invisible wall - they call it a NanoShell™. I rescued an old woman, I did, but we fell through the shield at the same time. I think that's why I can go into the Green areas.' He noticed a look on the Professor's face as if he was dubious. 'Then I tried to steal some food from the Grocery, but I got trapped in all this SecurityFilm™. I couldn't move. They released me...'

'Who released you?'

'Lizzie, Cain and a guy called Siddha. I'm a bit hazy on that.' He tried to remember but then decided it didn't matter, anyway. 'I went to this Town Hall meeting, and they showed a movie about the Revolution, and they did this science bit...'

'What was that?' Yuan said, eagerly.

'I fell asleep. I was never into that school crap.'

'Never mind. This is all very helpful, please, continue.'

'They all got to earn one-hundred Green credits to buy themselves a RedNanoSuit™. Everyone's going to get one. Apparently, it will make them indestructible.'

'They were developing Diamonoid Technology before even I was a mere student.'

'Next up, Professor, they will have to earn a thousand Green Credits for an OrangeNanoSuit™, and that will check them out for infections and diseases.'

'Who told you that?'

'A guy I met from the Highways Department. He was shoving abandoned vehicles off Highway 99. They were making Cycle Lanes - would you believe?'

'And this was after you'd left West McFarland?'

'Yes. I was heading down to Castaic - for business purposes.'

'It must have been important business to walk to Castaic.'

'What can I say? I'm an entrepreneur now. Anyhows, I got myself one of their GreenBikes™ - that took a load off. Then, after that, I came home.' *No way am I mentioning little black books and Small Hand Don,* he thought. 'Oh man, I nearly missed out the best bit. On my way home, there were these flying Green tankers. Well, they weren't green coloured, they were cream-coloured, not that that matters. Anyways, they were spraying every vehicle that had been shoved to the side of the road, and this silver goo was slowly rotting them away, and then POW - the tyres blew, like machine gun fire, and then BOOM the petrol tanks blew up, and man! You shoulda seen it when the petrol tankers went up - it was like the end of the world. And the NanoShell™ mirrored the flames and the debris, and the silver goo ate the smoke - it ate the smoke, man.'

He looked around, expecting his audience to love his crazy story, but they looked dejected.

'We heard the explosions,' Judge Jefferson said, 'and what we thought was gunfire. We hoped that the military were fighting back.'

'Ain't no military, ain't no police. You are the nearest I have seen to law and order anywhere. Sorry, your honour.'

'How are the other places you've visited coping?' Yuan asked.

'Bakersfield is chaotic - I don't think anyone's taken over yet. Castaic is probably ruled by the local Mafia by now. Alameda looked like a Green Town.' Brady was getting bored of talking, especially given his story about the exploding vehicles fell flat. 'Are we done here?'

'Thank you,' Yuan said. 'Your words have been insightful.'

'Do we have your word - for what it's worth - that you'll stay away?' Judge Jefferson said.

'When I get my stuff, yeah.'

'There's an old bus shelter, about half a mile north of your ranch. We'll collect up the CDs and DVDs, sort them out, and leave them for you by tomorrow evening.'

Professor Chu seemed to be deep in thought. He looked up. 'Brady, are you going to be doing a lot of travelling in your new business venture?'

'I guess so.'

'I would be most grateful if you could do me a personal favour.'

'And what's that?' *I like this guy,* he thought. *He treats me with respect.*

'Could you leave me notes about where you've visited and what the place is like? I don't need an essay, just a symbol to represent the area - with a tick to say it's like us, here in East McFarland, a cross if it's like Castaic, or a G to indicate that it's a green town. You see, if we find a way of communicating or travelling again, it would be nice for us to know where our future allies might be. You could leave your notes at the bus stop...'

'I get it. Yeah, I don't mind doing that - you can call it my civic duty.' He turned to the Judge. 'I hope you are going to get your little scribes to put that on the record.'

Judge Jefferson smiled warmly. 'Your assistance will be recorded.'

'One more thing. I was told that if a green space or maybe a whole block was vacated, the GreenNanoShell™ would claim the land. I saw it happening before my very eyes when I was travelling back.'

Some of the crowd were alarmed at this prospect and began scurrying back to their homes.

'Thank you, Brady,' Yuan said. 'You've been most helpful.'

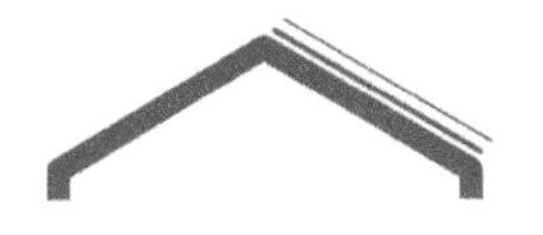

17.KING OF THE ROAD

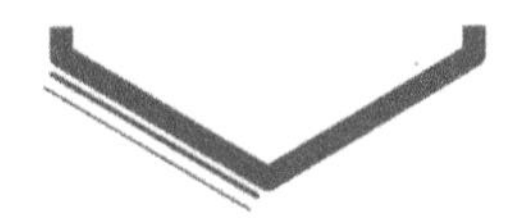

The townsfolk of East McFarland were as good as their word. Brady took along his bike and trailer to pick up the thousand CDs and DVDs. He could tell instantly that they looked clean and had been sorted into various categories. He felt as though he was evolving from a thuggish criminal into a semi-legitimate businessman.

When he got his stock back to the ranch, Lucian was ready and waiting to help Brady to unpack his stock. He removed Brady's overcoat and began transferring the stock into repurposed fruit trays. 'Hey, man,' he said, when he had finished, 'you'll never believe how hard everyone's worked to help set you up. Come with me, and I'll show you.' Brady followed Lucian into the barn. 'Here, we have the racking, and it's all, in alphabetical order, so we can find everything real quick. Archie sorted out the fixtures, while I put the stock in place - but that's not all. Mary-Lou has done an amazing job on the catalogue - the only trouble is that it's quite big. Take a look.'

He handed over a red binder to Brady. It was in sections divided by categories, and he could see that it couldn't have been made any smaller. He noticed each item had a reference number. He pointed at one. 'What does this mean?'

'Mary-Lou wanted to save you work when you got an order in.' He handed over a blue binder. 'And this is to take your orders. It's laid out so you don't forget anything. She took the inspiration from her Mom's business. It's got spaces for the name, address and payment information, but also, it's got a space for the reference number, so you don't have to write the whole thing out. Mary-Lou says that a lot of the descriptions can be very similar, so this will help us to pick you out exactly the right copy.'

Mary-Lou appeared and went over to Lucian's side. 'She's pregnant y'know,' Lucian announced proudly. 'She's having our baby. Can you believe that?'

Brady hugged his friend. 'Fuck me, you didn't waste any time. Congratulations Lucky, my best buddy, and to your good self, Mary-Lou.' She smiled bashfully, and Brady could see that Lucian hadn't prepared her for this moment. He diverted the subject away, a little. 'And thanks, Mary-Lou. The work you've done to help me is fantastic. I'd have never thought about all that. It's not as though I'd ever gone to business school y'know.'

Mary-Lou smiled. 'It's the least I can do after all you're doing for us here. I'm glad I can help.' Lucian put an arm around her and kissed her on the cheek. 'This baby is a sign of new hope. Amie needn't be alone if she has baby brothers and sisters to play with.'

'Whoa, how many kids are you planning to have, little lady?'

'I want loads and loads; I want to fill these ranches with children.' She laughed joyfully, and then she blushed as she realised that Brady would know what she was planning to do with Lucian.

Brady smiled. 'I mean it. I'm so happy for the both of you. It's going to make all the difference around here.'

Brady retrieved his coat which he had used to cover and secure the stock in his bike trailer. He put it on and then checked to see if the binders fit into the huge pockets at the base of his coat. 'They just about fits, one on each side, so they balance out. That's great if I'm walking and I need to keep my hands free. Otherwise, the binders would have to stay in the trailer.' He took out the binders and flicked through the pages, then put them into his bike trailer and removed his coat, placing it protectively over them. 'You know what I fancy - to celebrate?'

'What's that?' Lucian said.

'A barbecue. I'll be the chef-meister.'

THE WHOLE FAMILY ATE heartily from Archie's freezer stock. He had been keen to use this food since the power cut in the early days of the Green Revolution. It was a sunny afternoon, and they talked excitedly about plans for the future. Amie toddled around and picked daisies, which Mary-Lou made into a daisy chain. Towards late afternoon the clouds gathered in, and an almost inaudible droning sound could be made out when the trees stopped rustling. Then a delicate mist descended. It wasn't enough to make them head for shelter, so they continued their conversations. Brady rubbed the mist which that settled on his muscular arms, and noticed it felt dry to the touch - not wet, as he expected it to be.

'Fuck me,' Archie exclaimed. 'Did you see that?' He was pointing upward, but all they could see was low grey clouds.

'What did ya see, Pops?'

'A fucking alien spacecraft - that's what?'

'Oh, come on.'

'No. No. I seen it, I tells ya. Just keep looking.'

And then they all saw it. A long cream cylindrical vessel, with two hoses, swaying slowly underneath, and just as quickly as it emerged, it glided behind another bank of clouds.

The mist that settled on them didn't hurt them. Mary-Lou instinctively went to her daughter Amie and took her inside to bathe her and herself. Archie rubbed it and tried to smell it, but it was odourless. Brady prepared for the pain he expected to follow. He observed Lucian and his Pops carefully, wondering whether he might be immune as an honorary Green. He waited for a few minutes, as they all peered upwards, straining to catch another glimpse of the alien vessel.

Brady worried about the others. He remembered the bodies at the side of the Highway - the ones who were picking clean the vehicles, and who probably sheltered in them when the Highways Department and their vessels went by. *I wonder how long it took the goo to take effect,* he thought. And more darkly he considered. *How long did it take them to die?*

He looked over in the direction of West McFarland, and he was sure he could see a smearing effect on the NanoShell™.

'There it is!' Brady and Lucian followed Archie's outstretched arm pointing in the distance. It must have been a few miles away. It looked like a giant, slow-moving flying mammal taking a piss over everyone beneath it.

They watched it in silent awe for long minutes until it was too small a figure in the distance to see anymore. 'I've seen them before, or something very similar,' Brady said. 'It was breaking down the vehicles which were abandoned on the Highway. It ate into them. It wasn't like acid, but it killed people too.'

'Oh, fuck.' Lucian checked himself all over. 'I don't feel anything. I haven't even got it on my skin anymore. Do you think we're going to be ok?'

'It ain't just physical you got to worry about.' Archie said, pointing to his temple. 'It's up here as well. They might be pouring some of that NanoShit over the population to mind control us. That was crop spraying - pure and simple.'

Lucian tried to keep himself from panicking. 'You might be right about looking like it was crop-spraying, but maybe it was a health thing. Y'know, to protect us - or to stop the spread of disease.'

'Come on, boy. Those Green fuckers don't give a damn about us. There are only two options here. They're either trying to destroy us - or control us.'

Brady believed his Pops' version of events was closer to the truth. *We'll know it isn't about destroying us if we are still around by tomorrow*, he thought.

Brady couldn't sleep at all that night - not even for a few moments of shut-eye. He patrolled the grounds and listened nervously for sounds of pain - but his companions slept soundly. He then fretted about whether they were sleeping too soundly - but was put at ease when his Pops went for a piss just before dawn, before returning to his bed.

He might not have slept a wink, but by morning when all the family had woken up and were heartily tucking into a fried breakfast, he felt mighty fine as the weight of worry left his broad shoulders, leaving him with a profound sense of relief. He was looking forward to putting the strange events of yesterday behind him and embarking seriously on his new business venture.

OVER THE NEXT FEW WEEKS, Brady travelled up and down the Highways from McFarland and all the way down to Los Angeles, where he uncovered a lucrative market for his wares in the former Hollywood set. He was surprised that some of the wealthiest enclaves had turned to Green and not to rust – he'd always thought the rich were the most responsible for the planet's climate troubles. Instead, he discovered large communities of the old Liberal elites who seemed to have acquired a fortune in Green Credits in the run-up to the Revolution. As an added bonus, he seemed to find plenty of women who were as interested in him as they were in his catalogue. It certainly added motivation to his days of cycling to ply his trade this far south.

The more impoverished areas were the most troubled he had seen so far, as it had descended into anarchy and gang warfare, and large tracts of the city were left in a burned-out trail of destruction. Brady wanted to keep his tally of the state of play in various districts for Professor Yuan Chu. Brady, through a mixture of analysis and gut instinct, began to predict, with some accuracy, which towns and districts would fall into a particular category. If he saw offshore Intense Wind Farms, or the equally Intense Solar Farms, these would be a good indicator that they had turned Green – which meant the tiny villages nearby had a good chance of being next in line to be swallowed by the neighbouring NanoShell™. As he got closer, the Sattva Systems™ logos were the biggest giveaway. These were where his target market lived. The smaller towns contained the gentler systems like the one that was forming in East McFarland. The Highways and river boundaries often split the communities into two different types. The larger cities were the ones which struggled the most with the transition to the new order.

He got off to a slow start with his orders, as there was resistance to his pricing strategy. In the smaller towns, the people were busy saving for the RedNanoSuits™ at one hundred Greenbacks - as Brady began to call the Green Credits - apiece, and then faced the prospect of earning a further one thousand for the Orange™ health upgrades. He had three tiers of pricing dependant on the quality and quantity of the content of the item. He tried to go for five, ten and fifteen, at first. If using a water fountain was one Greenback, then five was cheap. But when he dropped the pricing structure to three, five and ten, he had more joy, and his order book began to fill up nicely. When he reached the old affluent coastal areas, west and south of Los Angeles, he reverted back to his original pricing structures, and he soon had an order book with a potential turnover of more than six-hundred Greenbacks. All he had to do now was head back to the ranch, fill up his trailer and return to his customers, fulfil the orders and collect his Greenbacks. Occasionally, he worried about running out of stock – but decided to give more thought to this problem when he had endless hours to pass on his days of cycling home.

HE MADE A DETOUR TO Castaic, to Small Hand Don's place. He had a virtually empty trailer to fill. He travelled there by night and went through nearby Green Communities, then took the most rural routes to get there. He was wary of the Cesares and how things might have developed in the time since his last visit. He had predicted that things were unlikely to have gotten any better.

He let himself in and headed quickly upstairs. He knew what he needed most urgently, and that was as many Blank Black Files as possible. He went to the storage area and rifled through some boxes.

He was in luck. He found a few boxes which he estimated contained around five thousand Files. *This guy was running a fucking industry from here*, he thought. He then found almost double that many with reference numbers on, not unlike the system which Mary-Lou had designed for his wares. *These must be already recorded on but maybe they can be overwritten. Won't do any harm to take them as well.* Back in the main bedroom, he noticed an old camcorder set up. He went to press the camcorder on, as it wasn't plugged into the dead electrical system, but the battery was flat. There were a few other Files placed near the camcorder, so Brady threw these into a box of tightly packed Black Files, and these were strewn over the top.

Flickering orange light lit up the road from outside. He looked out, and he thought he recognised some of the members of Cesare's crew. They were patrolling the area as though they were the new law enforcement. He instinctively knew that he shouldn't hang around for a second longer than necessary. He had what he'd come for. When the patrol had turned the corner and was out of sight. Brady loaded up his trailer and moved his GreenBike™ and trailer from the hallway of Don Pickerstaff's home and back onto the road towards the safety of Highway 5.

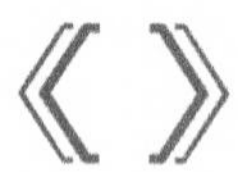

HE HAD STARTED HIS journey home when his Satt™ went off. He pulled over and took the call. There were only a handful of cream cars which passed him by and a few bikes. 'Mary-Lou has had a miscarriage,' Lucian said, as he answered.

'I'm real sorry, buddy. Is there anything I can do? Anything you need?'

Lucian cried. 'No. I just ain't got no-one else to talk to. It's messed up, man.'

Brady encouraged Lucian to talk. *I ain't big on sharing feelings and all,* he thought, *but he is my best buddy. I'll let him do all the talking, and I'll be the good listener type.*

THE RIDE BACK TO MCFARLAND seemed endless to Brady, and the thought of the atmosphere of sadness set to greet him back home took the edge off his feelings of success around his order book.

As he reached the outskirts of McFarland, he decided to drop in on Vance, to see if the middleman experiment was worth continuing.

He tracked him down to his home. He rapped on the door, and a young girl answered. 'Does Vance live here?'

'Yes sir. Who shall I say is calling?'

He noticed she showed no fear of him. 'Tell him it's Brady. Brady Mahone.'

Vance came to the door. 'Come in, man. Come up to my room, and we'll talk there.' A few people were chatting in the lounge, which had a similar vibe to the place where he shared the night with Lizzie.

'How's it going?' Brady said.

'Brilliant. I've made three hundred Green Credits in orders. It pays to know your audience, and not going door-to-door with only hope on your side.'

Brady wasn't going to divulge how much he had made himself, but he was impressed with the figures Vance was quoting - and all done without much effort. *I gotta admit,* he thought, *other people are better at business than me. What I need is a Vance in every town. I'll recruit when I deliver my products. I'm sure that some will work for my entertainments rather than pay me Greenbacks for them.*

'You've done well,' Brady said. 'Have you got the order details?'

'Sure thing, man.' Vance handed him wads of paper of assorted shapes and sizes.

Mary-Lou was right, he thought. *That's how I would have done it, and it's a mess.* 'I've got a proper order book. I'll bring you one to use. You'll find it easier to manage.'

'That's why you're the boss. Hey, so, I'll get my copies, y'know, as my payment - right?'

I'm going to need a bigger supply of Black Files at this rate. I might need Pops' little black book again, after all. 'Sure. A deal's a deal.'

'Great.' Vance smiled broadly, but Brady knew the relief of a fellow criminal when he broached the subject of being paid.

He held all the aces in this game, but he needed to cultivate his empire in these early days. He didn't like the guy, all the same.

'I need a vehicle,' he said. 'If I'm going to expand, I need to travel. Plus, I can't spend the rest of my days riding a bicycle like a fucking dork.'

'A Green Car, or FusionCar™ as we must call it, will put you back about two-thousand Green Credits.'

'What the fuck? For eleven hundred you can get both a Red™ and an OrangeNanoSuit™, but a car costs two-thousand?'

'It's three thousand for a FusionVan™.' Vance flinched as if expecting Brady to explode. 'They want you to obtain the Suits™. They don't want to encourage people to own vehicles. They say it's the vehicles that caused so much pollution.'

'Don't these cars run on...whatever power?'

'Yeah, but there's not many FusionPowered™ cars, so they're hard to come by. But the GreenRevs said that once we've got through the initial phases, more will be produced and then they'll become more affordable, and afterwards, they said that they will reintroduce FusionPowered™ consumer air travel, because they understand the human need to explore and feel free, blah blah blah. Right now, though... it is what it is.'

'Can you take me to an auto dealer?'

Vance shrugged. 'There's no point, man. There are only two designs available. One is a car like the one Cain has, the other is a van that's shaped like a hearse. You can have any colour you like as long as it's Ceramic Cream.' Vance laughed at his own joke. 'This isn't a material world, anymore. You can't change the design or customise them. Pride in ownership isn't encouraged.' He looked at Brady, who clearly was unimpressed. 'The good news is that they can run almost forever. No filling up, and no need for gas stations. Though they're not too quick - mind you.'

Brady had stopped listening. He was working out the fastest way to make more money. He thought about the notes he had made for Professor Chu and guessed they were of value to him. *But it's kinda one of those unwritten deals, a gentleman's agreement*, he thought. *I feel bad asking him for more stock. I always hated it when people did that to me.*

He then thought of another item which could be useful to a man like that, maybe valuable enough for the whole town to contribute

- if the Professor could persuade them. *But how do I get around the lack of working technology?*

'Hey, Vance. You know that movie you showed about the science stuff. Have you got a copy of that?'

'Every household has. Information is free to all.'

'Can I borrow a copy? I'll bring it back.' Brady peered straight into Vance's eyes, daring him to negotiate.

'Uhhh... Yes. Ok.' Vance went downstairs. Brady listened as Vance tried to explain to his housemates who Brady was, and how Cain had instructed him to keep Brady happy. *Why would Cain say that?* he thought. *Are they scared of me?* Vance returned with a Black File with a tiny label marked: *The New Green Deal.*

Brady took it from him and pocketed it. 'Thanks, man.'

After leaving Vance, Brady went to the bus stop near his ranch, and removed the old service information poster behind a soft plastic cover. He put in his notes and observations of the places he had visited or seen. It covered dozens of districts between here and slightly to the south of Los Angeles. He heard footsteps. By now, after all his travelling, he didn't want another confrontation. Brady just wanted to go home and check-in on his Pops, and to see how Lucian and Mary-Lou were coping. He went to get on his bike and started to ride away when a voice called out to him. 'Brady - please, wait.'

Brady stopped and looked back to see Professor Chu walk to the bus shelter. He was walking an old black Labrador dog. He watched as the Professor retrieved the notes he had left behind. The Professor sat down on the bench in the shelter, and the black Labrador sat beside him, obediently.

As Brady approached the bus stop, the Professor said, 'I was walking Bessie, and I saw you. I guessed what you were doing, and I wanted to say thank you - while I still had the chance.'

Brady bent over and stroked the old dog, while Professor Chu scanned Brady's notes. Brady said, 'Is it any use to you?'

'Yes, very much so - not in a practical sense just yet, but it's good to have a feel for what's going on elsewhere. It looks like a mixed bag.'

'Yeah. But it seems to be the more rural and isolated places are already Green - or at least more civilised.'

The Professor smiled warmly, not taking offence at the unintended slight. 'I agree. That's an insightful assessment.'

'Why is it that there are a lot of rich people around Los Angeles who live in Green areas? I thought they were the worst polluters, the most materialistic. Why save them and not people like you?'

'That is an excellent question. In another life, you would have had potential.' Brady laughed sarcastically, but the Professor added, 'No. I mean it.' He looked like he was thinking deeply. 'If I were to judge the venerable Bodhi Sattva - not his real name, by the way - as a human and not as a guru, or a cult-leader, I would suggest that he has protected the area where he was raised as a boy, and by extension, the family and friends of those who were close to him.'

'Makes sense,' Brady said, without irony. 'That's what I would do.'

The Professor stood up, as did Bessie. 'I better head back. I don't want them to send the search parties out for me. Thank you for these...' He held up the notes. 'And continue to have safe journeys.'

'To tell you the truth, it's not a happy place where I'm going home to. My friend's partner has had a miscarriage.'

'It's happened all over town. The GreenRevs are sterilising the population. I can't see there being any future pregnancies.'

'Holy fuck! They can't do that, surely?'

'It's their world to do with as they please. I'm not wholly surprised at what they are doing - just the speed of it. It's the opposite of my field of expertise – they're using Nano Technology to end reproduction.'

'Why didn't they just kill us all and be done with it?'

'They need to keep their own people on board. The Green Communities will be unaware, for the most part, though the leaders will undoubtedly know the plans. In their minds, the human race has always been the biggest risk to the welfare of the planet and its eco-systems. In time, the old ways of man will fade from existence, and the Greens will be a population who will be dedicated to using mankind's skills to help Mother Earth.'

'You almost sound like one of them.'

'It was the sort of topic we used to discuss at length. I just didn't foresee that they would acquire the means to implement it.'

Brady sensed an opportunity, but it seemed utterly selfish under the circumstances. Still, he couldn't resist. 'I feel bad saying this. I know I'm not a good person and all...'

'Go on. You can say it - the truth is powerful - or you can ask it, and I can always say *no*.' He smiled.

'I want to make another deal. I want another thousand CDs and DVDs.'

'I don't think there are that many left in the town. What are you offering to trade?'

'I'm not sure. I have some information that you, personally, could use, I think - as you could make sense of it - but you don't have the means to access it, so, it might be useless.'

'Tell me what you have, and I'll make the proposal to Judge Jefferson - if I deem it worth the price.'

Brady went to his trailer and rummaged around in the pockets of his crumpled Poacher's coat and retrieved the Black File. 'This is the movie they played for the Greens - not just in West McFarland, but in every Green Community across the world. It has all the scientific stuff they used in the Revolution and the plans for the future. You haven't got the power, or the hardware to play it on if you did have electricity, I'm guessing.' He paused for a few seconds. 'But would you want it?'

Professor Yuan Chu thought over the potential benefits of acquiring this information over the costs of handing over out of date, and useless discs. He also considered the problem of extracting the data from it. 'I can't promise you one thousand discs, but I could give you my word to give you every last disc in the town. I also wouldn't know if you already had a copy. You might receive duplicates.'

'Ok, but I'm not dealing for any less than five-hundred, minimum.'

'Let's say we have a deal. You would need to do some work to make it acceptable for me. The only problem is that it would mean a lot of writing, and I don't mean to be disrespectful...'

'I don't write much, but I have somebody who could do that. What are you thinking?'

'Somebody would have to play the movie and write down, word for word, everything that was said. Also, add in a brief description of the scenes.'

Brady didn't know how smart Lucian was in the words department. He'd had a computing job, once, but Brady wasn't sure if you needed writing skills for that. But Mary-Lou might be able to do it. 'I'm good at drawing,' he said. 'It would take time. But I might have someone who could write it out.'

'We would have to work harder to find the required CDs and DVDs than we did last time. I suggest that we leave each other notes, in this bus shelter, on our progress over the next couple of days - and when we are ready, we make the exchange. How does that sound?'

'Sounds good to me. Let's shake on it.' Brady was careful not to shake the old man's hand too hard.

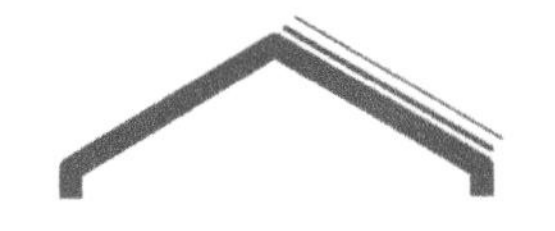

18.CODE BREAKERS

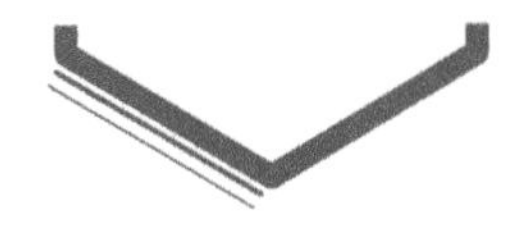

Brady's mood had darkened by the time he arrived home. He wondered about whether he would ever be able to have children. He considered Amie. Her future seemed over before it began. He decided against telling the family what he had learned. He thought about his Pops and how he hadn't been that far away from the truth, in his skewed worldview.

He put on a smile and used exhaustion as an excuse for his pensive mood. He hadn't intended to hug anybody, but they all hugged him, one by one, even Mary-Lou. He hadn't known a time in his life when he had been missed by anyone like this before.

'I'm sorry about, y'know, your news and all,' he said.

'Thanks, man,' Lucian replied. 'You look whacked. Let's get you inside and give you a chance to acclimatise. We'll get some food on, and we can all catch up over dinner.'

'I was going to put away the Files from my trailer.'

'I can do that for you - least I can do.'

Brady smiled. 'The ones with serial numbers are pre-recorded, and might not be any use, so put them away from the Blanks. If we get desperate, then we'll see if they can be wiped and re-used.'

They ate well - sat around the rough-hewn dining table in Archie's rustic but spacious kitchen area. 'Hey, Archie, old man, you certainly weren't planning on starving through the apocalypse,' Lucian said. 'You've got enough food to last you a hundred years at least.'

They all laughed as Archie's cheeks turned faintly red. 'When I was planning all this, I had a growing boy to cater for, and Jesus, it's just as well I did. Look at the size of him, now.'

Brady was relieved that the mood wasn't as gloomy as he'd feared. 'I know this ain't the right time and all,' he said, 'but I've got a job for Lucian and Mary-Lou - it could bring in up to another thousand discs. I'm sorry if I'm being insensitive, I'm not good in these, y'know, situations.'

'I can't lie,' Mary-Lou said. 'I'm feeling real low, but my life is so much better than the hell I lived in before. I'll always be grateful to you. In all honesty, I love the work, and if I can help you some more, then it will help to take my mind off things.' She looked away - Brady always made her blush a little, but she tried to recover quickly. 'What do you need?'

'I need somebody who's good at writing. I've got a movie the Greens played, showing how they made all this happen, and what they've got planned for the future. I met this Professor Chu guy over on the East Side, and he will pay for this in discs. Now they ain't got no power or equipment, so he asked for it - word for word.'

'A transcript,' Lucian added.

'Yeah. I can do the drawings because I remember a lot of diagrams were shown, and I think Professor Chu would appreciate that.'

'You always were good at sketching. I loved all those insects and animals you drew.'

'Thanks, Lucky.' Brady looked around the table and smiled. 'Can you do that?'

'How long was the movie?' Mary-Lou said.

'About an hour, I think. To tells you the truth of it, I fell asleep during it - I felt like I was back in school.'

Archie laughed. 'You ain't never been too good in the studying department, boy.' He reached over and ruffled Brady's black hair, which was beginning to grow out of the prisoner's crew cut. 'I sure would like to watch this movie of yours.'

Brady laughed. 'It was probably made just for you, Pops.'

'It'll take a while to do,' Mary-Lou said. 'There'll be lots of stopping and starting. And you'd have to stick around to do the drawings.'

'Not a problem. I'm sticking close to home for a while. The bike riding is killing me.' He looked around the table, 'I'm going to make enough money in the nearby town to buy one of the Green's vans. It means I won't be putting the Green Credits into here for a bit, as I got to save hard. I need three thousand Greenbacks. You'll be doing the work but getting no reward for a while.'

'I ain't got nothing better to do, buddy,' Lucian said.

Archie added, 'I ain't ever asked nothing from you, boy. You just make sure you stay safe.'

'Thanks, Pops. It will be worth it, eventually.' He turned to Mary-Lou. 'If we can get this transcript together, I'm thinking we could make lots of photocopies. Then I could sell it to other Trad areas when I take the orders back out.'

'That's a brilliant fucking idea,' Lucian shouted, before pausing. 'Sorry, Mary-Lou, I slipped up, again.'

OVER THE NEXT FEW DAYS, Brady and Professor Yuan Chu exchanged notes on their progress towards a deal.

Finally, Mary-Lou, Lucian and Brady finished the work on their document, and Brady settled for the eight-hundred and fifty-seven discs which exhausted the stocks in East MacFarland.

Brady travelled on his GreenBike™ with his trailer - the half-mile to the old bus stop to meet Professor Chu for the exchange. He saw he was accompanied by Judge Jefferson and a couple of men. He was wary of this apparent ambush, but not overly concerned. Still, he was hoping for a friendlier meeting. He dismounted his bike. 'Hey, Professor - what's all this?'

'It's nothing to worry about, Brady. I needed assistance with carrying this - I'm not as strong as you.' He smiled, warmly. 'Audre wanted to make sure everything went smoothly.'

'Hi, Judge,' Brady said cheekily.

'Hello, Brady. I never thought I'd be checking you've done your homework assignment.' She turned to her men. 'You boys can start loading the discs into Brady's trailer, if you wouldn't mind.'

'Yes Ma'am,' one replied, and began stacking the trailer neatly.

Brady handed his notes to the Professor, and the Judge moved in close to examine the documents with him. From Brady's perspective, they couldn't possibly be reading the pages that quickly, while talking at the same time.

'It seems the other thing they were spraying was fire retardant,' the Professor said, matter-of-factly. 'I'm guessing they were worried we would try to burn down our own buildings.'

'It's been done before, I suppose, in the good old days of riots and looting.' Brady laughed, in a needless attempt to show he was joking.

'I think it's their way of stopping us eating meat, and rearing cattle,' the Professor added. 'And reducing the risk of forest fires.'

Brady watched the way the Professor switched between the chat with him, and the intense scanning of the documentation. Professor Chu pointed to items which clearly fascinated him, and the Judge nodded in agreement. 'This is an excellent piece of work,' he said to Brady. 'Please, pass on my thanks to whoever did this.'

'Mary-Lou did the writing, and I did the drawings.'

'Really?' Audre said, glancing at the intricate drawings of Nanostructures. 'Truly remarkable - talk about hidden talents, Brady... I never knew you were so talented. I wish I had - I might have been inclined to punish you more constructively, instead of simply locking you up.'

'Water under the bridge, now. At least, you'll be reassured that I'll keep my word not to return to East McFarland. I know you haven't got any more CDs and DVDs.'

'I wish you no harm, Brady Mahone. Good luck in your business endeavours.'

The men had finished loading up Brady's trailer and backed away. Brady turned to Professor Yuan Chu. 'Give Bessie a pat from me - and thanks for not putting me down, and all. You're alright, y'know.'

'You too, Brady Mahone.' He held up the documents. 'This is straight A work and very much appreciated.'

19.SATTVA SYSTEMS™

Bodhi Sattva was the model of self-sacrifice. If his dreams of saving the planet from destructive climate change were to come to pass, then his home would be the most undesirable place in the world to live in.

He had little sense of pride in his massive industrial chemicals complex. The cream-coloured ceramic buildings, laboratories and enormous vats would have taken a day to walk around.

Bodhi managed his business by walking around. He was keen to be seen.

The old ways of doing business were an anathema to him, and he would only countenance them when it would have been utterly impractical to do it any other way. Bodhi Sattva's style was not to hold court in skyscrapers with highly polished tables with leather seats and giving his employees a bird's eye view of the kingdom he surveyed. Bodhi's style was pared back to all kinds of minimums. If there were trappings of success he enjoyed, then even his closest colleagues would be hard-pressed to name them, except for the unconditional respect and awe from his followers. His brand was an anti-brand, and yet it dominated every country in the world.

He walked for two hours, alone. He smiled and greeted every employee. He wore the same Sattva Systems™ overalls and hard hat that his workers wore - emblazoned with the moss green Sattva *S*. If they stopped and asked him a question, he replied truthfully - there was no sensitive information to protect in a world without competitors. He only held back if his management team needed to know first, as that was a matter of courtesy. He explained the need for civility to them when he denied them an answer. It was the civilised way to conduct his business. It only made them love him more.

Finally, he reached the transport hub of his Boulder Creek base. His visitors had requested permission to land near the Main Entrance of the Sattva Systems™ HQ, but he was eager to keep the trappings of hierarchy away from his front door. Bodhi held no possessions or trinkets of wealth to himself. He slept in a pod in the HQ, and he ate with the workers in the cafeteria.

The first of his visitors arrived in their private FusionPlane ™. Bridgett Tarnita brought the vehicle down vertically into the pre-allocated space. She was a continental Disciple for Europe, although her official title was only that of the Disciple for Green Malmo. Bodhi didn't want labels to become the new measure of wealth or self-worth - that was the Trad way of doing business.

Bridgett had been his person on the inside of the EU. She had first given him the indication that the climate change summit in 2050 would renege on all the climate change promises it had made a decade before. She effectively sealed the fate of the Trad world with her inside information, and she was now one of the most influential people in the new Green World except for Bodhi. Today she represented the Earth's Northern Hemisphere as she met with Bodhi Sattva to receive an update on the one-hundred-year plan.

The representative for Earth's Southern Hemisphere parked her private FusionPlane™ next to Bridgett's. Precious alighted her vehicle and went and stood beside Bridgett. They had to wait for two more visitors to arrive, and Bodhi would not want his next arrivals to appear to be at a disadvantage, so they all knew that he would greet them when they were all together. The tracking systems informed them that everything was on schedule, and they were due at any moment.

Precious hugged her ally while they waited for Glenarvon Cole and Rhea Laidlaw. Precious was the Disciple for Green Cape Town of Green South Africa - officially, but to Sattva Systems™, she was the continental Disciple of Green Africa.

Two more FusionPlanes™ came into land. Their gentle subsonic booms played like two heartbeats in competing rhythms. Glenarvon Cole was one person in the world who couldn't conceal his true stature. He was the Leader of the GreenRevs and the one person on the planet who could outdo the great Bodhi Sattva in the charisma stakes. He wore combat fatigues and yet seemed almost homely in his demeanour. The love of his fellow green warriors came from the knowledge that there was nothing he wouldn't do to protect them. He loved his soldiers, and they worshipped him in return.

Bodhi couldn't have completed the Green Coup without him, and Bodhi loved his revolutionary comrade. Glenarvon Cole was a man of his word, just as Bodhi Sattva was.

Rhea left her own FusionPlane™ and parked it next to the other three. The four vehicles looked precisely the same with their cream-coloured livery. The only difference was that Rhea's was a rental and not a private FusionPlane™. She could have had one, of course, but she played a winning card with Bodhi by eschewing ownership. Rhea had been given the small town of San Martin - a stone's throw from Boulder Creek - to administer as its Green Disciple. Its proximity to the Sattva Systems™ HQ enabled her to be Bodhi's eyes and ears in the outside world. She would jokingly describe herself as his Special Ops.

Bodhi smiled beatifically, and his arms outstretched, 'Welcome, friends.' They moved in for a group hug. This is how things worked when Bodhi held court.

'I'm going to give you the updates on the one-hundred-year plan. This means taking you to our esteemed Green Project Manager, Professor Pinar Dogan - you don't need me to tell you how difficult she can be.'

They laughed. Bridgett said, 'You provided us with the inspiration and the resources, but this is all hers.' She spun slowly around with her arms open wide to take in the surroundings.

'Ugly, isn't it?' Glen laughed.

Bodhi said, 'An unfortunate necessity.' He led them away, and he made a point of smiling at every worker, and the others followed his example in this silent training session.

It began to rain heavily, but the group hardly noticed, as the RedSuits™ repelled every water droplet.

Walking deliberately at the back of the group, Rhea over-rode her auto-settings by wanting to know what the rain felt like and instantly, she felt the cold rain in her hair and on her skin. Once it became uncomfortable, she turned the auto-settings back on again just by wanting it to happen. She still splish-sploshed through every puddle. *They all work so damned hard on being so self-effacing,* she thought, *I must remember to keep my sense of self within this Green cult.* Rhea knew there was little need for security, as the Greens were exceptionally well behaved, but it still perplexed her how they could enter any door at will. If there were warning signs, then that was considered ample to keep people from entering. Many doors informed them of hazardous or toxic materials, but workers wandered in and out of them without any protective clothing. She had to remind herself that she was now Red™ and that she had nothing to fear, but it was a hard habit to break.

I've never liked Bridgett, she thought. *Bodhi must have his uses for her - as her ruthlessness is way off the brand narrative of Sattva Systems™.* Rhea recalled Bridgett stating that eradicating the excess of humanity was the simplest solution to the climate change crisis.

She may as well have shrugged at the prospect for all she cared. She considered Precious in her African Print Rotta blue dress, she wasn't in Bridgett's fanatical league, but she was a skilled politician and arch manipulator. Rhea was never privy to the private discussions they had with Bodhi, but she shuddered at the breadth of topics under consideration. *It's unusual for Glen to be here. He always gives the impression that his work is done. The GreenRevs delivered the world to Bodhi, and now Bodhi's job is to fix it.*

She had a trained eye for picking out details, but the Green logistics were clever within their simplicity. Everything they designed was the same colour schemes of cream and moss green, even the office walls. It was proposed as being anti-Trad, anti-capitalist, and anti-materialist, and yet it was the branding of the highest order. The rooms had no tell-tale signs of whether they were more important than the next. One room could be working on a revolutionary new product, while the next could be a storage cupboard. Again, this was sold as anti-Trad, but in a complex of this magnitude, she decided it was a brilliant way of hiding secret operations.

They went through a door that opened out into a vast laboratory. She recognised the Turkish-looking woman in her trademark black leather clothes in deep, some might say, aggressive conversation with a couple of her colleagues.

Professor Pinar Dogan peered across at her visitors disdainfully and then continued to berate her subordinates. She marched over to Bodhi. 'I haven't got time for this.'

Bodhi smiled, 'Now, Pinar. Play nice. Our friends have travelled a long way to see you. This is a need-to-know situation. There is a big world out there to keep on board with our plans. These are the people to make it happen.'

'Fuck you, pay me.' She added at the looks of bemusement from the group. 'I won't allow the fucking Security Protocols™ to come within a mile of me. They are mine. If he...' She pointed at Bodhi, 'wants me to alter the settings, then he has to ask me, and then I decide - after I've made him grovel first.'

Rhea was glad she stayed at the back of the esteemed visitors because she wanted to laugh, and here, nobody could see her smile. Bodhi was non-plussed, he was either used to this; or could hide his discomfort with consummate ease.

'All in good time.' Bodhi said. 'Your selections have historical merit, and we can't allow them to become shrines to the Traditional Cultures.'

'You didn't say that.' She barked, 'I'll tell you how it's going to be from now on. I'm gonna be paid up front. Every time you want something from me, here's what I'm gonna say: Fuck you, pay me...'

'I thought you would be able to work that out for yourself. How could you reconcile your choices with our desire to relieve our followers of the need for nostalgia and painful memories.' He turned to the group and gestured an apology. 'We'll take that off-line if that's ok.'

'Fuck you. No.' Pinar moved in nose-to-nose with Bodhi.

Glenarvon Cole broke ranks and ushered Pinar away. 'After the Red Ceremonies, I will take you with me, all over the world, to help you select suitable properties. You have my word.'

'You, I trust. But him...' She made a dismissive sweep of her hand. 'Ok. Let's get this over with. I'm busy.' She called out to one of her colleagues. 'Have the reports ready on my bench.' Pinar's choice of standing around a bench in a laboratory was all the hint she needed to give that she had no intention of dragging this meeting out a moment longer than necessary.

She marched to the bench, and her VIPs were reduced to ducklings trailing the mother. She whipped a report open. 'We have manufacturing plants running across the world at full capacity to generate enough Red Nanomaterials for the Red Ceremonies. For the life of me, I cannot fathom why all the poxy Green peasants need to receive it at the same time.'

'For the sense of theatre.' Bodhi said softly.

'I always hated the fucking theatre. I didn't get it.' Rhea laughed, and Pinar laughed in response. Pinar's mood softened. 'We've had to manufacture enough for more than nine-hundred million RedSuits™ it's taken a vast amount of resources. At the moment, I have to say, our victory hasn't helped much in the impact of climate change.'

Bridgett intervened, 'There are still more than eight billion Trads in addition to the nearly one billion Greens populating Mother Earth. This is an unsustainable amount in a potential runaway Greenhouse situation. We could consider the possibility...'

'No.' Bodhi said. 'There is to be no direct harm to any living creature. Nature will take its course now that we have loaded the dice in Her favour.'

Pinar said. 'Just as well. I wouldn't have agreed to that. I'm a scientist, not a genocidal maniac.'

'Neither are we.' Glen stated.

'The sterilisation programme will cap the Trad population...'

Precious said, 'I need to work hard to sell this. Some have said that this has always been a white man's plan to reduce the population in Africa.'

'Do I look like a fucking white man?' Pinar joked aggressively.

'I'll work with you to recalibrate the Security Protocols™ to ease your burden. I agree we need to address all concerns of our Green colleagues with the utmost sensitivity. Historical and Traditional issues are of little help to us in Her hour of need.' Bodhi placed his hand on Precious' shoulder.

'Can I continue?' Pinar said.

'Please do.'

'The massive reduction in energy consumption will soon feed through into the statistics. There is no more Trad power, no electricity or power plants of any kind. All vehicles have been deactivated. There will be little capacity left to even create fire once our NanoFireRetardents™ complete their spread. However, we are continuing to allow the water system - as we don't want to spread diseases that could enter the food chains or harm the environment further. While this will allow the Trads to grow crops, this will be offset by the difficulty of surviving the winter months, especially in the harsher climates. Life expectancy will fall dramatically in the coming decades, and without the prospect of repopulation through childbirth, then within twenty years, there will be a massive improvement in the climate. But please, don't be fooled. This is still a race against time...'

Bodhi said, 'She's right. The one-hundred-year plan is sacrosanct. It has been precisely calibrated and signed off by myself and Pinar. We can do this if we all work together as a team.'

'What do you want me to do?' Glen said.

'You, our Green Hero. I can't think of anybody better to select the most Devout of our Green colleagues to help save the planet for thousands of years to come.' Bodhi flicked over the pages of the reports to a map of the world. 'There are twenty-six million square miles of hospitable land on the planet, and I want you to allocate the most Devout Greens to take a square mile each...'

'You want me to recruit twenty-six million volunteers...'

'Yes. It's a big world that needs micro-managing if we are to protect Her for eternity.'

'Ok. I'll start with the original GreenRevs and begin building from there. I was wondering about what their role could be after winning the war. When do they start?'

'June 2184.'

'But that's a hundred years away. You are confident the technology...'

'Yes.' Pinar interrupted. 'It would be a huge investment of resources, but my team are working on a NanoSuit™ variant which could enable its users to live for a thousand years - minimum. Why do you think I want to have plenty of places to stay in around the world?' She laughed, but nobody else did. They were stunned at this development, everybody except Bodhi Sattva.

Rhea asked, 'The Brady Mahone anomaly - are there any others like him?'

Only Glenarvon Cole, among this select group, seemed not to understand the question. 'Who is Brady Mahone? Have I missed something while I've been away?'

Bodhi said, 'It's nothing.' Rhea flashed a look of apology to Bodhi.

Glen looked at Bodhi, suggesting that this wasn't an answer.

'He's an escaped convict, a Trad. However, he can enter Green territory seemingly at will.'

Bridgett turned to Rhea. 'There have been no reports of any breaches in Europe or Asia.'

'Nor any from any of my territories. It seems he's a one-off. My guess is that he is Green, but maybe he doesn't know it.'

'Let's discuss the evidence,' Glen folded his arms, 'I don't like information being kept from me. I want to hear what you've got.'

'He's from California. He escaped from the Modern Ridgecrest Supermax Penitentiary on Revolution Day. He's a career criminal. However,' Bodhi attempted to appear serene, 'he wandered into the Green town of West McFarland unimpeded, but the Security Protocols™ apprehended him for attempting to steal groceries. He's nothing to worry about. In fact, he's become a little pet project of mine.' He touched Glenarvon Cole on his arm. 'Let me handle it. It's all under control.'

Glen looked at Pinar. 'How is this possible? The Shells™ have been tested for decades.'

'My team have their theories, but he seems to confound us at every turn.' Pinar laughed heartily, 'He's brought us much amusement. He's started up his own business selling entertainment to the people.'

Bodhi smiled, 'He's no threat. We have to learn from this specimen.'

'That's not enough.'

'It's not one Green area,' Pinar continued, 'nowhere is off-limits to him. We have evidence that he had been wounded on his travels. This would suggest that he is a Trad and, that he hasn't adopted a NanoSuit™. He is looking after a Trad family. However, he has murdered since his release...'

'And you say he's not a threat.' Glen said pensively.

Rhea watched on taking mental notes of the conversation.

'How old is he?'

'Forty-two? He was adopted by Archie and Edie Mahone - utterly unremarkable people.'

Glen said, 'The Security Protocols™ only intervene to save Greens. That's the whole point of the calibration of them. They prevent unlawful and disrespectful behaviour from one Green to another.'

Pinar laughed sarcastically, 'Of course. If we tried to rule over the Trads bad behaviour, the fucking things would explode in seconds.' Bridgett, Precious and Bodhi laughed along, but Glenarvon and Rhea didn't seem to find this observation particularly amusing.

Rhea smiled a little when she noticed Bodhi looking at her.

'So, the Security Protocols™ activated on the signals emitted by the Trad, Brady Mahone, to prevent him stealing...' Glen was thinking out loud.

'They also intervened when they detected sexual interference.' Pinar added.

'What the fuck was this animal up to?'

'Brady Mahone was the victim. He was touched inappropriately while suspended in NanoFilm™.' She shouted, 'Ha-ha! I got you. You should see your faces.'

'I don't think this is a laughing matter. It's a breach of security. We could...'

'No.' Bodhi said. 'We have a new world order. We cannot alter our core beliefs and principles for one man. We do not harm a single creature. He is one of Mother Earth's sentient beings. He should be allowed to try and survive like any other of Her creations. I will watch over Brady Mahone. I'm just trying to find a way where his uniqueness could be of use to me.' Bodhi smiled before adding, 'If he does anything to suggest he is more of a threat or indeed a potential enemy to our cause, then I'm sure that I'll have the wherewithal to deal with him.'

Pinar had lost interest and was flicking through her files, she still had to inform them about Destructive NanoEnzymes™, and they had already derailed the session with the talk of one rogue Trad. She wanted to bring this waste of time meeting to an end. She muttered, 'When a man plays God, is his enemy the Devil?'

20.ORDER FULFILMENT

Over the next month, Brady worked hard to supply his customers, and to deal his photocopied transcripts. He had set himself the goal of buying his FusionVan™ by Thanksgiving, and he achieved that and more. He checked his Distor™, and it informed him that he was now the proud owner of three-thousand and seventy-one Green Credits.

He went into West McFarland to pick up his van. He'd ordered it two weeks previously, as there was very little stock available anywhere in the state, apparently. He paid the GreenAutos™ owner the three thousand Greenbacks by dialling up the small ratchet on the Distor™ until the three-thousand glowed green. *I have to give this willingly*, he reminded himself. A green chip emerged from his Distor™ with the figure of three-thousand glowing on it. He picked it out between his thumb and forefinger, and it flashed as he handed it over to the owner who, in turn, placed it into his own Distor™.

'All done,' he said. 'She's all yours. She'll only respond to you, and she will send out sub-sonic signals when you are within range to ensure you don't lose her, or if you need to find her within a host of other FusionVans™. And you have full NanoShell™ protection within her, even if you go into the Trad areas.'

Brady examined his new car. It was an elongated van shape which Brady had already nicknamed the Hearse. It was ceramic cream, even the wheels and what he assumed were tyres. *It's an ugly sonofabitch fucking car*, he thought, *but now I can expand and make some real fucking money.*

He drove it back to the ranch. *It doesn't drive real fast, but it seems to know what to do before I do.* He celebrated having his new car at the family's Thanksgiving dinner, and even if he wasn't particularly proud of how it looked, he was proud of the fact that he had earned the money to buy it. He felt good about loading his stock in the Hearse. There was room in the back for his bike and trailer, which he figured he would still need in the Trad areas with barricades and roadblocks. There, he would leave his car in a green area and cycle.

He announced to the family that he would be gone for a few weeks but hoped he would be back for Christmas. He also asked Archie for his little black book. He didn't tell his Pops that this time he wouldn't be messing around trying to negotiate. He would take what they had and kill them if necessary. It was the obvious course of action, and if Archie was the only one to mourn them, then so be it.

Those fuckers don't deserve no mercy.

He appreciated the long drives down the almost uninhabited Highways. He also noted more towns had turned Green, though it was mostly the small hamlets at this point. He left the Highways to see how the streets were, there - and spotted the same patterns as on the Highways. The roads were cleared, the vehicles were *eaten*, (as Brady described it), and the buildings were sprayed, some already showing early signs of decay. Only the road infrastructure appeared to be protected. *It looks like they don't even want the Greens moving in there,* he thought, *although it's excellent for shortcuts.*

Brady switched into different personas as he went from place to place. He was threateningly charming as he recruited his Sales Reps, friendly and amenable as he sold his stock to new customers, and as upright as a citizen could be as he dealt with the great and the good when selling his documents. *I know these folks see me as nothing more than a snake-oil salesman, but as long as they pay me...*

He took his time exploring the formerly wealthy coastal areas. Some he had already visited as he now fulfilled his orders from a few weeks earlier, but now he explored further in search of the more well-heeled Green customers.

He was on his way back to the Hearse after a successful day's orders in Malibu when an old man in a suit - which gave him the appearance of a servant, rather than a businessman - approached him.

'Excuse me, sir. Libby Berrington requests an audience with you.'

I know the name, but I just can't place it, he thought. 'Is she buying?'

'I don't know, sir. She only said that she was sure you would want to meet her.'

'Where does she live?'

The old man pointed high up a cliff-top to something the size of an estate, rather than a home. 'I've got a lot of potential business down here,' Brady said. 'I'll see if I can head over this evening.'

'But sir, she said you would want to meet her. She sees very few people, and she is one of the most important people in California, maybe even the world, now.'

'I ain't got time for meets and greets,' Brady said. 'It'd better be worth it. Who is this dame, anyway?'

'Libby is the Mother of Bodhi Sattva. I trust you've heard of Sattva Systems™.'

'No fucking way am I walking into a trap. You must think old Brady is a stupid fuck. Step away old man, I ain't got time to be put away for bootlegging.'

A robotic voice stated from the ether - or from a speaker in a palm tree:

Increased stress levels detected. You may be contemplating committing an act which is not permitted in the Green Zone. Please accept our apologies if this is not the case. This message was brought to you by the Security and Protection Division of Sattva Systems™. Please enjoy the rest of your day.

The old man seemed ruffled. 'Oh, dear. Sir, I truly believe Libby only wants to meet you. I detected no trace of ill intent. Shall I inform her that you will meet her shortly?'

Brady tried to control his breathing and temper. He didn't want to end up wrapped in SecurityFilm™ again. 'Fine.'

'When you arrive, the guards will be expecting you.'

Brady drove up the snaking roads to the cliff-top mansion, and the gates opened without him even having to stop. The first thing he noticed was the fleet of ceramic cream cars. *In the old days, they were Ferraris and Bentleys,* he thought. *I miss those days - those cars had style.*

The threat of SecurityFilm™ reminded him that no one would be remotely scared of him in this place, not even the old woman who came out to greet him. She opened her arms. 'My dear Brady Mahone. Bodhi said that I really should meet you if ever you came to Malibu.'

The Palm trees stood like sentries as they walked together, down the long driveway to the main entrance, lined by garages on either side - with exclusive chalets above them. In front of him was a huge, glass-panelled entrance, and at the centre of the lobby was a spiral staircase of marble with ebony bannisters.

'So, which room are you staying in?'

Libby laughed. 'It's all mine, my dear. Trust me, I earned it.'

He studied her like he would an animal before he began to sketch it. He couldn't work out how old she was. Her hair was grey, but it was sleek and shiny, with traces of remaining jet-black strands running through it. She was slender and tanned, and her clothes were stylish and undoubtedly expensive. And, he thought, *she smells amazing.*

She guided him up the staircase to the gallery, which appropriately was lined with artworks from the late twentieth century. The place was so large that Brady lost his bearings, until he spotted the driveway he had walked down beneath him, the Pacific Ocean visible through the Palm trees. He looked down, and steps led to a sizeable open-aired jacuzzi only covered from the elements by a sloping glass ceiling.

Libby walked down the steps and her clothes melted away and now she was in a black swimsuit. Brady blinked, amazed by what he'd just seen. She entered the hot, bubbling water. 'Would you care to join me? We could get to know one and other a little better.'

After showering nude every day in prison with every kind of criminal, being naked with this old woman held no concerns for him – so he stripped. Libby looked at him approvingly as he sploshed down the steps, before lying in the pool like he was the master of the house.

'Could I get you anything?'

'A drink would be nice.' He chuckled. 'I don't suppose you've got any cigars lurking around the place?'

She rang a tiny bell which tinkled in the soft winter breeze. The old man appeared. 'Hunter, kindly bring Champagne for my guest and I, Brady...'

'Mahone. Brady Mahone.'

'And cigars. I think you'll find them in Freddie's old room.' She turned to Brady. 'One of my ex-husbands. I've had four - quite the collection. He was small for a Hollywood actor - but perfectly formed.'

The champagne and cigars arrived. Hunter helped Brady to light the cigar, and waited until Brady was content, then placed them on a wooden shelf which overhung the edges of the jacuzzi. Brady chuffed away at the cigar, blowing smoke rings. He gulped down a glass of champagne before retrieving the bottle from the ice bucket and pouring himself another. He positioned himself for the best view of the ocean, and then breathed out a contented sigh.

Libby sipped her champagne and smiled. 'I do like a man who can make himself at home. It shows confidence - and there is nothing more attractive in a man than confidence.'

'You have to take what you can while you have the opportunity. I'm not going to miss out on this. I've never been on vacation,' he added. 'I'm guessing this is what it would be like.'

'Yes. I suppose it would.'

They lay in the jacuzzi for more than an hour, barely uttering a word. Brady concentrated on the hot bubbles swirling around his naked body while drinking his champagne and smoking his cigar. The old man, without needing to be asked, brought out fresh bottles when required, and helped Brady to light his second cigar. Brady loved this place. The winter sun began its late afternoon descent, and he probably wouldn't have moved, even if Libby had suggested it. All he wanted to do was to feel the warm California breeze on his face and to watch the hazy sun sink into the sea in a display of fire-red against the backdrop of the wispy blushing clouds.

'Are you glad you came to visit me now?'

'Yes. I'm super-chilled.'

Libby laughed. She climbed out of the jacuzzi and was instantly dry, then instantly dressed in another set of clothes, as though she was about to attend an exclusive restaurant in the city, and Brady detected the scent of another sensuous perfume which was different to the last. Before he decided to leave, she returned with a white luxury bathrobe and slippers. 'I don't want you to slip on the marble floors.'

He pulled his naked body from the jacuzzi, and she held open the dressing gown for him to slip his arms into, and she tied the robe as if she were dressing a child.

Hunter appeared. 'Have Brady's clothes washed and take him to Xavier's bedroom,' she said. She turned to Brady. 'He was about your size when he was younger. Pick out what you want, and you can wear them this evening. Hunter will have your old clothes ready to take with you when you leave. Anything you choose - you can keep,' she added, smiling mischievously.

'Can your friend Hunter give me a tour of the place?' *I won't be able to steal anything,* he thought, *but there's no harm in scoping out the joint.*

'Of course, but don't be too long, as I was hoping you'd have time for dinner with me. Is there anything in particular you'd like?'

'Steak - well-done, with fries, mushrooms, onion rings and pepper sauce.'

Libby laughed. *I should have guessed,* she thought. 'I'll have my chef attend to it.'

As Hunter showed him around, Brady asked lots of questions. 'So, who's this Libby broad?'

'She was one of the most famous and glamorous actresses in Hollywood. I'm most surprised you hadn't heard of her.' Hunter changed direction and headed down another hallway, 'This way is Libby's bedroom.' All along the corridor was framed photos and movie posters. There were semi-naked poses in her youth, intermingled with costume dramas and serious poses through her middle-age.

'How many bedrooms does this place have?'

'Twelve, sir.'

'There seem to be as many lounges.'

'Yes, there are. There's also the games room, the cinema, the gymnasium, of course, and the kitchens. And before you ask, there's a private beach, four swimming pools and tennis courts.' He changed direction to head back to Xavier's room. Brady noticed a children's playroom, and it was full of toys and games for all ages.

'Who's that for?'

'It's for the visitor's children, to keep them amused while Libby is entertaining.'

'On the way back, I want to see the other bedrooms,' Brady said. 'The one Libby sleeps in, and the ones where her ex-husbands did as well.' While in Libby's bedroom he was struck by the beauty of one large movie poster. It was called *the Virgin* and was billed as an epic masterpiece. Libby was dressed in gossamer white and looked like an angel. She was playing the Virgin Mary. Brady gasped. 'Wow!'

'Everybody said she should have won her Oscar for that role,' Hunter said. 'It was a travesty. John Kane believed so and he used this to seduce her. She was outstanding in that role - utterly compelling.'

'So, why didn't she win?'

'The conspiracy theorists believe there was pressure bought to bear by the Catholic church. It is Libby's personal favourite image of her,' he added. 'John and Xavier loved it also. Xavier used to gaze upon it, just like you are now.'

Brady looked at it for a moment as if he was an art critic studying a masterpiece. 'I want to see the rest.'

'As you wish, sir.'

After a few minutes, they arrived, and Hunter opened the door for Brady. 'Here we are, sir. The walk-in wardrobe is over there.' He gestured to the left. 'And if you need to freshen up, then the en-suite bathroom is off to the right.'

Brady flopped down on the enormous bed and moved his head from side to side to take in the vast bedroom. There were a few photos of Libby - some with her son, and presumably, Xavier - AKA Bodhi's father. He got up, and went to the en-suite - another cavernous room with a golden bath at the centre, a sink area and a mirror above that both spanned the whole length of the room, as well as a gold toilet. If he'd had more time, he would have taken a bath, despite having spent all afternoon in the pool. He washed, and shaved, and then went over to the display shelves and put lots of aftershave on - just like he used to do with the tester bottles at the local drug stores.

He went to the walk-in wardrobe and flicked through the suits. He picked a dark one - this would be more practical in the outside world where he lived. He chose a silk shirt, but didn't want to wear a tie. In the drawers, he found expensive underwear and socks, and in a cupboard, he found expensive footwear of all kinds. He knew he should have chosen shoes to go with the suit, but the exclusive limited-edition sneakers took his eye, and they would be more comfortable to travel in.

When he was dressed, he left the room, and found Hunter waiting for him. 'Shall we continue the tour, sir?' he said stiffly, clearly disapproving of Brady's sartorial selections. He showed him the bedrooms, as Brady checked out whether there was stuff left behind in these vacated rooms, and he also took notice of any photos of the exes, especially the size and shape of them as they posed with Libby or Xavier.

Hunter guided him through the banqueting hall and through to a smaller dining room where the table was dressed as if Brady was a visiting royal. Hunter pulled out a chair for Brady, and he waited impatiently for Libby to arrive. *This is all good n'all,* he thought, *but I could have made some sales.*

He fiddled around with the heavy cutlery and ran his finger down the razor-sharp blade of the steak knife. He scanned the room and looked at the photos and expensive artwork. He saw Libby walk in with Hunter, who pulled out her chair. She sat, and whispered her instructions to Hunter. She didn't say anything to Brady, just gave a small smile of acknowledgement.

Then there was a burst of activity as waiters attended to them. She smiled at Brady. 'I didn't want to start a conversation, only to be interrupted by the staff. I do hope you understand. I think we should get to know one and other better.'

Brady drained a glass of wine with indecent haste, and a waiter refilled it immediately. 'Fine with me. Can I interest you in some of my Entertainment Files? I've got a catalogue in my Hearse - I mean, FusionCar™.'

How delightful, he's going to play the part of a low life travelling salesman, she thought. *My dear Xavier, what have I done to deserve this?* 'Sounds enchanting. I will peruse your delights after dinner.'

Brady ate well and drank a lot, but he didn't display any obvious signs of drunkenness. *I have to admit,* he thought, *that was the best steak I ever had.*

Afterwards, Hunter escorted them down in the elevator, which Brady hadn't noticed before. They walked over to a lounge area which overlooked the ocean. Brady gazed over the dark water and watched the moonlight fragment on the gentle waves.

Hunter was given his instructions, and a drinks cabinet was wheeled over, a cigar box was opened and left on the table, and some soft jazz music played in the background. Brady noticed the lights dimming. *If I didn't know better*, he thought, *I'd guess the old broad was trying to seduce me.*

'I can't say I ever saw many movies,' he said, 'so I can't flatter you by saying I loved a film you were in.' *It's now, or never*, he thought. *I need to make some sales before I leave*. 'But speaking of movies, I'll grab my catalogue and order books from my van.'

After a couple of wrong turns, he found his way back to the entrance, and then to his Hearse. He took a few deep breaths of the refreshing ocean air and fixed his eyes on a bright star until he could tune it from a blur in his eyes into a sharper focus - it made him feel like he could control his oncoming drunken state. *Whatever we are drinking, it's strong stuff. It's going to my head.*

He went back to join Libby and placed his Mahone Enterprises catalogue, with its amateurish-looking logo, designed by Mary-Lou, on the ebony and glass coffee table. Libby picked it up, and flicked through the pages, chatting in a distracted way, almost to herself. 'Nobody kept any hard copies. Everything was streamed, and to such high-quality - even my cinema is set up for streaming. I must get Xavier to arrange installation of some old-fashioned hardware. It would be lovely to use the cinema again.' She added, 'If ever you use my son's name be sure to pronounce the X as in X-avier, some try to say it as Zavier.'

I'll call him what the hell I want, he thought. Still, he played along. 'Why's that?'

'He was John's Project X. He used to joke that learning human nature was as easy as X, Y and Zee. Then he would say X marks the spot for perfection, Y is for the triers, and Zee is for life's losers. I can't say I understood him.' Libby looked away as if this was a memory she craved to delete. She moved back gratefully to a subject she could be distracted by.

She browsed his catalogue until she came to a section rich with movies which interested her. Brady moved next to Libby, with his pen poised over his order book. She looked at him, and her eyes sparkled as if she had transformed into the Hollywood starlet of her youth. It was as if another version of her had been switched on.

She continued her monologue while pointing at her selections, and Brady hurriedly copied the reference numbers into his order pad. 'Oh, such memories... She was such a sweetheart, but I couldn't say the same about her... That was one of my favourite performances... I was nominated for an Oscar in that role... That was where I met Freddie, we had such fun.' Libby continued her trip down memory lane for more than an hour, and Brady ended up with more than seventy orders in his book. He took the unusual step of asking for payment upfront. *She's loaded,* he thought. *She can afford to take the risk.* He wondered if the SecurityFilm™ would wrap him up if he displayed any bad intent in his vital signs, anyway. *It would be bad for business if I didn't deliver, as she would tell those wealthy friends of hers not to buy from me.*

Libby was merry from the alcohol, and in a dreamy state. She rang her tiny bell, and Hunter appeared with her Distor™. *He must be listening. She didn't even ask him for it.* She duly paid Brady the seven-hundred and fifty Green Credits. 'I'll bring them over in a couple of days,' he said.

She nodded. 'What kind of movies did you like?'

'Action movies, things with cool special effects. I used to like those Marvel comics ones. Were you in any of those?'

'No. My area was complex studies of relationships, and the occasional costume drama.'

'When was that?'

'At the turn of the century and through to the late twenties. The three great pandemics curtailed my career, somewhat.'

'So, how old are you then?' he said, bluntly.

'I'm one-hundred and fourteen years old.'

'Wow. I wouldn't have had you as a day over seventy.'

He would never know how much of an insult this was to Libby. 'One of the benefits of having a husband and son who led the world in cutting edge technology.'

'Like the clothes changes you do. What colour are you? That's what you Greens are into now, isn't it?'

She looked at him, still angry at his assessment of her as a woman - an old woman - but she had her assignment to complete. 'What have you learned about the NanoSuits™?'

'The Red™ one makes you indestructible. Professor Yuan Chu - nice guy by the way - said something about Diamonoid Shells. That kind of makes sense, y'know - diamonds and all.' *I miss those jewellery heists.* 'And then everybody has to save hard or work hard to grab one of the OrangeSuits™, which will look out for germs, and keep everybody healthy.'

'You've been keeping company with Professors?'

'Just the one. He treated me with respect.'

'And where was this?'

Brady didn't want her to know - he knew a potential undercover approach when he heard one. He wouldn't just lead her to the Professor, he would be leading them to his new family. 'Castaic - just south of Bakersfield. So, what colour are you?' He changed the subject as quickly as he could.

'Yellow™. It comes after Orange™. The textile industry uses so much water and resources... We just won't need it anymore. Personally, I welcome the return to freedom of expression through appearance - I was beginning to wonder if they were planning to eliminate style as well - which would have been quite unbearable.' Libby laughed at her own joke. Brady didn't think it was all that funny, but he smiled, anyway.

They talked for a couple of hours over brandy, while Brady chuffed away at his huge cigars. She spoke of her early childhood memories of London before moving to the States when her Hollywood career hit the heights. Occasionally, she mentioned how she met her ex-husbands, in no particular order, all were fellow leading actors in the movies she made with them. She discussed the merits of her movies, punctuated with, *I was nominated for this or that award, but I always just missed out...* And then she began to mention her first husband more, Brady guessed that the drink was talking now, *I thought this OrangeSuit™ would at least come up with a hangover cure.*

'I was Libby Skye, in my Hollywood glory days - such a lovely name. Then I became Libby Kane. John insisted that I take his surname. He was an industrialist with a vast fortune, and a man who was used to getting his own way.' Brady wanted to smile when she began to slur like an angry drunk as it revealed a Trad trait... 'But I drew the line at changing my name to Sattva. Libby Sattva, I mean, come on. I couldn't stop him changing Xavier's name to Bodhi.'

'Why did he do that?'

'John had one of those midlife crises and went all "Buddhist" on me. He wouldn't hurt a living creature, but he sure didn't mind hurting me.'

Brady thought about this. 'I noticed you don't have any of those Sattva Signs anywhere - not in your home, or in this part of Malibu at all.'

'This is my home. It's mine, I earned it. My home is not a damn corporation.' She closed her eyes, like a drunk trying to find a moment of clarity to re-join a conversation. 'Him and his visions, I thought meditation was supposed to bring peace. Anyway, after one of his interminable meditation sessions, he believed he was chosen to save Mother Earth and that a boy would be born at the turn of the Millennium to guide us to the New World.' Her demeanour darkened further. 'You look like him. He's playing games with me. How old are you? Where did you come from?'

'Me? I'm forty-two, I think.'

'You think?'

'I was abandoned as a baby outside a drug rehabilitation clinic. It was February time in 2042. Then I was in care, I was told, until I was fostered when I was four. I was kinda forgotten about, and just left there.'

'Nobody visited you?'

'Apart from the police, when they came to arrest me for something I *did* do.' He laughed. 'I hate it when the inmates squeal about the injustice done to them. I did it, I deserved it, but I got away with most of the stuff I did. When they caught me, I was unlucky, not because I didn't plan it right.'

'What did you do?'

He knew she wasn't scared – she was wearing a RedSuit™, and the NanoFilm™ would get him if a bad intention so much as crossed his mind – so he didn't mind telling her the truth. 'I was in for armed robbery, grand theft auto and assault. But I have committed murder, too. I just ain't been to jail for that - yet.'

She didn't seem at all fazed by his crimes. 'And nobody visited you - to check up on how you were doing?'

'Only my Foster Daddy from time to time. My Foster Moms drank herself to death when I was a young 'un.'

'I could look after you,' she said. 'I could pay for your NanoSuits™, all of them. Or any colour you like.'

Brady began to feel as if he had been suckered into being here. He heard his Pops' voice in his mind: *That's how they get you, son.* 'No. Thanks,' he said. 'I'm just fine as I am.'

'As you wish. Bodhi ensured I was a Green Credit millionaire before his revolution. I made sure my friends and neighbours were well compensated. I wasn't going to live here as a pariah. I need my friends.'

Brady made a mental note of the other Greenback millionaires he had to track down around here. 'What happened next, after the visions your husband had?'

'Pass me another drink. I think I'm going to need it.' Brady poured her another large Brandy. She sipped it elegantly, but Brady noticed that half the glass had been drained. 'John was a perfectionist. He wanted to run all kinds of tests on me to see how feasible it would be to conceive and have a son - it had to be a son - as close to midnight on the Millennial day as possible. You can probably deduce that John wasn't a particularly romantic person. I, of course, refused. I was a Hollywood Star in my own right. I had signed his prenup, and there weren't many upsides for me. Even if it had been possible, I didn't want to miss out on the party of the century to go into bloody labour.'

She took another sip of brandy. *He told me to tell him everything*, she thought. *He told me he could have anything he wanted, and if I refused, I would be punished.* 'John promised me anything I wanted, one thing - he specified, up to one hundred million pounds - which was a lot of money back then.' She laughed again at her own joke, but Brady didn't get it. 'And it would be entirely in my name and outside the scope of any future divorce proceedings. I did mention that he was a romantic, didn't I?'

Brady laughed. He was intrigued. He reflected upon all the things he might have chosen - the luxury high-performance cars, the massive gold chains, 'So, what did you choose?'

'This place. This home is mine, and mine alone. Even after the Green Revolution, Bodhi had to honour his father's promise to me. I gave him life. He only exists because of me. I have my home, and my friends and I earned it.'

Brady scoffed. 'You missed a party - you had a baby - but you earned all this? Get real, lady.'

'Let me tell you about that night. Pour me another.' Brady did, pouring himself one as well. 'I had been through all kinds of tests. My eggs had been engineered to ensure I would have a boy. The doctors and nurses had been well-rewarded for working on the Millennial Eve, but what I didn't know was that they were offered bonuses that would make them rich for life if they induced me to have the first baby in the world born on the Millennial Day. They even had a registrar ready. I should have wondered why I had to go to Tonga to deliver the baby. You could say that they were highly motivated. The only rule was that I couldn't have a Caesarean section, I must have a vaginal birth.'

Too much information, Brady thought.

She pulled her left hand to her face and breathed heavily into her palm. 'They were brutal with me. As the clocked ticked down, they tried everything to bring Xavier into the world, and then as the clock was about to strike twelve, the surgeon butchered me. He sliced me up. They used a ventouse and pulled him into the world on the first second of the new Millennium. I cannot find the words to describe the agony they made me endure. I suppose I should be grateful that they stuck around for the emergency surgery I needed afterwards. If I'd have known what John's plan was, I would never have agreed to it, not even for this place. I have massive scarring to this day - even after the best cosmetic surgery you could buy back in those primitive times.'

Brady wasn't overly interested, but he had learned that information had some value to the Trad areas, and it would give his business legitimacy if he could claim to be friends with Bodhi Sattva's mother. He thought it wise to keep her talking. 'What happened to Bodhi?'

At first, she scowled at the lack of interest in her welfare. *I suppose I shouldn't be surprised,* she thought. *He's a man, after all - and an uneducated criminal.* 'Xavier's education began even before he was born. John had his teachers come and talk to the baby inside me. Can you imagine how weird that was, having to let complete strangers hover over my stomach and recite science and business lessons to a foetus? Every single day I had to let them do that to me.'

'Was there nothing you could do about it?'

'I wasn't allowed to prevent this under the terms of our agreement. I did rebel in my own little way - I always do.'

'What did you do?'

'I talked to my unborn baby. He could hear me day or night. I used to say, "Xavier, this is your Mother. Whatever anybody should say to you, you must always protect your Mother." I must have looked like I was insane, but I talked to my boy, all the time, day and night. I had to keep my bond with my baby.'

'Did you have any other kids?'

'No. I tried. Freddie, in particular, was desperate for a child with me. That's why he left me, I believe. In no time at all, he was playing Daddy with my best friend. They were very dark days for me.' She sighed. 'I didn't even have Xavier for long. John took complete control over his upbringing. He was Daddy's little science project.' She waved her hand dismissively as if she were physically shooing away her memories.

Brady excused himself to go to the bathroom. Libby called Hunter over.

Libby was drunk. *I suppose I'd better get this over with*, she thought, *God only knows why Xavier insists on putting me through this ritual humiliation to play his little games.* She whispered to Hunter, 'I know I'm supposed to offer him the run of the place, and I'm not to suggest limitations, but I think I can bend the rules a little.'

'What would you like me to do?' Hunter said.

'Let him think that my personal and sentimental items are Film protected.'

'Which items?'

'Diaries, jewellery, artworks and photos...'

'I hope I won't be impacted.'

'Just do this for me, will you?'

'Yes, Libby.'

'Get others to help you. This one is going to be greedy.'

Hunter marched away, smiling at Brady as he returned. Libby stood up to greet him. 'I do believe it's Christmas in three days. We are not allowed to celebrate traditional date related festivals, here in the Green world – they're synonymous with materialistic indulgences and the depletion of the planet's resources. But no-one said anything about giving things away. I assume they are still planning Christmas festivities in the Traditional Areas?'

'Yes. Why wouldn't they?'

'Why, indeed. Hunter will escort you, but please feel free to take any items I own that could be of use to you. That will be my Christmas gift to you.'

I'm glad I asked for payment upfront, he thought. *Otherwise, I might have felt under pressure to give her the Files she ordered, free-of-charge.* 'Great, I mean - thanks.' He acted casually, but he was cautious, he glanced around for signs of a trap. However, the lure of free stuff was too tempting to pass up.

As Hunter and Brady left the room, Brady instantly began deciding how he'd make the most of this opportunity. He had robbed homes before, and he was thinking of the valuable items he could ram into his car. *The bike and trailer are taking up valuable space*, he thought. *I could leave the bike and pick up another rental later. But the trailer could be filled up. I need to organise the items. I could use sheets...*

'Sir, there is a trap within the request that you should be aware of,' Hunter said.

'Trap? Fuck.'

'You'll be able to take anything, but the artwork and jewellery are Film Protected, as are her personal objects, like diaries and photos. It wasn't intentional, but I think in her inebriated state, it slipped her mind. Bodhi had those things additionally covered.'

Brady was disappointed, but grateful for the information. He noticed a couple of men and a woman approaching.

'Michael, Jasper and Holly,' Hunter said, 'please assist Mr Mahone. He is very dear to Libby, and she has given him the freedom of the house to take away with him anything he needs. You can help take the items to his van.'

'Yes, Hunter,' they said, in unison.

'First off, I need a dozen sheets, some cords and cable ties, and a Magic Marker,' Brady said. 'I want you to lay them on the floor so I can sort things out. Is that clear?'

'Yes, Mr Mahone.'

Brady began with Xavier's room and rifled it for clothes, shoes, toiletries and aftershaves. He poised at the jewellery but left it untouched. He proceeded onto every other bedroom, followed by the kitchen. After three hours, his van was packed with wrapped up sheets, each full of luxury items. Then, he realised: he had more room on the passenger side. He asked for pillowcases and headed to the kitchens and utility rooms and stuffed these with food, alcohol, cigars, and even cleaning materials and detergents.

He finished packing the car, convinced he had used up every square inch of space when Hunter handed him his Catalogue and Order Book. He placed them under the driver's seat. *I should have thought about that before,* he thought, *but at least I don't have to give anything back*. 'I better go in and say thank-you. Goodbye, and all that.'

'There's no need, sir. Libby has retired to her bed. I fear she is going to have quite the hangover in the morning. Have a safe journey, Mr Mahone.'

21.HIDDEN WEALTH

Brady returned to the ranch; it was just before dawn. Archie heard Brady's car coming up the driveway and went out to greet him. There hadn't been any need for late-night watches, as the Trads couldn't enter, unable to pass the roads which surrounded the ranch, and the Greens had shown no interest in entering their land - the Sattva warning billboards of Lucian's seeming to do the trick. Archie was in his long johns, with a dressing gown wrapped around him, 'Hey, son, didja have a good trip?'

'Sure did, Pops. I would say get back to bed, but there is something you can help me with.' Brady pulled out the pillowcase sacks of food and homewares. 'I don't want this to go off. Could you help me to get it into storage and the freezers?'

Archie whistled when he saw what was inside. 'God damn it, son. This is some mighty fine shit you have here.'

When they had finished, Brady persuaded his Pops to go back to bed. He reversed his Hearse back to the barn, and then unloaded the rest of his goods into a corner, covering them with tarpaulin.

The next day was Christmas eve, and Mary-Lou was making an effort to make it memorable for Little Amie, as she was becoming affectionately known. Archie had dug out his old Christmas Tree, and Lucian and Mary-Lou had decorated it with tinsels and baubles. Mary-Lou was reading Amie Christmas stories.

As there was no TV stations or newspapers, everyone was desperate for news of the outside world and hung on every word of

Brady's trip to Malibu. He tried not to make them too jealous, as he worried about them being hyper-aware of what they were missing, and what they had lost, but it was impossible. His story - to their ears – couldn't sound anything but glamorous. Archie seemed especially interested in Bodhi's parents - John and Libby Kane.

There was a time, with so many distractions in the old world, when the life story of Bodhi Sattva might only have interested Archie and his conspiracy theories - but not now. They questioned every morsel of information and extrapolated it all into theories of what it could mean for the future. Brady knew he had a valuable commodity on his hands, and that if he chose carefully, he could gain a lot from the key influencers in the Trad Areas. *As long as I'm careful and don't get myself in a position where someone might choose to beat it out of me*, he thought, warily.

Archie spoke of the food and drink that Brady had brought home, and how they would have a proper Christmas feast tomorrow. Spirits were high at the Mahone and Lopez Ranches. It seemed no longer appropriate to call it the Hodgson Ranch, now that Mary-Lou and Lucian Lopez lived there.

Later, Mary-Lou and Lucian used the cleaning materials to scrub every surface clean. They had decided that the risk of infection was the most significant danger, but even the detergents were a welcome reminder of olden times.

Mary-Lou put Little Amie to bed, before drinking wine on the porch with Lucian. They had worked hard and talked themselves out after this busy day. They soon retreated into their homestead to get some much-needed rest.

Brady let Archie talk for hours. He had now decided that the doctors at Bodhi's birth were aliens, probing Libby and injecting her baby with alien DNA. That explained how he could do all this. 'It's all about alien technology. They've had it since Roswell, they were just waiting for the signal. I bet they ain't no real solar flares, that was their spaceships signalling the beginning of the invasion...'

Brady wished his Pops sweet dreams as he helped him to bed, but deep down, he knew his Pops' dreams would be like the sci-fi movies he was selling. He was happy for him – he guessed his Pops loved those dreams.

Brady went out on the porch to see in Christmas. In the very far distance, he saw a few fireworks explode. There couldn't have been many - as the display was over in a matter of seconds. He figured they must have found a few which hadn't been sprayed by the Greens. He kept his eyes peeled in case there were more. He saw a small ceramic cream airplane fly rapidly and quite low down and he assessed it was only a little bit larger than his Hearse. *I haven't seen one of those before*, he thought. He had a drink on the porch and reflected upon his life since escaping Ridgecrest. *It ain't been too bad really - not for the businessman of the year Mr Brady Mahone.*

After about an hour, everywhere seemed quiet and peaceful. Brady got up and went over the barn and quietly rolled his trailer to the tarpaulin in the corner. He removed it and then loaded up six loads of goods contained within the pillowcases. He checked his Magic Marker symbols and rubbed his fingers over the silk sheets. Even they would be useful for bedclothes, now they'd served their purpose. He didn't have his bike – he'd left it behind at Libby's Ocean view home - so he pulled it like a human workhorse. It was heavy, and the sheets looked like they were housing dead bodies as they hung over the edge of the trailer.

When he got to the Lopez ranch, he knew the door would be unlocked - there was no need to lock the doors anymore. *This will be a test of my skills. It's like a reverse robbery.* Before he went any further, he went from room to room to ensure everyone in the house was sleeping. He crept back to his trailer and then took the silken sacks one at a time and placed them at the bottom of the beds. He arranged them, with two on Lucian's side, two at Mary-Lou's and then he crept into Little Amie's and placed two outside her crib.

He headed back with his empty trailer behind him. *I still got it*, he thought, smiling to himself. *Not a peep from any of them. Just the old man to do and that completes another successful mission for top commando Sergeant Mahone.*

He knew his Pops was a light sleeper, but he also knew his single malt whisky should have knocked him out for the night. He had no problems completing his special delivery. His final act of the evening was to put the two sheet loads of goods at the bottom of his own bed. *I can't wait to check these out myself in the morning,* he thought. *I picked this stuff out in a hurry.*

It took a while for Brady to drift off to sleep, the adrenaline still pumping around his body - but when he did, he dreamed of being the richest man in the world, with a home like Libby's and his own private jet.

In the morning, he was woken by excited voices. He had slept heavily. Mary-Lou had bought over Little Amie holding a teddy, and in new night-clothes, which Libby had obviously kept aside for sleepovers, if her friends and family visited. Mary-Lou was in a new dress and shoes, and the smell of expensive perfume was almost overpowering. She had also made herself up with the cosmetics he had grabbed for her, while Lucian was in his smart clothes which Brady had assessed would fit from one of the photos of Libby's ex-husband. They were ecstatically talking of all the other luxury and practical items he had selected for them.

Archie came to join them in his designer and probably rare Levi jeans, and his new sneakers. 'These are the most comfortable sneakers I ever wore. Thank you, son - merry Christmas.'

They all joined in, 'Merry Christmas, Brady.'

'You all really came through for me when I needed you,' Brady said. 'You worked hard for me, and it was my way of thanking you -

but I can't promise this every year. I just made the most of a one-off opportunity.'

'This is delicate,' Archie said, 'and it don't matter to me one way or another, I just wants to know. Did you steal these?'

Brady laughed. 'You know I'd tell you if I did, but no, I didn't. Libby said I could take what I needed, so, I did. She gave them freely. You can't steal from the Greens. They wraps you up in SecurityFilm™ if you even try.'

Archie made them all breakfast as they talked excitedly about every item, and how much they would have cost in the old world. Brady went to help his Pops with the dishes, but his Pops sent him away. 'It's the least I can do, son.'

Brady went to his bedroom to put away his own things. He hung up the suits and silk shirts, and he displayed his array of luxury aftershaves on a bedside cabinet. He tried on an expensive full length Italian black leather coat which went down to his ankles. It had a large collar and deep pockets. He rummaged around in the pockets and pulled out a pair of calf-skin black gloves, and then a sizeable manly ring dropped on the floor with a thud.

He bent down and picked it up and tried it on, and it fitted on the third finger of his right hand. Brady knew his jewellery; it was his former profession, after all. It sparkled in the late morning light. There were many diamonds and inset was a letter S in the same font as that of Sattva Systems™, and this was made up of emeralds. *That Libby and her old creep Hunter fucking lied to me,* he realised. *I could've loaded up on all their jewels. They robbed me of my dream heist.* He paced the room as he plotted his revenge. He still had to deliver her movies. *I'll be ready if they give me another go.*

After a while, he heard the sounds of the family preparing the Christmas feast. *It doesn't seem that long since breakfast.* He looked at his old watch, and this irked him, as he had left behind a whole collection of vintage and designer watches. He realised he had been in his room for more than four hours, dwelling on his anger at missing out on his jackpot. *I got to get a grip. What good is jewellery in this world anyway?* He told himself. *There's no market for it.* He tried to make himself feel better by trying to convince himself that he had done right by the rest of them, but even that didn't entirely do the trick. *I still could have just replaced the one load, maybe, took one bagful of toys instead of the two. Little Amie would have been none the wiser, and you can get a helluva lot of jewellery in one of those sheets.*

TWO DAYS LATER, BRADY drove to Malibu in a sullen mood. He knew it was going to be challenging to maintain his composure to keep off the threat of the SecurityFilm™. To calm himself, he went around the other large houses and found a willing market for his wares. He soon picked up on the competitiveness of Libby's friends and acquaintances. They seemed to choose all the same movies as Libby - once Brady had informed them of her orders - and then chose one or two others, as though this would give them an edge of exclusivity. He had a full order book, which would mean another return trip in a couple of days. *I need a system or strategy to cut out all of this wasted time on the road. I've got my sales teams in the Green Communities, but I need to do something about the manufacturing side.* He laughed at himself, thinking like a big-shot businessman. *That would mean cutting out Lucky and Mary-Lou to a degree, but they are good at this kind of thinking - the strategy stuff.*

He put this to the back of his mind as he drove up the snaking roads to Libby's place. He arrived at the main entrance, but it was locked, and a security guard came over and asked why Brady was there.

'Libby is expecting me. I have her Entertainment orders.'

The guard said nothing but went back to his sentry point. He spoke into an old-fashioned walkie-talkie, before turning back to Brady. 'Someone, will see you shortly.'

Hunter came to the gates. 'Libby has requested that you give them to me.'

'I'll give them to her myself.'

'That won't be possible. You are to give them to me, freely, and then she requests that you never return.'

Brady handed over the Entertainment Files through a gap in the railings. As Hunter turned away, Brady shouted. 'Hey, Hunter. You fucking lied to me, man.' Brady held up his right hand with the Sattva ring on his third finger. Hunter turned ashen. Brady knew fear when he saw it. 'Seems you've made an enemy of more than just me; wouldn't you say. You have a nice day and all.'

After Brady walked away, Hunter smiled as if he was relieved. *I hope the ring is enough to save me.*

22.TIBERIUS

Brady kept his promise with Professor Yuan Chu and dutifully placed his update on the new areas he had visited. Usually, it would be the name of the district, with a tick against a place he had designated as civilised and well-ordered, a cross against the name if it was predominantly lawless, or a G to establish it as a green community - like the one on the west side of McFarland. For Malibu, he went so far as to give a further update.

He wrote:

Malibu - G. The place is full of liberal elite, wealthy bastards including Bodhi Sattva's Mother, who lives in a house that cost a hundred million dollars back at the turn of the Millennium. So much for principles - they can screw everybody else as long as they look after their own.

Look after yourself, Professor and give Bessie a pat from me.

Brady Mahone - Businessman of the Year!

He returned to his bland ceramic cream vehicle and directed it to home, having discovered the Sattnav™ and semi-autonomous functions. Once he fell asleep at the wheel, and it slowed itself. When he awoke, he felt the car avoiding obstacles and even wildlife on the road.

He explored the car, and as he moved his hands over the smooth, unblemished cream dashboard area, a cache of Files ejected. The current one installed had an inscription of Western United States of America with a small Sattva Systems™ logo underneath. Alongside this was a batch of other files with areas such as Mainland Europe, China, Australia, and dozens of others, which he guessed covered the entire planet. *Does that mean Satnav is operating*? he thought. *I suppose the Satellite Phones still work.*

By Californian standards the weather was miserable, the slate grey sky soaking everything with its cold drizzle. Brady strode into the house, not in the mood for idle chit-chat. 'Hey, Pops. I've got a full order book. Can you go and bring Lucky and Mary-Lou over? I need them to get on with making the next batch.'

'Boy, have you seen the weather out there - it's real miserable.'

'I'll do it myself then, shall I?'

'No. I'll do it.'

Brady watched in gloomy silence as Archie retrieved a rarely used raincoat and trudged across to the Lopez Ranch. He then went to his van and retrieved his order book. It was raining harder now, and the cold wind picked up. He went to the barn and waited and waited.

After about an hour, Archie, Lucian, Mary-Lou and Little Amie arrived. 'Why the fuck did it take you so long?' Brady snapped.

'Little Amie was having her bath - we had to sort her out first. We came as fast as we could,' Mary-Lou answered. She wanted to show her anger at being treated like this, but she was grateful for everything Brady had done for her. 'Sorry, Brady. We didn't mean to keep you waiting. What do you want me to do?'

Brady smiled grimly. 'There are hundreds of orders to do. I need the Files completed for me to deliver tomorrow.'

Lucian gave Brady a look of concern, but he followed Mary-Lou as she scurried away to begin work.

Brady turned to Archie. 'I want that book back - the one with your contacts.'

'But you said...'

'I don't want to fuck about. They've got what I, no make that we, need.'

'Ok, boy. No need to get all uppity about it.' Archie left Brady alone in the room. 'Jesus, what's eating him?' he muttered to himself on the way out.

Brady made himself a coffee and sulked. He took out his Sattva ring and examined it, squinting as he looked for hallmarks or other tell-tale signs, but he couldn't find any.

After a while, he realised Archie hadn't returned. *He's had second thoughts*, he thought. *I wonder if he's looking through that fucking book checking if there's anything even more incriminating in there. Does he think I wouldn't know he'd do exactly that? Anyways, they couldn't possibly be any worse than Small Hand Don.*

He went outside to check that Lucian and Mary-Lou weren't slacking. They weren't. The machines were blinking away, and the barn rang to the sound of spinning discs. Lucian looked around, having been engrossed in the DVD filing system of the racks, and smiled at Brady. Brady gave him a thin smile in return and then returned to the kitchen table.

He took out the ring and fiddled with it for a few more minutes before decisively placing it back in his pocket.

Archie returned clinging to his little black book. He gave it to Brady. Archie turned to leave, but Brady stopped him. 'Hold on there, Pops.'

'I got things to do, son.'

'You can do them later. Sit down.'

Archie scowled. 'What's gotten into you, boy?'

Brady said nothing. He flicked through the pages, one by one. He examined the seams minutely before moving on to the next page. This process continued for a few minutes. 'Hand it over, Pops,' he said, finally.

'Hand what over?'

Brady moved his chair next to Archie. 'Look, here, see that? It's a fresh tear in the page. You ripped it out. Judging by the letters, I'm guessing it's a J or a K.'

'You're mistaken, boy. That page coulda fell out years ago. This book is at least sixty years old by now. C'mon, give your old man a break.'

'Do I have to search you, for it?'

'No. Of course, you don't.'

'Then fucking hand it over. Now.'

Archie reached into the back pocket of the Levi jeans Brady had given him for Christmas and gave Brady the missing page. The first names on it would usually be significant enough - there was Judge Almeida, followed by Justice Santos, but it was the final name Brady's eyes narrowed on: John Kane.

'What the actual fuck, Pops? John fucking Kane. You ain't going to tell me it's not the same one - like it's some kinda fucking coincidence, are you?'

'No.' He looked away, as though he thought Brady might peer directly into his brain and see all his darkest secrets.

Brady slammed his fist on the table. 'I think it's high time you told me the whole fucking truth, you degenerate old bastard. Otherwise, I'm outta here, and I ain't coming back. You can rot for all I care.' Archie looked at him, tears running down his face. 'And don't think you can come on with all the waterworks. It don't work when some girl tries that on with me, and it sure ain't gonna work with you, you old fucker.'

'Ok. Ok. John Kane was the money man. He was a cold fish - lordin' it about over us, like he was something special. If he wanted something -particular, like. Then we could get it for him. I don't like to go into details...'

'I've been locked up for fucking years, with every kinda criminal you can imagine,' Brady snarled. 'You don't think I haven't heard stories about the fucking paedophiles who were in the same jails as me. Just spit it out. It's not like any of you lot are going to be brought to justice in this world - is it?'

Archie grimaced and licked his old lips. 'Oftentimes, it was runaways we'd collect, or we'd have people placed in care homes or even schools - the church was good hunting ground. However, sometimes kids were stolen to order. John Kane had the money to pick any kind of kid he needed when he was hungry - like.'

'Hungry?'

'Sorry. It was a term we used.'

'Go on.'

'Well, we were kind of immune. If one of us got caught, then we always had connections to get us out of trouble, and John Kane had deep pockets.'

'And what was in it for you?'

He sighed. 'Ok, son. I'll tell you it all, but you ain't gonna like it. You'll probably leave anyway no matter what I says. But when I tell you that I left it all behind me, and I did nothing since I had you, you gotta believe that too. Do you promise to believe that?'

Brady reflected on this. He went back as far as he could, searching for signs, but he couldn't find or recall anything. 'Ok. I promise.'

'I used to make money from the kids I found - big money, and a percentage of the earnings, you know, porn films, prostitution... And I used to get a taste... Y'know - of the action.'

'Why did you tear this one piece of paper out? Is it because I mentioned his name?'

Archie sighed, and his shoulders sagged. Brady knew this look. He did it himself when he knew he was outplayed by a detective, and he was ready to confess, just to get it over with. 'It was a big story, back in the day, big shot industrialist vanishes. It went on for years, it did.' Brady practised what the police used to do to him - he didn't say anything, just leaned in, encouraging Archie to speak more. He did. 'I did it. I killed him. I garrotted him with a cheese wire. Damn near took his head off, I did. And then I buried him, deep in the forests. I knew the cops would be swarming all over this.'

'Why'd you do it?' Brady's tone was cold, still imitating police procedure, and not showing signs of understanding - which Archie hoped for.

'He came here to take you away from me, boy. He wanted you, but I loved you, and I wasn't going to let that happen - not for all the money in the world. I ain't ashamed to say it, but I loved you, son - always have - always will.'

Brady's mind was in a whirl. Pops... John Kane... Libby... Bodhi... Take what you want... Unexpectedly fostered... Foster Mom's drinking herself into an early grave...

A loud scream came from the barn. Brady followed more slowly as Archie rushed out to investigate. Brady guessed his Pops would have used any excuse to pull himself away from this interrogation. When Brady reached the barn, he found Lucian consoling Mary-Lou. She was shaking. 'What is it?' Brady said, rushing over. 'Has there been an accident?'

'Your Father is a monster,' Mary-Lou yelled. 'Keep him away from my child.' She sobbed, tears of rage streaming down her face. Brady was utterly confused. *Was she listening?* he thought. *But if she was listening, why did she go to the barn to start screaming? Maybe it was because Lucky was there...*

Lucian held her tightly as she buried her face in his chest as if she couldn't bear to look at Brady. 'We ran out of blank Black Files, so, we checked out the pre-recorded ones you brought back. On the top of the box were a few scattered about. Mary-Lou thought that maybe they weren't as important as the neatly stacked ones, so it wouldn't matter if we broke a couple by using a screwdriver on the button which looked like a flip switch...'

'But she wanted to see what was on them first,' Brady said, filling the gaps. His mind went back to Don Pickerstaff's place, he recalled the camcorder and the Black Files next to it. He must have been watching them the night I was there until the battery died.

'She was doing it for you and the business - there might have been something useful on there. She wasn't going to just destroy them without checking.'

'I can never unsee that filth,' she yelled, 'but at least I'm aware of the monster who lives here. He is a threat to my child, my poor baby.' She was weeping, but Brady could sense her disgust. He didn't want to ask her what she had seen, and he didn't want Lucian to let her go.

Archie had listened and watched what was happening through a crack in the door. He didn't want to inflame the situation. He watched Brady with an overwhelming sense of dread as he wandered over to the Black File player.

Brady stopped. He went through a box of accessories and found a pair of headphones. He plugged them into the player. Brady positioned himself to block the screen from Lucian and Mary-Lou. He pressed Play from Start. The title credits rolled, but it was evident to Brady that the names were pseudonyms, and then a banner appeared stating proudly that this was an *All Friends Together* production.

Then a serious-looking black screen with writing appeared. *In Ancient Rome on the heavenly isle of Capri, Emperor Tiberius is entertaining guests from the senate...* Brady guessed the delay was a ruse to make it look like a historical costume drama if the viewers needed to explain what they were watching. *Just hit Play from Start and it makes you look like you're watching the History Channel.* There was more historical context before the first punchline for the dickless wonders - he knew these nonces had an awful sense of humour to match their god-awful personalities. *Do I think that about Pops? I know others would - and I wouldn't blame them.* Brady ground his teeth as the title appeared: *Orgy Porgie Pudding and Pie.*

The faux movie opened with Emperor Tiberius declaring that today's indulgences were open, but he must take the virgin first. There must have been thirty or more children, and as many adults. Of course, they were nearly all men, but there were a couple of women present. He watched a boy of about seven being selected and being stripped and presented to Tiberius. Brady turned away as the boy was about to be raped, but he couldn't escape the sound of it happening and the encouragement of the crowd.

Outside the barn, Little Amie toddled over from her playpen and was heading to the barn, she smiled at Grandpops, as they were teaching her to say. He smiled grimly.

Brady wanted to stop watching, but he had to know whether Archie was there. There had been only rapid cuts of the crowd so far. *Maybe he wasn't there? Perhaps it only looked like him? What if he was there but didn't take part - could that be excusable? For the love of God give him plausible deniability.*

After the red-faced Tiberius had finished, he looked at the crying child and smiled broadly as if was reliving his sexual gratification. He raised his arms and declared: 'Let the games begin!'

The adults rushed over and grabbed the children. Some fought over the same angelic girl. And then he saw a close up of one of the child molesters slobbering over a young girl. It may have been more than half a century ago, but the face which leered into the camera proudly couldn't be denied.

It's Pops.

He didn't need to see anymore. He ejected the File and put it in his pocket, almost absentmindedly as he fought to control his emotions. *Should I try to explain it to Lucky? Comfort Mary-Lou? Confront Pops? What do I do first?*

Little Amie tottered into the barn. Mary-Lou broke free from Lucian's loving arms and picked her up and hugged her protectively. 'My baby, what was I thinking? Leaving you to play with that monster on the prowl. I'm so stupid.'

'It's ok,' Lucian said. 'She's fine.'

'No. It's far from fucking ok. I can't leave. I can't take Amie out of harm's way, and he will be waiting and watching, every day and night, waiting for his moment. He'll be fantasising about her until one day he will act - and do those terrible things to my daughter. That is my life from now on, dreading the moment he takes her for another one of his victims.'

Brady observed Mary-Lou and put himself in her position. *I'd think that if I was her*, he thought. *I can't change her way of thinking. If it was me, I'd kill him*. He then remembered that Archie wasn't in the barn - but he should have been there before him. *Where is he*?

Before he reached the house, he scanned the ranches - but if Archie was out there, he couldn't see him. He went into the homestead, and searched from room to room, but Archie was nowhere to be seen. Then Brady went into the bathroom. He found Archie in the bathtub lying fully clothed but in a pool of blood.

'Pops! No, Pops!' He tried to lift him, and Archie groaned. 'What have you done, you...?' He was a dead weight, and in an awkward position, so he put him back down. He went to the airing cupboard and tore off strips of linen to bind his wrists. He spotted the cut-throat razor which had slipped beneath Archie when he had attempted to lift him. The wounds on both wrists pumped out the blood at an alarming rate, and as he tried to clear the blood away, Brady realised how deep the wounds were. Archie had sliced through the veins and arteries the whole length of his forearms.

Archie gasped. 'Ain't long to go now, boy. Nothing you can do for me. Don't blame...' His eyes closed, and Brady already feared he was dead, but Archie made an effort to open his eyes. It looked to

Brady like his Pop's eyelids were heavier than any lift he had done in the gym. Archie whispered, with his last dying breaths, 'Tiberius...' He gulped. 'Is John Kane.' And then he slumped into Brady's arms.

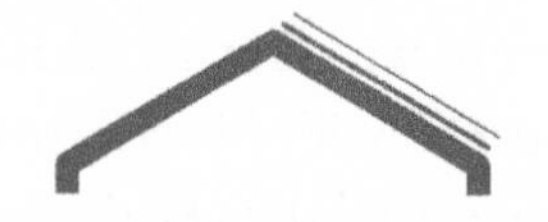

23.NIGHT ON THE TOWN

Only Lucian and Brady attended the burial and funeral of Archie Mahone. Brady had dug the grave alone. It was an act of penance, though for what, he wasn't quite sure. *I should've done something. It was my fault bringing those Files back from Castaic. I should've checked them myself.*

He thought about what he needed to do next. *I'll deliver the completed orders to Malibu tomorrow, and then I've got to dig out some Blank Files - I might have to start exploring north of here - up to San Jose. I'll make a plan for the new year.*

He went to the barn and gathered up the box of pre-recorded Files, retrieving the ones that lay next to the File player and taking them back to his bedroom. He intended to keep them from causing any further damage until he had checked them out. He knew what John Kane looked like. *I ain't looking forward to going through them, especially if Pops is on them, but they could provide leverage if I'm in a tight spot.*

One thing's for sure, they ain't for sale.

He went through to Archie's bedroom. He ached to cry when he saw the pile of presents, he had given him. *I ain't crying,* he told himself. *I don't cry for no one.* He took a deep breath and set about tidying up his Pops' room for one last time. After he had finished, he sat on his Pops' bed and tried to compose himself, but he felt like going out and getting drunk and picking a fight with someone. He wanted someone to fight back, just so he could feel something, but the options were virtually non-existent around here. *I don't want to hurt Lucky or Mary-Lou - it ain't their fault.* He thought about going into the Eastside, but he experienced something he rarely had for anything or anybody - respect. *I like it that Professor Chu treats me like a real person. I don't want to let him down.* He then thought about the Green community on the west side, he considered Vance. *I don't like the guy, he ain't got a RedSuit™, but surely that fucking SecurityFilm™ would activate and then I'd be fucked. In any case, it ain't good for business.* His anger rose when he thought of Siddha, Cain, and Lizzie. *They would just stand there laughing in their indestructible Suits™ - smug bastards.*

He took a last look at Archie's room before closing the door gently. He considered checking in on Lucian, Mary-Lou, and Little Amie, but decided to let them have some space to deal with the day's events. He thought about Lizzie. He didn't want to be alone this evening. *Not tonight. Not here.* He laughed bitterly. *Make love not war - isn't that what those fucking hippies always used to say.*

He shuffled to his own bedroom. He picked up the Sattva ring and fiddled with it until it caught the light and sparkled. *I'm gonna get dressed up for a night on the town and take the car.* He selected the most expensive and luxurious of Bodhi's old attire. The handmade black suit, the silk shirt and even a bowtie, even the underwear and socks exuded quality. He had showered, shaved, and sprayed himself with deodorants and lavished on large quantities of aftershave. He laughed. *They could smell me coming from here.* He didn't care that he would look insanely out of place in the understated to the very soul of West McFarland. *That's the whole fucking point. Let them see me in all my glory. A successful Trad with all the trappings of success they left behind. I'm going to strut my stuff. Let them laugh if they want. I can outsmart them. I am Brady, Brady Mahone. King of the new frontier. They'll rue the day when they decided to fuck with me.*

He wasn't going to spoil the look this time by wearing sneakers with a suit. He selected a pair of shiny black shoes. He examined the label which informed Brady that these were limited edition handcrafted Italian leather by Gucci. He put them on, and they fit perfectly. In the full-length mirror, he pasted back his black scrub of hair with moisturising hair cream from a golden pot. *I never looked so good, and on a day when I never felt so bad*, he thought. *Wish me luck, Pops.*

As he cruised West McFarland unhindered by any other vehicles, he pulled up frequently to check out what was passing for entertainment in this joyless fuck-hole. He saw plenty of recruitment centres. They advertised jobs ranging from wildlife census clerks to a myriad of work under the banner of Operation Clean-up. He liked the idea of a HeavyLoader™ FusionPlane™ operative. *That woulda suited me*. He saw other signs as he passed more recruitment centres, they seemed celebratory as they implored:

You've earned the Red™ - now go for the Orange™.

He drove down to the New Green Hall. He watched dozens of volunteers putting up environmentally friendly banners and bunting, for the *Freely Giving of the Red Ceremony. All are welcome. This is the New Green Years for the New You.*

He reflected darkly on their New Year, a stark contrast with the tough times for those not in the GreenShells™. It seemed a good time to wander around in and among the volunteers. He looked like a visiting President, and the volunteers weren't sure how to react. His aftershave wafted after him. He looked wealthy, whereas, by comparison, they appeared poor. Some smiled politely, but nobody laughed. Even though their minds informed them that they were protected, they couldn't reconcile this powerful looking Trad wandering around showing not one shred of fear, though he could be stopped in a heartbeat. Brady owned the room. He had star quality, and the spotlights of their eyes followed him everywhere until he, and not they, decided it was time for him to go.

He got back in his car and headed over to Lizzie's place. When he arrived, he knocked on the door, and she answered. Her frown was enough to let him know he wasn't welcome. She looked him up and down and smirked. 'Sorry we aren't buying anything. Goodbye.'

He put his foot in the door before she could close it. A teenager was walking up the road and called out, 'Are you ok, Miss?'

'Yes. Thank you, Dawson. Have you completed your homework assignment?'

'Nearly. I'll hand it in before the Red Ceremony tomorrow - promise.' Dawson smiled and headed on his way.

'Who is it?' a voice called out from the lounge.

'It's Brady.' She sighed. 'You may as well come in - seeing as you've obviously gone to a lot of trouble.'

Cain came out to the hallway in his white robe and bare feet. He looked over Brady. 'Business is obviously going well. Congratulations, my friend.'

You ain't no friend of mine. 'Thank you. Us Trads aren't beaten, yet.'

'We are not in competition with you. I wish you every happiness,' Cain said, without a hint of sarcasm. Siddha came out to investigate but said nothing. He looked over Brady's clothes and bowtie without disguising his utter contempt. Cain said, 'Come, Siddha. Let's take an evening stroll and talk about our plans for the next few days. We'll give Lizzie some privacy.' Lizzie glared at him as if she'd been given an order she wasn't allowed to refuse.

She went up the stairs without offering Brady a tacit invitation, knowing Brady wouldn't wait for the courtesies of polite company. *One thing I like about these Green Girls is that they are so easy - no messing,* Brady thought.

Lizzie did her duty and let him make love to her. She even adjusted the settings on her RedSuit™ to set her own stimulation levels to maximum. *If he deems me to be exceptionally responsive, it will play to his ego and vanity*, she told herself. *If I'm doing this, then I may as well extract as much information from him for Cain and the cause.*

Brady left the bed and showered without asking or waiting for permission. The soap was basic and reminded him of the bars they were allocated in prison. He wished he hadn't washed his aftershave away. He began to get dressed when Lizzie said, 'So, you're not planning to stay?' Lizzie was naked but had pulled up a sheet to cover herself.

'I didn't think you'd want me to.'

She knew she was intellectually light-years removed from this thug, and yet here he was treating her like a groupie. He carried on dressing, he fiddled around with his bowtie until he gave up and shoved it in his pocket. Then, he made a show of putting on his ring. He looked up - knowing she would be curious. 'I'm sure you recognise the design,' he said. 'Isn't this where you ask me how I got it?'

'And why would I do that?'

'Come on, lady. I know you think I'm some kinda dumb fuck.'

'That's the most insightful comment you've made. Congratulations. I'll give you a B+ for effort.'

She expected Brady to get angry and storm out, maybe even to slam the door behind him, but he didn't. He smiled. 'Maybe you're right. After all, this whole Green mess proves it. You've won, and now you get to treat the losers like shit.'

There was a glint in his eyes which made Lizzie wary. 'No. We don't gloat.'

'Are you sure? There was a guy on the TV. I remember - Glenarvon Cole. He was with a pretty red-headed reporter. He was surrounded by some of your GreenRevs - that sure looked like some heavy-duty gloating to me.'

'That was in the heat of celebrating the victory. I can assure you, we are far too busy repairing the damage left behind to spend precious time on pontificating and gloating.' Lizzie enjoyed debating. It was a specialism of hers in school, and it felt good to cross swords with someone again, even if it was with an old-fashioned meat-head jock like Brady Mahone. First, she had to get him off balance and lower his guard, and then she would be well placed to go in for the kill. 'Why, apart from the obvious, did you come over here tonight? And what's with the dressing up for the occasion? You didn't think it would impress me - surely?'

Brady sat on the bed next to her as he was lacing up his shoes. When he had finished, he swivelled around on the bed to look at her. 'My Pops died today.'

'Oh,' she said, briefly taken aback. 'I'm sorry. I'm sure he will be a significant loss to society, I mean, he brought you into the world, and that's quite an achievement. What happened to him?'

'I'd rather not say.'

Ooh, he's displaying sensitivity, she thought. *I'm not sure how I feel being his sympathy screw for the evening.* 'Did you love your father?'

'Yes. Pops wasn't a good man, but he was to me.'

'I'm sure he was.' She paused. 'What's your earliest memory of him?'

Brady thought for a moment, and then lied. 'There was this nursery rhyme he used to sing to me, but I can only recall the first line.'

She smiled. 'I used to teach kindergarten; I might be able to help.'

'Ok, it went something like - Georgie Porgie...'

She picked up the rhyme. 'Kissed the girls and made them cry. When the girls - or boys...' She laughed. 'Came out to play, Georgie Porgie ran away.'

'What does it mean?'

'I wouldn't want to say. It might tarnish your precious memories of your Father, and I wouldn't want to do that.'

'Please, I insist.'

'Well, let me say firstly, your Father wouldn't have looked into the rhyme in any other way than it just being a popular children's rhyme. However, it was banned, quietly, because of its potential body image connotations, and of course, due to its hints at shaming children for having latent homosexuality traits. Of course, no decent person would agree with that in these more enlightened times, but back then...'

'It was seen as being kinda funny,' he said.

She nodded and smiled. Brady frowned and considered his next move. 'Where are Cain and Siddha going?'

'Nowhere in particular. Cain often takes one of us out in the night for a long walk and a chat. He likes the peace and quiet; it helps him to concentrate. When I'm with him, I find I listen more intently, without the distractions of the daylight hours. I wouldn't be surprised if they headed to the Town Hall to see how the preparations are going for the Red Ceremonies,' she added.

'That's where the rest of the people get their RedNanoSuits™, the things which make them kinda indestructible?'

'Yes.' She wondered if she had given something away, but then she remembered the SecurityFilm™. In the old world, this would have been the time to plan a terrorist assault, before the population was fully protected. However, the SecurityFilm™ would detect any ill intent, and why would anyone target an outpost like West McFarland and not the more significant Green Communities across the globe? *Nobody could plan an attack of that magnitude.* Lizzie was shaken that she still felt insecure, even in this impregnable fortress. She wanted to change the subject – even if it was only in her mind. 'It will take all night for Cain to give out the RedFiles™, but it will be part of the New Green Year festivities. The townsfolk are very excited, despite the hard work which lies ahead of them next year.'

'And then they'll all work like slaves to earn enough Greenbacks - I mean Green Credits for the OrangeSuits™ - like the one this Bodhi Sattva has?'

'You've been listening and learning. Well done, you.'

Her patronising tone was not lost on Brady. *That's just fine by me, Little Lady Lizzie*. 'And you are all equal under the Green sun and sky like some big happy-clappy collective. Everyone working together, sharing each other's homes, and eschewing the trappings of capitalism.'

'Eschewing is a big word for you. Have you been moving in educated circles?'

'Professor Yuan Chu is a mate of mine. He thinks I'm smart. I'm sure you know him.'

'Of course. Everybody in McFarland knew Professor Chu. He should have been with us.'

'He worked on NanoTech™, helping couples with fertility issues. He told me that his work went against the doctrines of Sattva Systems™, so his expertise wasn't welcome.' He peered into her eyes. 'You know that, though, don't you? You are happy to let Sattva Systems™ sterilise the planet - even me?'

'I'm sure you've sown your seed around the Western Seaboard, and I'm sure you haven't bothered to find out if there are any mini-Mahones out there,' she joked. Still, she was rattled. She'd underestimated him. 'The last thing this planet needs at this time of crisis is more humans using up the last of Her precious resources. We haven't hurt or directly harmed anyone...'

'My friend has had a miscarriage since being crop sprayed by your Green goo.'

'That doesn't count. Any babies who went to full term were unaffected.'

Brady laughed darkly. 'I'll go and give your condolences to Mary-Lou when I get back. My friend, Lucky - I mean Lucian - was the father.'

They both lay in silence. Lizzie was still under the covers, while Brady was in his expensive suit and shiny shoes, on top of the bedclothes beside her. She wanted him to leave but didn't make this request because Cain would need more information. She hadn't got to the bottom of his impeccable - though strange, on him - collection of clothes... or the ring. She had lost one round with Brady, but the fight wasn't over.

'Where did you pick up those clothes? I assume you broke into a tailor store on the Trad side?'

'I was given them - *freely*.' He emphasised the word to draw her in. He was still in the same wrecking mood as when he left the ranch. He couldn't wipe them out physically, but he was confident he could mess with their smug attitudes and assumptions. 'I know what you are up to. I've had girls like you, when I pulled off a big jewellery heist - who'd let me sleep with them, hoping to get something sparkly and nice out of me. You ain't no better than them, except you want Greenie points from your boss - or are you being paid in Green Credits to sleep with me and gather information?'

Bless him, he honestly believes that he has played his killer line in the debate - as if I care what this lump of Traditional Meat thinks of my motivations. 'Of course, you are right. I don't want this to come across as being laced with sarcasm, but yes - the only reason any woman would sleep with a lowlife like you is to get something out of you. For some, that might be jewellery or money. I mean, nobody in their right mind would want to have a long-term relationship with you. I mean, what have you got to offer but a life of pain and misery and punctuated with an occasional slap to keep the little woman in her place?

'So, in answer to your question, I am sleeping with you for information, though for the life of me - I don't know why, it's hardly likely you would have anything particularly insightful to bring to the party. And no, I am not being paid in Green Credits because I am a veteran GreenRev. I don't need Green Credits to receive my upgrades. I've witnessed, first-hand the hellish tactics you brutal Trads used to repel us. They were happy enough to use children as their human shields, so don't come at me with this *won't someone think of the poor children crap.*'

He was delighted she was getting angry. 'The clothes I'm wearing were given to me by a woman who is one-hundred and fourteen years old - her name was Libby. I can't remember her current surname - she seems to have gone through a few in her time - but she was married to John Kane. Am I ringing any bells?'

This did shock her, but she attempted to cover it up, 'Please don't tell me you slept with her, like some tawdry gigolo.'

'If I had, then I could have persuaded her to turn up her NanoSuit™ to maximum pleasure. I know when I'm being played. There's a Cain, Siddha and a Lizzie in every Green Town, except some of the Green Girls talk a lot - and I mean a lot - about the fabulous innovations the Suits™ have to extend sexual pleasure. Some of them seem very keen for me to get a NanoSuit™ of my own...' *That's how they get you, son.*

'Did you have sex with Libby?'

Brady roared with laughter. *I might leave that question hanging.* 'So, you do know her?'

'Of course, I know her. She's Bodhi's mother.'

He leered at her, 'And you recognise this ring, don't you?' He put his hand near her face and waggled his finger - the diamonds and emeralds sparkling in the dappled moonlight through the gaps in the curtains.

'Yes. That is the same font as used by Sattva Systems™. It must be either Bodhi's or John Kane's.'

'I'll give you a chance to escape now, with all your pretty preconceptions still intact,' he said, playfully. 'Do you want me to leave right now? Because I can – it's no skin off my nose. Or shall I stay, and tell you all the juicy stuff? Cain will probably take it quite calmly, but Siddha, he's a creepy bastard, by the way, he will go absolutely ape.' He sat up, as though he was going to leave anyway. He did it to toy with her.

There was no point in hiding her true intent, any longer. 'No. I've gone this far. Cain would never forgive me if I didn't find out everything.'

'Ok, but you have been warned.' He paused and then showed her the ring. 'This...' he said, like he was reciting a bedtime story. 'This is a magic ring.'

'Oh, please.'

'Ok, it might not make magic, but it does have the power to break spells. Is that magic?'

'It's a profound question, but let's just say I have no idea and cut to the chase.'

He exaggerated his disappointed slump, like was a child, and she'd told him she didn't want to play anymore. 'You've told me these fairy stories about your magical world, where you all share everything with each other, and in your Green World you don't see the need for the finer things in life because those things represent the Old Order of capitalism and materialism...'

'Thanks for the history lesson. I am a teacher, remember.'

'Well, this is where it begins to unravel for me. I was invited to visit Libby. I didn't stumble upon her by accident. She got her servant to seek me out and bring me to her.' He waited for the word servant to land. He knew precisely the effect each revelation would have on her. 'Anyhows, he accompanies me up to her enormous house in Malibu, set on a clifftop and overlooking the Pacific, with its twelve bedrooms...'

'I don't need the full realtor spiel...'

'This house was worth one hundred million dollars back at the turn of the Millennium, and it's still hers - I'm putting Greenbacks on Bodhi having kept the paper deeds to this one.' He went on. 'She wasn't sharing this palace with any other needy and worthy Greens - it was all hers. Oh, and she didn't lose any friends as they kept their luxury condos because Libby would be upset if she had lost her friends.'

Lizzie resorted to lying about how she felt. 'So, Bodhi is looking after his Mother. That's understandable, I suppose.'

'Did you look after your Mother?'

'That's none of your business.'

Brady snorted. 'I'll take that as a No, then.'

Lizzie was reeling. 'Why would she want you to know all this? It doesn't make sense.'

'Who cares? All I know is it was a very profitable day for me. And looky here - I've got Bodhi's ring or Xavier as his darling Moms insisted on calling him. And your SecurityFilm™, which you place so much faith in, is doing nothing at all about it.' He held up his hand triumphantly, and said to the darkness, 'Hello. I've got Bodhi's ring. Come and get it.' He paused, 'Nothing. It must be his night off.' He looked at her, like an opponent in a boxing ring, checking they were in precisely the right position to receive the knock-out blow. 'But you're right. Bodhi's a terrific guy, and upright citizen and all that jazz.'

'Is that it? Is that all you've got to tell me?'

'I'm curious. What would Cain, and Siddha make of this?'

She knew he wouldn't believe her if she tried to pretend it wouldn't be of concern to them. 'They would be disappointed, but I hope they would treat it as a human flaw with Bodhi. After all, he is a man and not a God.'

'I think you had him down as the Perfect Man. I've never heard any of you mention flaws before.' He deliberately slowed the pace. He needed to draw out the justifications from her now - to leave her spent, when the final moment came. 'I had a wonderful time at Libby's. She made me feel like an honoured guest. She gave me brandy and Cuban cigars and then invited me into the hot tub with her.'

'She sounds like a very nice woman. I wouldn't have expected anything less from Bodhi's Mother.'

'For a broad of one-hundred and fourteen, she didn't look a day over seventy. She kept herself in good shape. And by the way, I didn't have sex with her. She was out of my age range,' he added. 'There was something else. Something she said, which didn't make sense.'

Lizzie leaned in, sensing that this was she was meant to find out. If Brady didn't understand it, then it was probably something good. 'What did she say?'

'She said she was *Yellow*™.'

'She can't be. That's impossible. Even Bodhi is only at Orange™ - and he only tries the new NanoSuits™ on himself before letting anybody else have them. It's a matter of ethics. If there is any fault within the technology, then only he would be harmed. You're either lying or badly mistaken. You said it yourself. She's positively ancient. She might be coming to the end of her extended life...that's it, she's confused, and she got her colours mixed up. I mean, Orange™ is only a shade away from Yellow™.' She paused. 'The YellowSuits™ are still years away.'

'You're probably right. I've been in a few courtrooms in my time. I'm probably one of those unreliable witnesses. However, the sight of her did take my breath away.'

'What do you mean?'

'The way she was fully clothed one second, and then as she glided down the steps into the pool, her clothing transformed into a bathing suit.'

24. RED CEREMONY

Cain walked through the adoring crowds on New Year's Day. It was 2085 and the first New Year of the Green Revolution. They cheered him as they passed. It was the day when the Green Community of West McFarland would be issuing its citizens with their new RedNanoSuits™. Most had worked hard to earn enough Green Credits to pay for the suits, but for those who were less fortunate, through no fault of their own who found they had missed the deadline, others contributed the Credits for them to receive them on this auspicious day. It was an act of kindness and charity which was embedded into the very souls of these caring people. They were sacrificing everything to save the planet from climate extinction, but today, they would be receiving their just rewards for their generosity of spirit.

They were at one with all the other Green Communities from West McFarland to Malibu to New York, and from London to Singapore to Sydney, in celebrating the Year of the Red™.

Cain was contemplating the phone call he made at his allotted time the previous evening with Bodhi. He had been honest and brave as he informed Bodhi of every detail of Brady Mahone's encounter with Libby Kane - Bodhi's Mother. He expected denials, excuses and justifications, but all he received was praise. All Bodhi asked of Cain was that he should trust him and that it was all part of the overall plan. He also informed Cain that he should keep this to himself, for now, and that Cain would be rewarded for his work by being the first of all the Green Community leaders across the globe to be invited to receive the Yellow™ - when it was ready and available. Bodhi didn't state the obvious rebuttal regarding Libby's account. Cain was happy to be elevated, and he hadn't hidden anything from Bodhi - and therefore, he had nothing to fear. He had faith.

Cain wove his way through the bustling crowds of the New Green Hall, which the older residents still preferred to call, simply, the Town Hall. He went backstage to greet his closest friend and confidante Siddha. They hugged warmly. Cain patted Siddha heartily on his back. 'We have come through so much together and this year has been tumultuous, but now the hard work begins.'

There were no chairs - it was standing room only in the New Green Hall, with thousands more in the grounds outside. Lizzie went to Cain to affix a microphone onto his robe, while Siddha brought over the two RedDistors™.

'I'm sorry, Cain,' Lizzie said. 'I didn't expect him to be so brutal.'

'And I'm sorry for placing you in such an insidious situation. If it makes you feel any better, then Bodhi says that Brady has a function to perform, but even he admitted that he had underestimated Brady Mahone's intelligence levels.'

'I suppose even criminals have intelligence...'

'But he's hardly a criminal mastermind. He's been captured and detained on so many occasions.'

Lizzie laughed. 'We caught him stealing fruit from the GreenGrocers™.'

Cain held out his arms. Lizzie took this as a sign she had been forgiven. She moved in for a hug with the man she most admired in the world. 'I want you to be at my right-hand side today,' he whispered.

'Is Siddha ok with that?'

'Of course. He will be at my left.' He looked around the hall and through the open doors of the main entrance. The sun was shining brightly against the azure sky. 'I think we are ready.'

Lizzie moved to her position on the stage and Siddha gave her a warm smile as she passed him. 'I've dreamed so long of days such as this,' he said.

The applause and cheers were almost deafening as Cain moved to the centre of the stage. It was daylight, but still, Vance shone a spotlight on Cain before moving back to the edge of the crowd.

Cain opened his arms in the universal gesture of greeting, his white robe hanging from him like a holy man. He scrunched his Nano protected toes on the wooden stage. His crystal green eyes sparkled as he addressed his audience. 'Today is our Red Day. Are you ready to receive?'

The audience cheered. 'Yes. Yes.' They whooped and hollered, and this mixed with laughter in the jubilation of the day.

Cain waited until the din subsided. 'The next few years will not be easy. There is much work to do beyond the NanoShells™. We have to clean and rewild America, and our fellow activists across the globe will be doing the same in their lands. Together we will restore Mother Earth to full health. We will end, once and for all, the devastating impact of man on the planet. Remember this, when you are challenged by the Trads in the old world - the planet and every living thing that relied upon its bounty was in its death throes. The Trads would have destroyed not only us, but also, themselves. Just because they didn't understand, doesn't mean it wasn't so. We took direct action, and now we'll make the world a better place, not just for mankind but for all Her creatures. We – you – won!'

There were more cheers. 'To go out in the world you will need to be protected. The RedNanoSuits™ you are to receive today have been battle tested by our glorious GreenRevs.' The front rows of the audience were reserved for the GreenRev veterans, who roared and jumped up and down furiously like a mosh pit from the old rock concert days. Some waved at Lizzie, and she beamed and waved back. Cain and Siddha laughed proudly.

'With these Suits™, they cannot hurt you. They even anchor through the floor, so you are immovable. But they also come with responsibility. You cannot use them to hurt another living thing. You cannot even use them to deliberately embarrass an enemy. We will not hurt the feelings of another. If you do, the Security Protocols™ will be alerted, and your Suit™ will be withdrawn. We are not here to harm - our whole reason of being is to save.

He let the warning hang for a second before continuing, he shouted at the top of his voice: 'Are you ready to receive?'

His audience clapped and cheered. 'I want all of you to hold the hand of whoever is next to you. Please look around and ensure that nobody is left without a partner. While you are doing this, the GreenRevs will form a human chain to Lizzie on my right and Siddha on my left.'

There was much shuffling, and quiet chatter as people linked up. They knew what to do - it was a similar ceremony they had taken part in a few short weeks after the Revolution, when they had all received the InfraRedPrimerSuits™. These were only an outer coating, but they did speed up the healing process if they were injured in any way. This gave them all the reassurance they needed - nobody had acquired any ill side-effects. In fact, quite the opposite was noted, as many had stated that they had never felt better. After a few minutes of checking and double-checking that nobody was left out of the human daisy chain - a reverential calm descended. All eyes were fixed upon the stage, where Cain stood as the only broken link. He held up the two red tubes - the RedDistors™. The crowd waited for the new holy words of the Green Revolution. There was utter silence as Cain built up the tension like a consummate showman.

'Our Mother.

Who art Heaven on Earth.
For what we are about to receive
May we be truly grateful
And lead us not into temptation.
Show us the way.'

The audience murmured in reply, 'Show us the way.'

Cain held the RedDistors™ above his head and then lowered them into the waiting hands of Lizzie and Siddha. There was a frisson in the air as a soft red glow passed slowly from one audience member to another, as if each were gaining a visible aura. Cain reminded the audience, 'Do not let go of your hands until everyone has received.'

They held hands in a meditative silence. Cain looked right, and then left at the RedDistors™ until a message in Red appeared. *All Given Freely.*

25. ALL IS QUIET

The Mahone Ranch didn't merrily greet the oncoming of the New Year. Lucian, Mary-Lou and Little Amie remained in the Lopez Ranch. They felt they couldn't conspicuously celebrate in the light of Archie Mahone's suicide - and they wanted to give Brady some space to grieve his Pops death.

Brady did mourn his Pops - in the time-honoured tradition of getting drunk. It didn't feel right to drink the alcohol he had acquired from Libby. Instead, he drank copious amounts of Archie's homemade Moonshine. He couldn't ever remember getting so drunk.

He awoke next day to the mother-of-all-hangovers. He scratched around for whatever breakfast would take the least effort to make, poured himself and chain-drank black coffee, and then he fell into a sleep full of headaches again. He dreamed of his Pops and his Foster Moms, even in this dream state he began to understand her attraction to the thought of drinking the pain away.

He roused himself at midday. He looked over to West McFarland and was sure he saw the barely detectable clear GreenShell™ turn to a reddish glow for a few minutes. *With a bit of luck, they've blown themselves up.* He smiled and then winced at the pain in his head. He walked around the Ranch to try and get a bit of fresh air. He then went into his barn and looked at the empty boxes which used to be home for his Blank Black Files, and then the DVDs and music CDs awaiting his next deliveries. He was taking stock.

He went to the catalogues and order books. *Jesus - he's a smart kid, that Mary-Lou. I still need her*. He looked at the strewn tarpaulin with which he'd used to cover his Christmas gifts. Already, that day felt like a lifetime ago. He shook his head ruefully.

I'll go and see Lucky tomorrow. I'm not up to it today.

He strolled back to the house, and he drew in deep breaths of fresh air, but instead of reinvigorating Brady, it only added dizziness to his list of drink-related symptoms.

He lay back down on his bed and stared up at the ceiling. In his pocket he toyed with the Sattva ring he now carried around with him. *I need to look after this,* he thought. *I can't wear it all the time, but I can't have it falling out my pocket*.

Brady wandered into to Archie's room and went to the bedside table. He opened the drawer and pulled out the thick silver chain he always used to wear around his neck. It was only then that Brady remembered that he wasn't wearing it when he slashed his wrists. He didn't know why Archie had done this. *He musta had his reasons*. He slid the Sattva ring over the chain and slipped it over his head. He went to the bathroom, and he checked to see how it looked. The ring seemed weighted to hang with the *S* the right way up.

He twisted the silver chain between his thumb and forefinger of his huge hand and then pulled the chain around until the catch was hidden at the back of his neck. He removed his T-shirt and examined himself, and even in this hungover state he concluded that he still looked good for his age - younger than his years. He looked over his tattoos from the weird Hawaiian guy in prison, and he examined himself for scars, but there weren't any.

I always did heal real quick.

Brady put his T-shirt back on and went to the porch and sat next to the Old Marvin machine gun. He playfully aimed it in the direction of the dissipating redness from the Shell™ over West McFarland. He knew this was just the beginning.

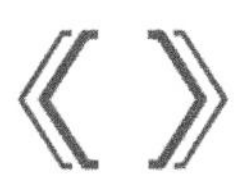

THE END

ACKNOWLEDGEMENTS

I'd like to give my heartfelt thanks to my family, Cathy, my wife and my daughters, Beck and Katie, for their love and support while writing (and recording) this book.

A Small Request...

If you have enjoyed this book, do please help to spread the word by putting a review or a rating on your favourite bookseller or Goodreads; by posting something on social media; or in the old-fashioned way by simply telling your friends or family about it.

Book publishing is a very competitive business these days, to a saturated market, and independent publishers such as ourselves are often crowded out by big business.

Support from readers like you can make all the difference to a book's success.

Many thanks.

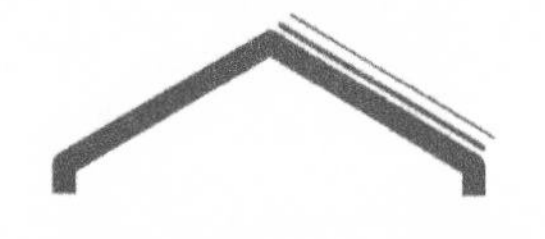

MORE FROM JIM LOWE

The Green Deal Quartet contains the following titles:

BOOK ONE: 2084 - New World Man

Brady knew two things:

It was the end of the world, and the Greens had won.

2084 was going to be an interesting year. All he needed to do was break out of jail first.

Sattva Systems™ had transformed Nanotechnology and Fusion Power in a bid to avert the oncoming climate change catastrophe. Still, they were thwarted by the old industries at every turn. Leaving Bodhi Sattva - its charismatic owner with no choice but to team up with the Green Revolutionaries to bring down the internet and capitalism. He would lead them into a new era with his one-hundred-year plan to save the planet.

It was all going so well.

Then Brady discovered he had a unique ability that he could exploit to establish a criminal enterprise for himself and his adopted family of misfits and conspiracy theorists.

The Greens saw Brady as a threat to their project but not Bodhi Sattva. He had plans for Brady. But nobody could imagine how devastating these plans might be...

This science fiction series is captivating and chilling in equal measure.

Order your copy today.

BOOK TWO: 2100 - Crime of the Century

BOOK THREE: 2142 - The Revealing Science

BOOK FOUR: 2184 - Twenty-Second Century Man

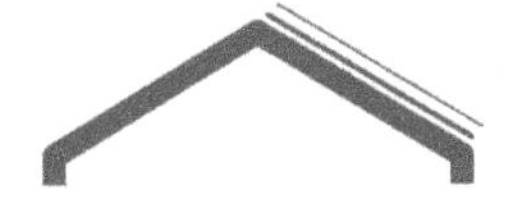

Previously published by Jim Lowe: The New Reform Quartet

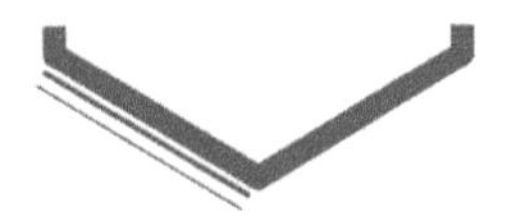

Book One: New Reform

Tatum had learning difficulties and had a brutal home life, but one thing to emerge from her living with a family of gun runners was that she learned to shoot with unerring accuracy.

When she finally escaped her family, she found friendship and camaraderie with a sisterhood of feminist activists until many of her friends were killed in a deadly terrorist attack.

It was then that Tatum spiralled into a state where the only solution was to take revenge on their killers...

THE NEW REFORM SERIES was conceived in 2013 (before Brexit and Trump) and was a darkly satirical look into future political influences.

Not only did it play with the idea of corrupt populism, but also militant feminism, marketing, hacking, viral content, social media influencers, new money combined with dark desires - and even what could happen to the latent power of the aristocracy and the liberal elite if their power was turned inwards to ignite a potent force.

The four books have different themes but are interlinked, and by the end of the final book, all the plotlines are neatly gift-wrapped and presented with a tightly knotted jet-black bow.

Set in the fictional city of Arlington, this alternative history spans decades beginning in the eighties.

The story begins with Tatum waiting and watching - something she is exceptionally good at. In fact, she could watch and wait for England - and beyond...

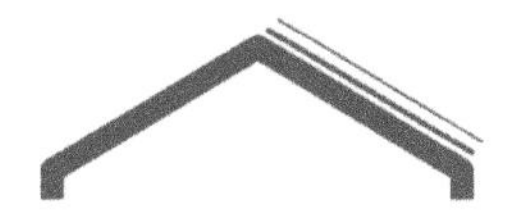

Book Two: The ODC (The Online Death Cult)

Denise was a soulless sociopath with money to burn and urges to satisfy, and then she met Brandon. He was a celebrity seeker with a love for her, but with no regard to the trail of destruction, he would be willing to cause to make her his own.

Book Three: With Two Eyes

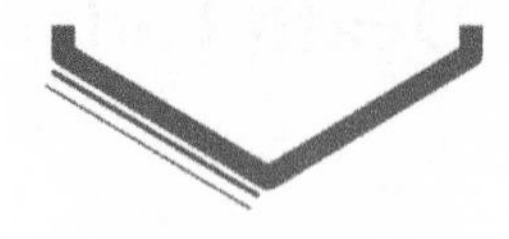

Nadie was only seeking the truth for the family of the man she had loved, but instead, she found herself treated as a travelling freak show. But as she doggedly continued in her lonely quest, little did she know that she was changing the world one step at a time.

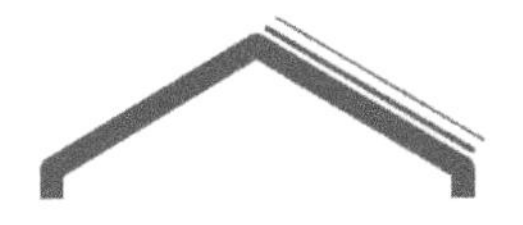

Book Four: Fourth Room.

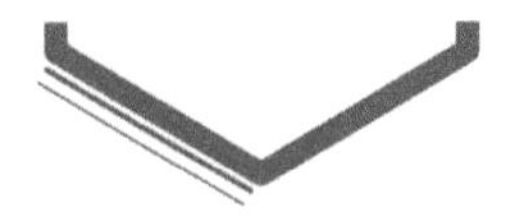

Bob had all the power and money he could want, but all this gave him was boredom and frustration at his perceived lack of freedom. Would he stand in the way of those who would use his position to start a new world order in his name...

All titles will be available, wherever possible, on eBook, paperback, hardback, and audiobook.

If you want to know more about my writing and recording, please visit my website at **jimlowewriting.com.**

Thank you.

Don't miss out!

Visit the website below and you can sign up to receive emails whenever Jim Lowe publishes a new book. There's no charge and no obligation.

https://books2read.com/r/B-A-KPCR-DKCUB

BOOKS 2 READ

Connecting independent readers to independent writers.

About the Author

Jim Lowe was a bookseller for a UK retail chain for forty years but has now taken early retirement. He loves books and the creative arts.

He is married to Cath and has two grown-up daughters, Beck and Katie.

Jim is an active - some might say, an over-enthusiastic - member of his local community in the Worcester area and runs Facebook groups for musicians and writers of all backgrounds and levels of experience. He has also worked closely as a volunteer for BBC Introducing as a filmmaker, and his niche YouTube channel for local artists has had over 300,000 views.

He has lived and worked in many locations in England including, Ashbourne, Braintree, Burton-Upon-Trent, Bury St Edmunds, Chelmsford, Derby - where he was born and remains a lifelong Rams fan - Great Yarmouth, Lowestoft, Tewkesbury and Worcester, where he has lived for more than twenty years.

Read more at https://jimlowewriting.com/.

Lightning Source UK Ltd.
Milton Keynes UK
UKHW010746151222
413978UK00001B/217